swallow

Sefi Atta

Interlink Books

An imprint of Interlink Publishing Group, Inc.
Northampton, Massachusetts

For my families: the Attas, Thomases, and Ransome-Kutis

First published in 2010 by

INTERLINK BOOKS
An imprint of Interlink Publishing Group, Inc.
46 Crosby Street, Northampton, Massachusetts 01060
www.interlinkbooks.com

Library of Congress Cataloging-in-Publication Data
Atta, Sefi.
Swallow / by Sefi Atta.—1st American ed.
    p. cm.
ISBN 978-1-56656-833-3 (pbk.)
1. Female friendship—Fiction. 2. Mothers and daughters—Fiction.
3. Nigeria—Fiction. 4. Domestic fiction. I. Title.
PS3601.T78S93 2010
813'.6—dc22

                        2010013252

A portion of this book previously appeared in *Sable* and *Per Contra*.

Photo © Frenk and Danielle Kaufmann

Printed and bound in the United States of America

swallow

PART ONE

On the morning that Rose was sacked she and I could easily have been killed, and that wouldn't have been our first brush with death on our way to work.

I remember clearly that this time, our bus was not even speeding. A group of pedestrians was running across the expressway. One of them lagged behind the others. Our bus driver punched on his horn and then he braked. Our bus swerved, the conductor almost fell out of the door. He was holding on and whimpering, "*Sanu mi*," mercy. His legs were swinging this way and that, passengers were colliding with each other, a woman in front was screaming that her enemies had succeeded in smiting her, her basket of oranges rolled down the aisle.

Rose and I were trembling by the rear window as the driver steered us back on course. We thought our bus was about to overturn. I caught a glimpse of the slow crosser; he was safely on the other side of the expressway now and shaking his head as if someone else had almost caused the accident. As usual, onlookers were gathering around the scene and pointing. Within seconds, passengers on the bus were scrambling for seats and the conductor was collecting fares as if nothing had happened. Even the oranges were back in their basket, sitting upright like us. At that time of the morning, our bus was full and once we recovered from the shock, we were more concerned about having to stand than surviving the rest of the ride.

"What were we saying again?" Rose asked.

"Sanwo," I reminded her.

We always spoke in English because she couldn't speak Yoruba and I couldn't understand her own language, Ijaw. Today, we spoke between gaps to hide our conversation from our fellow passengers: secretaries, clerks, couriers, security men who worked in the city center and lived on the mainland. Most of us had roots elsewhere. My hometown, Makoku, was west of Lagos, and Rose had grown up in Port Harcourt in Rivers State. Some of the other passengers we knew from our daily commutes. We greeted them at the stop every morning and ran together when our bus arrived. Inside, we shared seats, sweat, and gossip. Passengers were always staring ahead or out of the windows, but they were listening, despite the rumble of the bus engine. "Oh yes, my sister," Rose said. "That Sanwo of yours. He's not serious at all. Every day he's promising and still no dowry. The way things are going with that man, you're heading for a black hole."

"Why?"

She counted on her fingers. "No house..."

"Has a house, Rose," I said.

"One room in his uncle's quarters? Let me finish. No house, no job..."

"Has a job," I said.

She nudged me. "Business for his uncle? You see? That is the problem. You're always defending the man. None of us enjoy working and I don't see you sitting around telling long stories like him. No house, no job in Lagos. Straight into a black hole is all I have to say. He says he wants to marry you?"

I nodded, in case she'd forgotten that other passengers were listening.

"How long since he's been promising?"

"Don't know."

"How long, Tolani?"

Two years. I could barely open my mouth to tell her.

She clapped. "So. Don't ask me again if you're not prepared to take my advice. Six months and no marriage, I'm free to meet someone else is my rule. See you on Friday night. Take me to parties and nightclubs. Buy me beer and don't wake me up asking for yam and eggs. Understand? Six months maximum."

"Ultimatum?" I asked.

"Yes," she said. "He's blocking your way and he's not delivering, so he can forget about any lovey-dovey treatment. No woman can afford to be nice in this place. It's a war between men and us. A war, you hear me? So face the *bobo* squarely, make sure your demands are met. If not, you're a fine chick, you'll find someone else, plain and simple."

She sucked her tongue through the gap between her teeth. She was proud of that gap; it was a sign of beauty, like a birthmark.

Rose had been with eight men in the time I knew her. She had even been with a Lebanese. One man threatened to pour boiling water on her; another kept coming to our office to see her, until she called his house to tell him to stop and discovered he had a wife. But what was the sense in changing them like that? Men who beat, men who stole, men who could kill. You could never guess what they were really like by looking at their faces. They were all over Lagos and I did not want to know them.

I'd met Sanwo in the same year I arrived in the city. The worst about him was that he worked for his uncle. He had been working for his uncle for as long as I'd known him, managing government contracts for which he received a percentage cut. The contracts were not regular, so he'd never earned as much as I had working as a secretary in a bank.

Our bus stopped for more passengers. They looked exhausted and vexed; some were in uniform.

Those in traditional wear were mostly traders. There was no space left to stand in the aisle. The air was full of exhaust fumes and body odors. The bus smelled as bad as manure.

"This dowry business," Rose said, "is primitive anyway."

"How so?" I asked.

She shook her gold bangles and stared out of the window. "Me, I like the way the *oyinbos* do it— diamond ring, 'I do, I do.'"

Rose often complained about being a Nigerian. She thought she was born in the wrong country. She wished she had been born in Czechoslovakia because the name sounded sophisticated. Nigeria was uncivilized, she said.

"A diamond ring is like a dowry," I said. "And we do 'I do, I do' over here."

She nodded. "Yes, but we add our customs to it, letter writing, engagement, all that. Aunts, uncles, cousins, everybody involved. By the time you've finished, you've married a whole village. Rich people, the same thing. They want to wear their diamond rings and they still take dowries. Me, I think it is all primitive rubbish."

The man seated next to her eyed her. Rose didn't notice. In one way she was a patriotic Nigerian: arguing was her favorite pastime. Today, the dowry could be a great custom; tomorrow, it could be the worst.

"You-sef," I said. "You change your views faster than you change boyfriends."

"It's true," she said. "We never think. And why do we still follow such a foolish tradition? It's unfair to women. You might as well sell somebody like a cow."

I laughed. "You're for women's liberation this morning?"

"I'm for sense in the head," she said, tapping her temple. "I don't know anything about any women's liberation."

We passed National Stadium, a series of concrete structures higher than the surrounding billboards and palm trees. The houses of the neighborhood were grayish-white with corrugated iron roofs. There was a light morning mist, and the sun was rising a fierce orange. By the main entrance of the stadium, a group of highway administrators were sweeping. Around them was enough litter to keep them working for the rest of the week. They swept slowly. The wind blew what the rain had soaked and the sun had dried.

Dowries were unfair to men. These days, to marry a woman, a man had to present all sorts of gifts to her family. If the woman was wealthy, her family could demand a car. I'd heard of families asking for brassieres if she was poor. What used to be a tradition was now a means of extortion. The women of the bride's family drew up a list and presented it at her engagement ceremony. Sometimes, families stated exactly how much naira they wanted. More and more in Lagos, every relationship began and ended with a question of money.

I had told Sanwo this much: I had a savings account at the bank. It was gathering more dust than interest. I could withdraw the money and invest it in one of his trading consignments, and we could use the profits toward my dowry. He said that was like telling him he was not a real man, even though he talked and talked about a wedding until I agreed. I preferred a registry service and was not interested in a church ceremony. Sanwo said he wasn't either, but his family expected one. I was beginning to doubt his sincerity.

"What time is it?" Rose asked.

I glanced at my watch. "Seven thirty sharp."

"Hunger is killing me."

"Me too," I said.

Our bus pulled away. The vibrations from the engine tickled my ears.

You should have seen us that morning, thinking it was just another working day ahead. Rent took up half our salaries, but no one could tell from our appearance. Rose's face was fresh with powder, like a proper Lagos *sisi*. She had no eyebrows, though. She'd shaved them and drawn two thin black lines over her eyes. I couldn't convince her those lines made her look angry, which she often was. Her blouse was rumpled, and her black skirt was too big, so she had on my favorite red belt. She called me a corporate executive because I wore a beige skirt suit and had a matching beige clip in my hair. Women like us, we did not play with fashion; wearing the cheapest and latest was how we indulged.

We bought fried yams as soon as we got off the bus and ate them out of newspaper pages. Federal Community, our bank on Broad Street, was one of the small buildings in the city center. I worked on the second floor in the Loans department; Rose worked on the ground floor by the banking hall and Cash and Teller department. The bank was chartered in the year of independence, to cater to the masses. Now, almost twenty-five years later, profits still went to military governors, government ministers, and ex-politicians. They were on our board of directors. The government was a majority shareholder; we worked as slowly as civil servants, shifting paper.

All morning I typed bad debt notices. Some dated so far back I wondered why our department bothered to send them out. We never got replies. I began to imagine the showdown I would have with Sanwo over the weekend. If I gave him an ultimatum, he would only laugh. He took my loyalty for granted. He would also say Rose was jealous that she couldn't keep a boyfriend and was always trying to drive a man to his early grave.

I did not see her that morning and never even asked after her, which wasn't unusual. We lived together, and at work, kept to our separate departments. It was our way of preserving our friendship. Rose found me reserved and, as far as I was concerned, she talked too much, even though I was grateful for her advice that morning. She'd told me exactly what I needed to hear and more: I was to withhold all affection. She was ruthless with men. She didn't discriminate and that was the problem.

I was getting tired of typing those bad debt notices when Ignatius from Personnel came to my desk with news, just before lunchtime.

"My sister," he said.

"Uncle," I said.

Ignatius was the oldest employee in the bank. He had a white patch on one side of his hair and was distinguished looking with a turned-up nose. He settled arguments between employees and gave advice if we had problems with management: suspensions, probations, cautions. Like Rose, he was from Rivers State. He called her his country-woman. Rose laughed at him behind his back. "The village he's from," she'd told me, "they shit in the creeks they bath in."

"They've sacked Rose," he whispered.

"What?"

"Insubordination."

"Eh, why?"

"She slapped Salako."

"Ye!"

Rose was Mr. Salako's secretary. Ignatius lifted his hand to calm me down.

"It was from Franka I heard," he said.

"When did it happen?"

"Thirty minutes now."

"How did Franka find out?"

"I don't know. I don't know, but all the news in

the office comes out of that woman's mouth."

"She is a liar."

"She swears she saw it with her own two eyes."

I glanced at Alhaji Umar's door. Quiet as he was, Alhaji Umar, my manager, was a strict follower of the government's War Against Indiscipline. Lateness to work was "unaccep-a-table." Personal phone calls were "unaccep-a-table." Idle talk was also "unaccep-a-table." He stuttered over certain words and was in favor of adopting military-style punishments like frog jumps and squats to discipline the bank staff because such punishments had been "effec-e-tive" within the civil service. His door was shut.

"Rose has left?" I asked.

Ignatius shook his head. "I don't know. I only came to tell you as her friend."

I imagined Rose walking to the bus stop and cursing Mr. Salako.

"Thank you, Uncle," I said.

"My sister," Ignatius said, tapping my back.

I continued to type my bad debt letters, looking over my shoulder for Mr. Salako.

Mr. Salako was our branch manager, the most senior manager in the bank. Rose had complained about him many times before, how he'd passed comments about her body, grabbed her hands and tickled her palms. A few times, he had tried to hug her and she pushed him away. But to slap him? What was the sense in doing that? Mr. Salako would sack her and no one would question him. Mr. Salako was the board of director's messenger boy. He told them exactly what they wanted to hear and came back to tell us lies. His last lie was that he valued each and every employee.

I was beginning to get tired of looking out for him when he appeared, clutching the banister. He was sweating and panting as usual. Rose once said that Mr. Salako could eat five hundred donuts in one sitting. Her nickname for him was "Mr. Biggs." He was not that big, only around his stomach; consequently, his trousers were buckled high — almost up to his chest — or below his waist. Today, he was riding low. He waddled to Alhaji Umar's office and shut the door behind him. The news spread before he came out. Rose had insulted him in front of everyone downstairs, including the customers on the banking floor and security guards. She'd called him a bloody bastard and slapped him.

Ignatius thought she would never have done that had he been around to calm her. "She's my countrywoman," he kept repeating, as if they were the closest of friends.

I wondered why he thought this was the right time to brag about his association with Rose. Rose had no time for Ignatius. She didn't even respect him, despite his age. She said he had been trying to chase her from the moment he handed her an employment contract to sign, that he was an old goat, and a real goat stood a better chance. Ignatius was married with two children in university.

Those of us who broke for lunch at twelve o'clock were standing outside the bank in line to buy groundnuts from the hawker who sat by the entrance. The hawker measured each portion in an empty milk can. The sun was hot and I shut my eyes to a blanket of red as I listened to what the others had to say about Rose. Hakeem from Customer Services thought her outburst was due to her upbringing. He'd never cared for Rose, and as usual, typical Ibadan man, he was dropping and picking up his H's.

"Yes. I hexpected it sooner or later. It was a matter of time. That woman does not know 'ow to control 'erself, and Salako 'as been letting her get away with it. Now, see what she's gone and done, disgracing 'im in public like a small boy…"

Godwin said he would pray for Rose.

Franka said Rose had to be Mr. Salako's girlfriend. "Otherwise why would she…" She turned around to check and when she saw me said, "Hey-Hey, Tolani. I didn't know you were here. Why so quiet? Haven't you heard?"

"Heard what?" I asked, shielding my eyes from the sun.

"Ah-ah? You haven't heard already?"

I'd heard that Franka's husband often beat her for gossiping. No news ever escaped her ears and the bigger the news, the wider her eyes became. Sometimes her eyes filled up with tears when she was overcome from gossiping. We called her "Radio Nigeria."

"Rose," she said. "Her boyfriend Salako has finally sacked her."

Godwin, who was ahead of her in the line, leaned back and said, "Thou shalt not bear false witness."

"Face your front, Mr. Pastor," she snapped.

Godwin took a step forward with his hands over his groin. He was one of those born-agains, and I never really had problems with him.

"It's Rose's concern," I said calmly. "No one else's."

"But it's a pity," Franka said, with a smile.

When I wouldn't confirm, she turned her back on me.

For the rest of the day, I ignored the talk in the office. The story had changed. People were saying that Rose tore Mr. Salako's shirt in the banking hall, and the security guards dragged her out of the building, and they set their Alsatians on her, and one of the Alsatians bit Rose, but no one was sure if it was her left or right thigh, or how deep the bite was.

On my way home I passed a beggar with no legs, sitting on a wooden tray with wheels. He maneuvered himself so skillfully that I gave him my spare kobos. Normally, I pretended not to see beggars: it was almost like seeing my future.

Every morning at five thirty, when the air was cool, Rose and I caught a *kabukabu* from the end of our street to another district. There, we waited at a stop for our bus named "Who Knows Tomorrow?" If our bus arrived on time, and if it didn't break down along the way, we arrived at Tafawa Balewa Square in the city center at quarter to eight. Our bank was another fifteen-minute walk away.

During our morning walks, we looked out for taxi drivers who sometimes drove along the sidewalks. I'd seen street traders fight until they drew blood. I'd also seen a crowd catch a thief and beat him to death, throw a tire over a pickpocket and set him on fire. If someone pointed at a person in the city center and shouted, "*Ole*," thief, that was the end.

Rose and I would eat fried yams on our way to the bank; it was our main meal for the day. On our way back from work, when we were hungry and our shoes pinched, we walked huddled over. "Hurry up with your high-and-pointeds," she always complained about my pumps. "You and your flat-and-wides," I would answer. She was almost thirty, two years older than me, and she still couldn't balance on high heels. Her feet were huge for a woman's, so she preferred men's loafers.

In the evenings, our scramble began at the bus stop. We elbowed and pushed people out of our way. We woke up early in the mornings to avoid the crowds. After work, the crowds were there, waiting for the same buses, heading in the same direction of the mainland. Quarrels, plenty. Chaos, unbelievable. Sometimes, the police showed up and horsewhipped people. They had always done that, but the government's War Against Indiscipline gave them a legitimate reason. Now, they could say it was part of their duties to ensure the public behaved in an orderly fashion. They treated us like cattle. The bus terminal was like a market. If we managed to get on a bus on time, we watched the exodus in the evenings — people at bus stops, along the bridge, some with sacks on their shoulders and baskets on their heads, school children carrying books and chairs — everyone's eyes as red as the sun.

Lagos. The street on which we lived was named after a military governor. Our neighborhood smelled of burned beans and rotten *egusi* leaves. Juju and apala music, disco and reggae music jumped from windows, and fluorescent blue cylinders lit up the entire place past midnight. Ground-floor rooms were rented to businesses like tailors, notary publics, and palm wine bars; families took rooms upstairs. There were no telephone lines and we had regular power cuts. At the bottom of our walls were gutters, heavy with slime. On our walls we had pee stains over *Post No Bills* signs. Our sidewalks were blocked with broken-down cars, cement bricks, and rubbish piles as tall as trees. Street hawkers sat between them selling Coca-Cola, eggs, cigarettes, and malaria pills by kerosene lanterns. If we ventured on the street, even a bicycle could knock a person over, and we wanted to get home alive and on time. Most days, I barely saw the people I greeted along the way: "How now? Good evening. Long time." I was in a trance. My mind was fixed on the place my shoes would come off — our sitting room. Over the years, Rose and I had acquired two green garden chairs and a brown velvet sofa. In the center, we had an oval-shaped table; it was wooden like our side tables and had water stains that looked like burn marks.

She was lying on the sofa when I walked in. I told her exactly what Franka had said. She said, "That woman is very lucky I wasn't there to handle her."

She had been sleeping. As she sat up, she accidentally elbowed the photographs of herself posing in different outfits at Bar Beach. I picked them up and rearranged them on the side table. I still couldn't believe she'd lost her job; the thought alone made me nervous.

"How can he sack you like that?" I asked.

She wiped her mouth with the back of her hand. "He is a bastard and his whole life will spoil for what he did to me."

"What happened, eh?"

"No justice. No justice for people like us. You hear? Only for the wicked and the corrupt in this country. Look at Salako — everything he steals from the bank, taking money from customers, taking bribes. The same thing with that sneaky little Umar."

"Forget that foolish one. What happened between you and Salako?"

"Umar is part of it. Can't you see? Look at all

those bad debt letters you've been typing. You think the loans were ever meant to be repaid?"

"All I know is Umar is a useless manager."

"He is fraudulent! And he's trying to cover his tracks! He and his accomplice, Salako! Everyone knows! Salako opens an account for Big Man. Umar gives Big Man a loan. Big Man gives Salako and Umar a cut. The loan is never repaid, and that is just the beginning. All those dormant accounts, I know Salako is using them as his personal accounts. He's a thief, like everybody else in this godforsaken country. Read the papers every day. Our oil revenues are missing. Where are they? Under my pillow?"

I kicked my shoes off as she continued to rant. She was not telling me anything new, and we'd had the same discussion about Mr. Salako and Alhaji Umar before. Rose thought they were partners in a banking scam. I couldn't imagine how. They didn't trust each other. Alhaji Umar was a Hausa man and Mr. Salako was Yoruba. They were both Muslims, but they were typical tribalists as far as I was concerned, and I was fed up with talking about corruption anyway. People talked nonstop about corruption, and their talk changed nothing.

"Government minister steals," she carried on. "State governor steals, contractor steals. President steals. You work, work, work. Can't even afford meat to eat at lunchtime. Taking insults from one manager. I swear to God, if I ever see that man again, by the time I finish with him, he will think he's in Armageddon."

"Take it easy, my sister."

"My job for seven years. Show me one person who can type faster than me in that bank. One person whose shorthand is better…"

She held her head and rocked. Rose never cried. News came from her hometown — her cousin was dead, her aunt, her brother — she ended up drinking beer to recover. She had been drinking beer. The empty bottle was under the sofa. I didn't know how to comfort her.

After a while I asked, "What will you do now?"

"Don't worry about me," she mumbled. "I can take care of myself."

She had no savings and her rent was due.

"Have you eaten?" I asked.

"I don't want to eat."

I walked into the kitchen and found that she had helped herself to my yam pottage anyway. The lid of my pot was in the sink; my spoon was on the kerosene stove in a pool of palm oil. She had burned the bottom of my pottage while heating it. I was tempted to call her and order her to clean up.

Rose had been living in the flat when I started work at the bank. She was looking for a roommate because hers had walked out after a fight. I told her I needed a place to stay.

"Come," she said. "So long as you're not like that witch from Calabar." When I moved in, I saw why her roommate, the witch, had walked out. Rose ate and left plates on the floor. She asked to try food from my pot and cooked only once a month: pepper soup. She threw in double the peppers people normally used. Her eyes and nose would stream as she ate. She would slap her forehead like a drug addict and beg me to join her. "You have to! Oo, it's sweet, my sister! The sweetest I've ever made. This one will cure your cold, cough, burn out your germs, jealousy, temper. Try just a little."

She was an awful cook and had a sensitive stomach. After she'd finished her pepper soups, she would run to the toilet for the rest of the week and swallow all sorts of pills to settle her insides. I'd seen her argue with neighbors because she didn't like the way they looked at her. She sometimes borrowed my clothes without asking. She never paid back loans. The men she brought home; the problems they gave her. She cursed their great-grandfathers when she broke up with them and she could drink beer like a soldier, but she paid her rent on time and didn't go around telling my life history to strangers.

She was loyal. No one could say a word against me when Rose was around, and when she was in the mood to tell a story, especially when she spoke in pidgin, twisting and turning her mouth, she would make me laugh until I begged her to stop. Her stories were vulgar. Totally. She had a temper all right, but she'd never lost it with me, and I was surprised that she would at work; after all, she was used to office politics. In my department, people were subdued by Alhaji Umar. Downstairs, they were in contact with customers and were always competing for "Christmas gifts" all year long from their wealthy account holders. Rose was unpopular because she was a barrier between the staff and Mr. Salako. At the same time, she was trying to avoid Mr. Salako's advances. The stress of doing her job would have finished me.

She did not tell me why she had slapped Mr. Salako and she had not denied that she was his girlfriend either, but that was Rose, five times a girl, no explanations or apologies. She was always having her way and didn't care about consequences. She took chances without thinking, never regretted the choices she made. In that respect, she was a fearless woman and tough, unlike me.

Sanwo came to see me that weekend. He had been supervising deliveries of printed stationery to local government offices and making sure the deliveries were not stolen before they were accounted for and receipts were signed. He came directly from the domestic airport. We ate *dodo* and beans for lunch. He was exhausted and fell asleep sitting upright on the sofa. I turned the table fan toward him and watched him snore for a while. His new polka-dot tie reminded me how much he had changed from the day I met him at the College of Technology.

I was in my first year of commercial studies back then, and Sanwo had just graduated with a diploma in business administration. He'd come to the college to visit his friends who worked in the students' office. They were teasing him about the tie he was wearing. One friend said his tie was the color of an unripe lime; the other said it was the color of a sick man's tongue. The tie was truly ugly, but I couldn't understand why they were laughing so hard, and Sanwo was the loudest of the lot. He wheezed and slapped his knees, almost fell to the floor, then clutched his throat: he had choked on chewing gum. I slapped his back; he coughed it up. A week later, he came back to the campus to thank me. "You're an angel," he said.

"You'll spend your whole life saving that one," Rose said, when I told her the story.

He had such a fresh face in those days and was full of useless economic and business theories by Keynes and Galbraith, talked about boosting national exports, utilizing natural resources, diversification and feasibility studies. "Mr. Monetary and Fiscal," I called him. I was sure he would make an excellent teacher. He had enough interest in his subject, more than enough knowledge and patience. He was always giving his nephews and nieces tutorials, even when they didn't appreciate or care for them; he was not interested in applying for teaching positions because he couldn't bear the idea of being stuck in a classroom, or waiting for the government to pay him pittance in arrears, which I understood. What I couldn't understand was why he'd chosen to work for his uncle, whose main business was with the government. Now, his forehead was permanently creased from the stress of worrying about one contract or the other. He traveled too much and didn't have time to rest or cook himself meals.

What Sanwo loved was business, and he believed that business dealings should be legal and efficient. He disliked waiting for government officials to show up for meetings, or coaxing them to sign documents, sometimes having to bribe them. The practicalities of doing business Nigerian-style had caught up with him.

I let him sleep in peace and thought about how to bring up the question of our wedding without causing an argument. I had a tendency to bully him about our wedding plans and he always managed to joke his way out of giving me answers. I didn't want our conversation to end up that way, so I waited patiently as any sensible woman would.

The moment came after he had woken up, after I'd told him all that had happened to Rose. As I had expected, he didn't have much sympathy for her. He went on and on about how unprofessionally she had behaved and how there was no justification for her actions. "It's enough," I kept saying to make him stop; he was distracting me and I was preparing for the long speech I'd memorized. Sometimes, Sanwo nagged like a woman.

Toward the evening, I reminded him that he had to leave before the traffic from the mainland became congested. For once, I was eager to see him off and that should have alerted him, but he was still too tired to notice. We walked to the gates of the block of flats where I lived. I thought it was the perfect place to give him the ultimatum. Neighbors and passersby were walking the street, talking, laughing, and buying food from street hawkers before sunset. Sanwo wouldn't argue with me knowing that they would probably stop to watch us. He leaned against the column by the gates and crossed his arms.

"Who cut your hair?" I asked.

"My barber," he said.

I preferred his previous haircut. This one was too square-shaped for his head.

"He must not like you," I said.

He yawned and patted his crown. "Is it that bad?"

"Listen," I said, switching to Yoruba: there was a seriousness I could never achieve in English. "This wedding of ours."

"Yes?"

"You asked me to give you time. That was two years ago. I don't understand. My family is not greedy or hungry. My mother will not ask for much. I've told you one way we can raise money for my dowry and you have refused. I don't want to be one of those women who..."

"Who?" he interrupted.

I lifted my hand. "Just listen. I don't want to be one of those women who ends up old and dry because a man disappointed her, you hear me?"

He frowned. "What brought this on?"

"I'm just telling you. My eyes are watching you from now on, and the way I see it, time is running out."

"Running out how?"

"I'm young. I don't have to commit myself. I may not have a lot of money, but money certainly doesn't rule my life."

"What are you talking about?"

He was transforming already, and I could hear it in his voice. He was the same man who had bought me more necklaces and bangles than I could wear, ironed my work clothes if I asked, and nursed me through bouts of malaria, but the moment he heard the word "marriage," he was on defense; I was the enemy. How could the word alone bring on such a reaction in him? And what would I do then? Remain his girlfriend forever?

"You're acting strange again," I said.

"You're the one acting strange," he said.

At least he'd noticed, and I was ready to bargain. "Set a wedding date and everything will be back to normal."

"What, you're blaming me for the delay?"

"I'm asking when, that's all."

"But you talk as if you don't know who we are and how much we earn. Where will we live?"

"Together. Like every married couple."

"But you can't move into my uncle's quarters and we can't afford to rent."

"I'm renting now."

"Do you know how much it costs to live in this city?"

He was trying to provoke me. I stayed calm.

"What difference will marriage make? We will manage as I am managing now."

"How?"

"Cut down on unnecessary family charity, for one."

He wasn't generous with me alone; whenever he made a profit, he gave too much money to his sisters who had marital problems. They called him until he sent them "a little something" and then they were quiet again. They had heard we were planning to get married. "What does she do?" was the first question they asked. "Hope she works," was the one wish they had for me. Sanwo also gave his parents a monthly allowance, and they were thankful because they got nothing from their daughters but complaints.

"What brought this on today?" he asked again.

"I don't want to be one of those jilted women."

"Who's jilting whom?"

"I'm serious."

He smiled. "I mean, can't a man rest? Every time I come here it's marriage, marriage, marriage."

"What!"

"Why are you so desperate?"

I poked his shoulder. "Who asked me to marry him? Who harassed me? All I want to know is when, and instead you give me stories. I'm ready to move out of this place, that's all I'm saying. Rose can bring a killer home and not know the difference. I'm fed up with living here. My reasons for marriage are practical, not like yours, love and romance."

I said that to spite him, and also because I didn't want to appear desperate. He wheezed and slapped his knees. Sanwo's laugh had not changed over the years. He still sounded like a man of about a hundred years and it was hard to keep a straight face, but I did.

"Rose agrees with me," I said. "She thinks I should give you six months maximum."

He stopped laughing. "That one? She's just jealous."

"Of what?"

"She can't keep a man. All those funny-funny fellows she ends up with. She sees you in a steady relationship and she can't take it. She's always been jealous. She wished us bad from the start."

"And your uncle, this man who hasn't helped you? He hands you small money here and there and sends you around on errands. Whenever he travels to England and America, he goes first class. Whenever he needs to take a trip within Nigeria, he calls you. Why?"

He shrugged. "Ask him."

"I'll tell you why. Because he's scared the planes will crash."

"Who isn't?"

"Is that someone who wishes you well?"

"Please, leave the man out of this."

"Think! He wants to keep you as his messenger boy and you're so grateful you can't even see. If he really cared about you, he would like you to be independent. He would make sure you had enough to start a business of your own."

"It's his wife."

"Oh, yes, his wife, the corrupt woman."

She was one of those Lagos socialites who had eventually married his uncle. Sanwo believed she didn't want anyone to share the man's wealth and whenever his uncle refused to back his business propositions, he blamed her.

"She is corrupt," he insisted. "She's still sleeping around. She's very lucky I don't tell him. You would think she would be grateful. Instead she's become an enemy of progress."

I held my head. "Sanwo Odunsi, the only son of your father."

When would he ever stop setting high standards of morality? Standards I wasn't even sure I could keep up with.

"It's true," he said. "As for that Rose, she should worry about her own life, not ours. She deserves to be sacked without severance for what she did. I knew she was behind your change in attitude. I just knew."

His main grudge with Rose was that she had introduced me to Ladies Night at Phaze Two Disco. He would never admit that, but he was scowling at our balcony as if she was standing there. Only her laundry was in sight. She had left home in the morning to visit her sister Violet, the one person in the whole wide world who could lend her money for rent. I didn't offer. I knew I would not get my money back.

"She's giving you advice," Sanwo said, "yet she can't even manage her own life. Let's see how long it takes her to find another job. Maybe then she'll realize she needs to hold on to her source of income like everyone else in Lagos. Even my uncle's wife knows which side her bread is buttered."

I eyed him. "It's time you moved out of their quarters. You should be grateful that she has tolerated you living there for so long."

"She's not tolerating me. We are tolerating her — we, the Odunsi family — and the day my uncle is fed up with her, she will be out with those bony buttocks of hers, and no one will beg for her."

It was no use. He was trying to change the subject or at least turn it into a joke.

"I'm not here to discuss that woman," I said.

"So what are you here to discuss?"

"You know."

"Aren't discussions supposed to be two-way? You've said your speech. Can't I say mine, eh?"

He pulled my ear until I smiled. I couldn't help that whenever I was irritated. My cold act was making me tired anyway.

"Talk then," I said.

"Good," he said. "I know you're frustrated. I know. But I am an honest man. I have nothing but kindness in my heart. I may tease you, but that doesn't mean I'm not serious. I want to provide the best for you. I will provide the best for my wife and the mother of my children. Nothing can stand in our way."

"I want facts, not stories."

"I've been working on a deal."

I turned away. "No more business deals."

"*Haba*, let me finish. This one is different."

"Different like the shea butter?"

He waved his arms around. "There is a market for shea butter overseas! It's a question of bringing the product to the buyer!"

Sanwo was still sensitive about his first business venture, a shea butter export business that had never taken off. He'd gathered the women in his hometown and told them he would act as their agent. They would be rich. Women abroad were begging for shea butter for their hair and faces.

I continued to taunt him. "You are lucky the women didn't mob you. Very lucky they didn't tear you to pieces after raising their hopes so high."

"All I needed was an investor."

"Your uncle, don't tell me."

"It was that woman. She said my idea was nonsense. It was the best proposition I ever had. That's the problem with this country. You have a good idea and you can't get the financial backing."

"What is this new business deal?" I asked, lowering my voice.

"Never mind."

"Tell me."

"No. I'm not saying a word. That's another problem over here. People are always ready to give you reasons why your business will fail. No one ever wants to give support or encouragement. All you need to know is that it's risk-free."

I patted his shoulder. He was clever though

unrealistic. Over the years, his business ideas had come and gone. The problem of how to raise money was still there and I didn't know why it wasn't clear to him that I was supportive. In the end, he should have been a teacher. He wasn't ruthless enough to be a Lagos hustler and was too fair to cheat. He had the right qualities in a man, but he was definitely in the wrong line of work.

"If your uncle really cares," I said, "he will provide the money for your business. If he doesn't this time, don't come back here without a proper job."

"I'm not an office man."

"Is it my nature to be in an office?"

"I'm an entrepreneur. I can't sit behind a desk pushing paper."

"Call yourself what you like. Just find yourself a job."

He frowned. "You. You always want to behave like somebody's mother."

"Yes," I said. "Because I'm surrounded by people who behave like children. You and Rose." I pointed at her laundry on the balcony. "You don't face reality. I have to. It's me looking after my mother. Me alone sending her money. No father, rich uncle, sisters with their one million problems."

I was practical in that way. My responsibility was to take care of my mother and myself after she was widowed. I came to Lagos to get an education and to earn a living. If I acted like Sanwo's mother, it was only because I was tired of having the same argument with him.

The seamstress across the street waved. She was sitting on a wooden stool on her veranda. I could tell she had taken her evening bath. Her neck and chest were white with talcum powder. I waved back, feeling embarrassed. I was sure everyone on our street had heard us.

"Why can't we just go to a registry?" I asked.

"I can't," Sanwo said. "You know I can't."

"You must be the only man on earth who wants a church ceremony."

"I'm the only son in my family."

"You please them too much."

"How?"

"Your sisters especially. You're always catering to their needs."

"Who else will if I don't?"

"Maybe you should marry them."

He shook his head. "You this woman, I'm in trouble with you today. I come here to relax and all you give me is a headache."

This time, I laughed. He looked like a trapped bush rat, especially with his new haircut. Perhaps I'd gone too far. Face-to-face he seemed incapable of letting me down, and he had family pressures I didn't have. Everyone expected him to be their benefactor because he was close to their one rich relation. They took advantage of Sanwo because he found it difficult to say no. He never complained, and the truth was that I felt guilty about adding to his stress. Our argument seemed ridiculous now, unnecessary. He placed his hand over his chest like the man I trusted.

"Give me time," he said. "That's all I ask. I will not disappoint you. I am not a bastard."

We walked to the end of the street holding hands, and I was still not sure he was being sincere.

I hated my job at Federal Community Bank, couldn't stand my daily commute. Sometimes, on the bus, I imagined my hometown Makoku as it was when my mother was a girl, with yam and cassava farms, streams where children bathed, and rocks over which women beat their wrappers clean. Men fished where the riverbed dipped, and all around were bushes and plants, most of which were unnamed, but people knew which leaf was bitter, which leaf looked like chicken feet, which leaf held poison, and which leaf, if brewed with peppery tree bark, could break a fever.

My grandmother cooked vegetable soups over firewood. The fire was their light at night; the smoke was the smell of the compound, a small clearing of six homes. Those who lived there belonged to the same family: aunts, uncles, cousins. They were my mother's people. Women traded and elders watched over children, so children were not afraid and had to keep out of mischief. At dawn they woke up and swept the grounds. They made half-moon patterns in the soil with palm fronds and at night, they listened to stories. They began and ended the stories with a greeting.

Alo o
Alo

That was the Makoku of my mother's childhood. My own Makoku, the one I grew up in, was more modern. The path of red dust was now a wide tarred road — Market Road. I walked it with my friends as a girl. We kept to the sides to avoid lorries. We did not go as far as the farming settlements. Too big for staying at home and too cool to eat local snacks like *kulikuli* and *gurudi*, we knew just where to find foreign foods in town and laugh at grownups behind their backs. Good Health Chemist stocked provisions we couldn't find in the marketplace, like lemon and honey throat lozenges and powdered milk. Niger Hotel sold Coca-Cola. The Mobil station had a hot curried meat pie. National Electric Power Authority had opened a branch nearby. Mr. Kolawole who worked there spat as he spoke: "Good day to you!" "Happy night rest!" always keeping an eye on someone. English was his downfall, my mother said. My friends and I called him "Mr. Never Expect Power Always."

Those of us who attended Baptist Missionary School were not interested in becoming farmers or traders like our parents. We had all learned the words of our morning chorus:

Education alone
Without a cutlass or hoe
Isn't good enough
Farming is the work of our land
He who doesn't work will steal

We sang the words without understanding. Each time I returned to Makoku, I noticed that the towns-people were providing more and more services: car repairs, tailoring, photocopying, and hairdressing. The farming settlements my mother grew up in were shrinking. Loggers had chopped down half the trees in the surrounding forests. What would the townspeople eventually eat? I thought. Car spare parts? Watches? Videos, clothes, shoes, bags, and children's toys from Taiwan?

There were more goods traders than food traders in the marketplace. I stopped recognizing faces whenever I visited Makoku, and it seemed to me that as people like me left their hometowns for Lagos, so Lagosians came to neighboring towns like mine, to avoid the crowds. I heard their voices calling out: "Original Ro-less watch! Pee-geot car sparks!" Not until I got down from the stop at Mount Olive Maternity and took the road up the hill did I ever hear familiar voices calling out to me: "City girl. You are back? How long are you staying this time?" "Ah, it's Tolani Ajao, the drummer's daughter. Welcome home."

My father was a drummer in Makoku. His father was and so on. He had visited Lagos many times and other cities especially in the Southwest and performed at music festivals: Ife, of the bronze and terra-cotta masks; Oshogbo, of the shrines of the Yoruba gods; Oyo, of the carved calabashes; Ogbomosho, where missionaries had founded a settlement for lepers. He told me stories about his tours. He didn't like Lagos because Lagosians were warped, he said. They threw money at juju bands, danced until the sun came up and went straight back to work for more money.

My father was always reluctant to travel to Lagos, but one of the band members would come to our house in Makoku to persuade him: Uncle Festus, "Mr. Conga-Bongo-Samba Drums," or Adeoye, with his tambourines, or Uncle Segs, who shook the shekere like no other. Sometimes Tunde Twinkle, the maestro juju bandleader himself, came to our house. He said my father was one man who understood the language of the talking drum and no one else could play that instrument for his band. But Tunde Twinkle was a businessman before an artist. During the seventies, he began to bring in new instruments like drum sets and electric guitars, to compete with the newer juju bands. He expanded his band to become an orchestra, brought in younger men who knew how to play these instruments. My father could no longer be persuaded to go on tour with the band. He did not recognize the music they were playing.

Tunde Twinkle became a big star in Lagos, signed record deals and made millions of naira. Fatai Rolling Dollar, Ayinde Barrister, Emperor Pick Peters, King Sunny Ade, Admiral Dele Abiodun, he was as popular as any of these musicians. His band members shared in his wealth. My father, meanwhile, stayed in Makoku, getting rid of the money he had earned with the band. Anyone who visited our house left with a small gift like yams, palm wine, kola nuts, something for the children, or something for the wife — that always annoyed my mother.

There was once I thought my father was the most generous man in the world; then I saw how my mother struggled after he died and I wondered. He was killed on his way to Lagos. He was going for a band reunion. Tunde Twinkle had asked him to come urgently. The truth was that he had heard that my father was broke again. The taxi my father was in skidded off the road and rolled into a ditch. It was a few days before they found his body. I was eighteen and ready to follow him to his grave rather than come to terms with my loss. I could not believe I would not see him for the rest of my life. Then, to have his memory tarnished by some foolish family rumor that I was not his child. Of course I dismissed what I'd overheard. Of course I wanted to trust my mother. I couldn't accept she was keeping such a secret from me or capable of betraying him in that way. After all, they'd known each other from childhood. That long. She'd told me herself. Her first recollection of him was that he had dust in his hair, bruised legs, and red mud on his feet.

His shorts fell below his waist and the way his stomach protruded, I was sure he suffered from worms. We were just ten years old. He was standing at the entrance of his family compound, pounding a tin can he used for a drum. He'd been sick with measles and his family had taken him to the baba-lawo and now that he was well again, he bragged about his spiritual powers.

"*What's that foolish thing?*" *he asked, as I hurried past.*

I was carrying a wooden doll on my back. I treated it like a real child in those days. From a distance I called out, "Heathen!"

He said, "Me, a heathen? Wait until I get my hands on you."

I ran from him. His family were Shango worshippers and mine were Christian converts, so he was like dirt to me.

I headed straight for my aunt's compound. In those days, the main street in Makoku was a path that had red dust in the dry season and mud in the rainy season. On either side were bushes above which palm trees grew. Palm wine tappers climbed to the top of the trees and I sometimes watched them, trying to imagine the beginning and end of our town. There was the diocese on the hill, the palace near the marketplace, the cemetery by my aunt's compound, the farm settlement where my family lived, forests and streams.

My wrapper was slipping off as I ran. I could hear your father's voice getting louder, "My father is the son of a drummer. The son of a drummer, who was the son of a drummer and so on before the oyinbos *came here and handed you Bibles. Who is a heathen? Wait till I get my hands on you…"*

I rounded the bend and my doll dropped from my back.

"My future has been decided for me," he said, "by our forefathers, not by any Christians. I know what I'm going to be when I become a man, a drummer like my

father, and I will have a girl like you..."

I stopped to pick my doll up and he ran into me. We both fell on the path. At first the pain shocked me. I couldn't breathe, but somehow, I stood up, tightened my wrapper and faced him. I began to hit him over his head. "You fell me down! You fell me down!"

"I'll marry you," he cried out. "Yes, I will. And you will cook for me all day long. Yes, yams, since that is what your father grows."

I kicked his legs. "Don't ever mention my father's name."

"I know your name. It's Arike."

"Heathen."

I fought back so hard, as if I was defending Christ's honor. He was hopping around, using one hand to shield his head and the other to shield his legs. "I'll marry you whether or not you like," he said, gasping for breath, "and at night I'll lie on top of you and do what men do to women..."

I ran all the way home. I couldn't believe what I'd heard. My family asked why I was crying and I told them I'd come across an evil spirit. It was nighttime when I remembered my doll outside.

Next morning, I went to look for my doll and it was gone. I never forgave your father for that and I beat him up that day because I thought the worst thing for a woman was to be married. Yes, I knew I would be one day. All girls did. You reached a certain age and you were married off. Your family arranged that. They received your dowry: cloth, yams, palm oil, goats, or whatever your husband's family could afford, to show his appreciation for your upbringing. It was a token, nothing more. You moved into his home, had children, and took care of them.

But I'd heard my own mother complaining how she had seven mouths to feed; how, if I hadn't been born a girl to save her, she would have lived a terrible life cooking on her own. And I'd seen my aunt, Iya Alaro, as everyone called her. She was a master adire *dyer. She had pretty facial marks on her cheeks and tattoos on her arms. She was a widow and had no children, so she practically adopted me as her daughter. She headed a co-op of cloth dyers who worked in her compound. During the day, I watched as the women painted patterns on cloth using chicken feathers. There were no stencils or imported dyes to work with in those days, no candle or beeswax, and each pattern was painted on separately. The women used a cassava starch mixture on the bales of white cloth and dipped the cloth into the vats of indigo.*

Three yards of cloth could take four days to dye and when shoppers came to buy finished cloth, money passed without the women raising their heads from their work.

My aunt, Iya Alaro, was my mentor. She trained me to be a cloth dyer. She taught me the secrets I was not supposed to know at such a young age. My left hand barely touched my right ear and I knew which elu leaves to pluck, how to sieve the pulp through cocoa ash, stir the indigo juice, taste, feel, until the dye was ready for use. The one thing my small hands could not do was to keep still while painting, so I was only allowed to watch. I liked the smell of the indigo in the vats, the patterns the women painted: rings, stars, petals, cowry shells, pestles. I especially enjoyed their gossip, which they tried to disguise as proverbs: "Point one finger at me, you're pointing three at yourself." "That's right." "If you keep calling your calabash useless, why won't everyone else?" "Of course they will." "Continue digging holes for others and one day you will eventually fall in." "True, true."

I could almost always guess whom they were talking about. It was not that difficult. Not many people lived in Makoku, not many could escape the women's eyes once they raised their heads from their work, and they were watching like domestic vigilantes. For instance, if a child looked unkempt or unfed, they would arrange a family meeting to discuss the custody of the child, or if a man beat his wife, a silent mob would blindfold him at night, drag him into the bush and give him the beating of his life. The very next day, if he lifted his hand to his wife, the same thing happened, over and over again. Even the most foolish man would eventually begin to make the connection.

Women were not allowed to form secret societies as men did, but my aunt did as she pleased. People were afraid of her. They said she was a reincarnation of a witch who had long ago terrorized our town. The witch had no husband or children to speak of and was driven away to the forest. They claimed she'd brought bad luck, caused illness, and destroyed crops. Utter nonsense. They also said my aunt had offended the witch's spirit by converting to Christianity, so the witch punished my aunt by killing off her husband and unborn children, but if my aunt was angry enough, she could summon the witch's destructive powers.

The rumors made no sense whatsoever, but my aunt used her so-called powers. She protected women and children in our town with the help of the women of her co-op. Strong men, heads of compounds and elders even, hurried past her compound for fear of being targeted. So while the ruler of Makoku, our great, most revered Oba and his court were busy raising taxes and squandering them, passing edicts and banning women and children from festivals, threatening even the smallest baby with a barren womb if her mother dared to break a taboo; and while people thought the royal court had all the power in our town, elders and men in that order, it was the women of my aunt's co-op who were busy policing quietly and silently. I saw that and thought I would be exactly the sort of woman my aunt was when I grew up. I told her, "I want to be a widow, just like you."

You can imagine. I had no idea that would be my fate.

On Monday morning a man had a seizure at the bus stop. He fell to the ground, a crowd formed around him. I joined them to watch. The man's eyes rolled back and his teeth were clenched. People who didn't know better began to cry out, "It's the devil! The devil has got him!" Those who knew what was going on said, "It's *warapa*."

"Epileptic feasts," the man next to me explained. "Where is a spoon?"

A spoon, a spoon, everyone was searching for — to slip into the mouth of the convulsing man. No one had the courage to touch him. As soon as our bus "Who Knows Tomorrow?" arrived, we dispersed and began to scramble. The bus driver, angry that we had been preoccupied with some other event, drove off fast to teach us a lesson. I sprinted down the street, nudged one skinny man out of my way. My shins were scratched by the time I hopped on that bus.

I got to work on time though and Mr. Salako seemed to be celebrating. He was laughing louder than normal, slapping men on their backs. Perhaps he expected the usual begging scene. Whenever someone was sacked, their relations came to see him. They knelt, cried, and hung around the banking hall until they were driven away by the security guards. No relations came for Rose, and people at work were no longer talking about her, as if she had never existed, or as if she had died. I continued to type my bad debt letters, taking a break mid-morning when Alhaji Umar called me into his office.

"Yes, sir?" I said.

Alhaji Umar was a small man who looked taller than he really was because his body was so narrow. He wore glasses and never seemed to see beyond the frames. A man from the North, his accent always sounded foreign to me.

"Mr. Salako," he said, "has requested zat you be trans-a-ferred downstairs to work for him."

I was certain I had not heard him right. Apart from his stutter and accent, his voice tended to trail into a whisper.

"Sir?" I asked.

"Mr. Salako," he said, "has requested zat you be trans-a-ferred downstairs imme-e-diately."

That was Alhaji Umar's way; even when he was punishing an employee, he would repeat himself without raising his voice. I imagined myself grabbing his narrow shoulders and shaking his voice louder.

"Sir," I said. "Why?"

He adjusted his glasses. "He has terminated his secretary Rose Adamson, as you know."

"Yes?"

"He wants someone from within za bank to replace her. I have told him you will be avail-a-able from tomorrow. I want you to clean out your desk today and report to him downstairs."

"B-but I am typing letters."

"Letter-ers? What letter-ers?"

I could tell from his expression he couldn't remember he had given me the assignment. I was a little confused myself, and now I imagined Salako downstairs and his plump fingers tickling my palms.

"Bad debts," I said. "I have several left. Please, sir, I like it here in Loans."

Alhaji Umar nodded. I thought he might be showing sympathy.

"Mr. Salako," he said. "Has requested zat you be trans-a-ferred."

Rose once told me that Hausa people, you could not trust them, most especially when they smiled. The minute you turned your back, they were ready with daggers. To people who were of no benefit to them, they did not bother to smile; their faces were like walls. They could be plotting your death meanwhile, she said, even their pretty women who pretended to be innocent in purdah, and their men were all secretly homosexuals. "I'm not a tribalist," I had told Rose then. She had also said I was the only Yoruba she would consider living with because Yorubas were cowardly and sycophantic by nature. We put on the finest clothes, yet our homes were always filthy.

I cleaned out my desk and said goodbye to my colleagues in Loans. I felt as if I was being trans-ferred to a war zone. Downstairs, I looked out for my twelve o'clock lunch mates. Ignatius gave me a signal, opening his palms. I wanted to speak to him and listen to his usual counseling, but Franka was hovering around his desk, keeping an eye on the line of customers in the banking hall and at the same time watching my movements. I wouldn't survive a second around office gossips like Franka.

Mr. Salako answered after my first knock.

"Yes, yes," he said. "Miss Ajao? Alhaji Umar already briefed you? I had, eh, a meeting with him regarding your new position, on the morning that Miss eh, eh, what's her name again?" He scratched his head.

"Rose," I said. "Adamson."

Mr. Salako's face was easy to read. He flaunted the fact that he was acting, as if he was trying to test people's intelligence. I smelled boiled eggs in his office, but I could not be sure.

He bared his small, pointed teeth. "Her name is funny isn't it? Rose Adamson. It's typical of those Rivers people. They have one silly foreign name or the other. Have you ever been there? The whole place is full of the descendants of *oyinbo* sailors."

"Rose is not one," I said.

"I'm aware of that," he said.

"And I'm not a tribalist," I added.

He cleared his throat. "We are of different ethnicities, Miss Ajao, not tribes, and I hope you're not implying that a harmless jest is in any way prejudicial. Animosity between Nigerians ended with the Civil War."

People said Mr. Salako was scatterbrained. I thought it was part of his act to appear that way in order to avoid his duties. It was there in his good English; Mr. Salako could suddenly become alert if he needed to.

"Your father was with Tunde Twinkle's band?" he asked.

"Yes," I said.

"A renowned drummer or something."

"Yes."

"Rose told me. She told me a lot about you."

I did not believe him.

"You are from where?" he asked.

"Makoku Town," I said.

He pushed his lips forward as if he couldn't pronounce the name. "Ku? Ku?"

"Ma-ko-ku," I said.

"Ah, the interior. I thought so."

Even if it were the heart of the bush, who was this downtown Lagos man to look down on me?

"It's not far from Lagos," I said in Yoruba. "We are Egba, not interior people."

"At least," he said, "you are Yoruba, and your appearance is always neat. I appreciate that in a...eh, a secretary. How is your diction by the way?"

"My diction?"

"Yes, your English. I want to know how you speak and write it. Whatever one might say about Miss Adamson, her diction and grammar were excellent."

Who cared? Was English my mother tongue? I stepped forward. "My diction is fine. What about my job, sir?"

"Yes, yes," he said. "I want you to eh, I want you to eh, I want you to clean out Miss Adamson's desk. Yes. Clean it out. I checked myself and found all sorts of horrors. I did not touch any of it because I'm not sure about the juju from Port Harcourt."

"Juju?"

"Yes. I don't want anyone jazzing me up. Since she's your friend, you are safe. I want you to clean

52

the place out. Fumigate it if necessary."

His phone rang. Mr. Salako raised a finger to silence me. I smoothed my skirt down as he answered the call and noticed his gaze followed my hand movements. He was scared of juju, this man with his good English? He was scared of being jazzed up?

"Hello?" he shouted.

Another thing Mr. Salako did, Rose said, was shout on the phone. Despite his education, he was a bushman. He stood up. "Chief? Yes, of course! This is Salako, sir!"

I looked downward to hide my smile, which, again, came from irritation.

"Yes, sir," he said. "An unfortunate incident. Miss Adamson left us. Yes, yes, I'm answering my own phone now. Government austerity measures. It catches up with us all eventually. No, no, sir. We are well. The family is well..."

He was ducking, as if the caller was standing before him. The caller was definitely a director or a Big Man, the kind who walked through the banking hall in white lace robes with an entourage of managers ducking as Mr. Salako was. They never joined the customer lines full of poor people. They were ushered straight into cool air-conditioned offices and offered cups of hot tea.

"How can I be of service?" Mr. Salako said even louder, with a big smile on his face and signaled for me to leave his office.

Outside, I found Rose's desk drawer full of notepads, a toilet roll, a Vicks inhaler, Tiger Balm, sachets of pain relievers, a packet of peppery sausage roll, a leaking Bic biro, groundnuts wrapped in newspaper. I found what Mr. Salako thought was juju from Port Harcourt, a dried-up chicken bone, and threw it in her dustbin.

Rose. I was furious after cleaning up her mess at home and at work. She was back from her sister Violet's house. Violet had given her lunch and she had developed stomach cramps.

"She's trying to poison me," Rose said. "And she didn't even give me any money."

To cure her stomachache, she'd swallowed aspirins, dewormer, laxative, malaria pills, and half a bottle of children's cough syrup.

In Rose's family, there was Violet, the eldest daughter. She was dark and beautiful like their mother, with a mouth just as sharp. Rose said she'd worked as a prostitute in Rome. Now, she was back in Lagos, running a hair salon. Violet's father had disappeared during the Civil War. He was also father to Lucky and Hope, the first and second sons in their family. After Violet came another daughter, Christie, whose father was a Scottish sailor. Christie fled to England as soon as she was able. Rose was the third daughter. Her father was Mr. Adamson, a local headmaster who was married to some other woman. They called him "Daddy Adamson." Rose's mother they called "Sisi." Sisi's last child she nicknamed "Somebody." Somebody suffered complications when he was born. Lucky took care of him after Hope died.

Rose spoke well of her family, except of Violet who lived in Lagos. They argued a lot because Violet was always trying to provoke Rose. One day on our balcony, I witnessed their worst fight and feared Rose might push Violet off. Sisi had been sick and Violet said she would not contribute a kobo toward the cost of buying Sisi's medications. In fact, she swore that she would only ever contribute toward Sisi's casket.

"Sisi disowned me," Violet said. "She should have thought of her old age beforehand."

Rose forgot about her sister's seniority. "You're rotten," she said to Violet. "Rotten to the core. You would do anything for money and you're selfish. If Sisi were bleeding to death you would walk straight past her. Sisi said it. She said it."

"Ugly face," Violet said. "Ugly like Daddy Adamson. Look at your face like a horse."

Violet galloped, horsey-horsey style, from one side of the balcony to the other and galloped back again. Rose grabbed her neck and tried to strangle her. Violet freed herself from Rose, then threw herself back at Rose and demanded to be killed. A week later, they were together in Simpatico hair salon, because really, they had no other blood relations in Lagos.

I could not understand Rose's relationship with Violet or their relationship with their mother, Sisi. Sisi taught her daughters how to attract men even before their bodies developed. She sent her sons to beg their father's relations for money as soon as they were able to walk. Somebody was Lucky's child, she told everyone. They all talked far too much in their family and the difference between theirs and mine was that they were useless at keeping family secrets.

On my way home from work I kept shifting away from the woman who was seated next to me. She was sweating on my sleeve. The more I moved, the more she pressed against me so I had to keep still. She was as hot as if she had malaria and I resented her. Lagosians had ways of making other people share their suffering. I cared only about the scratches on my shins. I'd even forgotten about Rose and her job until I arrived home and saw her lying on the sofa in our sitting room.

Her skirt was halfway up her thighs. A bottle of beer was on the side table, almost empty. Our sitting room smelled of her sleep and the television was loud. I woke her up gently.

"What!" she exclaimed, when I told her about my new position.

"I can't believe it either," I said.

She sat up. "What do you know about my job? You don't even have direct customer experience."

I was surprised by her tone. "It's not my fault Salako wants me there."

"But you're not used to dealing with custo-mers," she said. "You don't know what my job entails."

"Nothing," I said, shaking my head. "There is nothing in that bank that entails anything. Today, all I did was clean desks. The work I was doing last week, Alhaji Umar didn't even know I was doing it. What can the job entail? You see the customer, you say hello, they say hello. Finish."

"You have to make them feel welcome, when they phone, when they come in. You have to make them feel good. It's what I did."

I pushed my shoes into the corner. She was angry, of course.

"I don't want to work for Salako," I said.

"Tell him then."

"How?" I asked.

"The same way you told Umar."

"Did Umar listen to me?"

She began to talk to herself: "He's doing this to pepper me. He knows we live together. He wants me to go back to him and I'll never go back..."

Perhaps she was involved with Mr. Salako after all, I thought, as she continued to talk about him as if he were her ex-lover rather than her ex-boss. I crossed the room in anger and remembered the dried-up chicken bone in her desk. Then I felt bad for her. Truly. She had no job, no savings or relations to depend on. There was a month's difference between her and a beggar.

"Rose," I said. "Is Salako that scared of juju?"

"More than an illiterate."

"The smell in his office. What is it?"

57

She shrugged. "He spoils the air. You'll have to get used to it."

She turned to watch the television, and I, too, watched in resignation. There was a government advert we normally recited together, because it came on so often, like the War Against Indiscipline adverts. In this advert, Andrew, a Nigerian who just arrived from the United States, complained about life in Nigeria. "No water, no light," he said. "I'm checking out." The voice-over followed like a fed up father, "ANDREW. Nigeria is OUR country. Let us STAY and salvage it TOGETHER."

A jingle ended the advert, "Save Nigeria today..."

"Andrew" had become the national nickname for Nigerians who lived overseas. They were not good citizens like those of us who stayed and suffered.

Our flat was number three. The flat next to ours, number four, was occupied by the Durojaiye family, a mother and her three young sons. What had happened to their father, I did not know, but I hoped he hadn't abandoned them.

Mrs. Durojaiye was a midwife at a teaching hospital in Lagos. Every morning I saw her getting into her old Peugeot. She was always in her starched white uniform and her hair was neatly sectioned and threaded. She was immaculate, the one tenant in our block with a car, even though it had broken reverse lights. She must have bought it when times were good.

Mrs. Durojaiye never greeted Rose, and Rose never greeted Mrs. Durojaiye. I greeted Mrs. Durojaiye, because I knew something must have happened to make Mrs. Durojaiye as she was. She walked with her back stiff, never smiled, and her mouth was permanently turned downward. She was short and carried her weight behind. Her arms were thick and muscular. Sometimes, from our flat we could hear her beating her sons. "Please, Mummy!" they would be crying out. "We're sorry, Mummy! We'll never do it again!" We could also hear their footsteps running from her switch — never a sound from Mrs. Durojaiye herself.

When I first moved in, I introduced myself to her and she glared at the door of Rose's flat and said, "Hope the situation next door improves."

"What situation?" Rose asked, when I repeated the comment to her. "That frustrated old fowl. I'm going to her place to find out what situation she means. She's been looking for my trouble since I came here, and today, today, she'll see my red eyes."

I tried to stop her. We struggled by the door and collapsed over each other. From then on, I wouldn't tell Rose a word Mrs. Durojaiye said.

Then Sanwo started visiting. I was always embarrassed whenever Mrs. Durojaiye saw him, the way she looked at him, judging his appearance. Sanwo's sense of style had improved from his college days, but he was still color-blind and could wear a red shirt and green trousers and walk around confidently. Mrs. Durojaiye never greeted him and I would nudge him to greet her, because Yoruba people loved respect more than fine clothes. Mrs. Durojaiye eventually accepted Sanwo because he greeted her the proper way, bowing with one hand behind his back and pointing his forefinger to the ground. Still, Mrs. Durojaiye would not smile at him.

Then he began to stay overnight. I would have to check that the corridor was clear before he came out. Sanwo would stand behind the door and I would stand in front. I would knock on the door to tell him when he was free to come out. Sanwo would hurry down the stairs and I would follow. Once, Mrs. Durojaiye appeared at the same time Sanwo was hurrying down the stairs. I caught up with him after she had driven off to work and asked him, "What did she say? How did she look?" I was holding his collar so tight I almost cut off his air supply.

I never cared to show off Sanwo in front of Mrs. Durojaiye. I began to because I decided that what God had seen, Mrs. Durojaiye would have to get used to. Yes, I was committing fornication. She was like a Sister Superior really, and the only neighbor I became close to eventually. The other tenants avoided us after Rose and Violet fought on the balcony.

I went downstairs that night to empty our dustbin. Rose had gone to bed early. She was drinking more than usual and beer made her drowsy. We had had a power cut at the time we expected one. The street was dark and within our compound were battery and kerosene lanterns, visible in several windows. My flashlight was switched off. Mrs. Durojaiye was driving in as I emptied the dustbin in the dump near our gates. For a moment, the headlights of her Peugeot blinded me. I waited as she parked.

"Ah, Tolani, it's you?" she said.

"You're late today, ma," I said.

She slipped her car keys into her handbag. We always spoke in Yoruba, Mrs. Durojaiye and I. If I didn't, she would be offended: English was not polite enough. I noticed her hair was disheveled. Normally, her threads were tighter. Tonight, her bases were puffy and one end was loose. It made her look kinder.

"I've been at a union meeting," she said.

"Hope all is well."

"No. We've decided to go on strike in support of the doctors."

"Ha," I said, clapping my hands in sympathy.

"Yes," she said. "Again. The last time we did this, the government threatened to stop paying our salaries. This time they say they will arrest us."

"Arrest?"

"They are just boasting, you know these army men. They think because they are military they can command us and we will obey, but they cannot intimidate us, not this time. We stand with the doctors."

Her voice trembled. Mrs. Durojaiye sounded much younger and more nervous than she actually was.

"They will have to consider your pay demands," I said.

"Let them pay us regularly first," she said. "That's what we need. Don't delay our salaries, and improve our working conditions. They tell us that patients will die if we go on strike. We say they are dying, anyway, no beds, this and that. The government says it's our fault. We are not managing our facilities and supplies well. Can you imagine that?"

I couldn't imagine going to the hospital she worked in. If I were dying, I would rather die at home. Patients had to buy their own medications, IV drips, and bandages. There were never enough beds and during operations they had power cuts. Patients died from a lack of simple oxygen. They had to pay deposits before they were admitted and they were given oily meals and slept on dirty bedsheets. To top it all, the nurses were rude. The hospital was, of course, not private but government-funded. One of our very best.

As we walked toward the block, Mrs. Durojaiye lifted her chin in the direction of our balcony. "Your friend upstairs, I saw her walking around yesterday afternoon. She's on leave or something?"

Mrs. Durojaiye never called Rose by her name. It was her way of showing she didn't approve of her.

"She lost her job."

Rose would be angry I told Mrs. Durojaiye, but Mrs. Durojaiye would find out anyway and come back to ask why I hadn't told her the truth. I couldn't take that risk.

"Hm," she said. "What a pity. You'd better hold on to your own job then. Me with no pay and your friend with no job. We might be coming to ask you for rent money at the end of this month, eh?"

I smiled. "That will never happen, ma."

As we approached the stairs leading to the first floor, I switched on my flashlight. In the dark, with the lanterns in the windows, our block of flats looked like a normal place to live. During the day the building was as it really was, as though it had barely survived a fire. The green paint had a smoky gray film; the mosquito netting over our windows was ripped and brown with dust. There was laundry hanging on our balconies. The compound was cemented and had pockmarks from past rains. Around the compound was a wall about eight feet high, spiked with broken glass to prevent thieves. Our landlord had had the block built as close to the wall as possible to accommodate six flats. Every month he arrived on time to collect his rent.

Mrs. Durojaiye turned to me. "Have you heard any noise from my sons this evening?"

"No," I said.

"This new girl I have looking after them, Philomena, I think she is lazy. Watch them, please. I don't want them running around and getting into mischief."

"They are good boys."

"No one is born bad. You have to watch them."

She had been fighting for a long time, to feed her sons and keep her job. She had probably fought her husband and in-laws. Why else was she alone? What I knew for sure was that I didn't want to be like Mrs. Durojaiye, that tough and lonely. She was so tough, the government would be a small foe for her. She was some sort of senior official in the nurse's union. I wasn't sure what her exact title was.

"I don't know," she murmured. "I will have to send them to their father for this period of the strike. Maybe I will keep my youngest, Ayo, here with me. His brothers are getting to an age when I can't handle them anymore. I beat them these days and my arm begins to ache."

The beam of my flashlight danced as I laughed. Mrs. Durojaiye beat her children like no other mother. I let her walk up the stairs first. The woman scared me, and I, too, was on my own strike until Sanwo met my demands.

No one in the world loved shoes more than me, no one, and the higher and sexier they were, the more I cherished them, quite frankly. I polished all my shoes and kept them in a row under my bed, stuffed them with old newspaper sheets and walked softly, softly so they wouldn't scuff. When my soles became worn down, there was an elderly shoe repairman down our street who replaced them. "Papa," everyone called him. He sat on his bench with his jaw jutting out and was forever going on about backlogs. Whenever I handed my shoes over to Papa, I had anxiety from thinking that he might lose them or ruin them. I'd actually pray that he wouldn't. I once confessed this to Rose. "God forbid bad thing," she said. "You treat those shoes like pets."

She was quiet for a few days after I started working for Mr. Salako. I'd ask her a question and she'd answer with a grunt, which didn't surprise me. What I wasn't prepared for was to come home in the evenings and find her lying on the sofa like some rich madam, watching television. She was drinking beer like water now, drinking and falling asleep. We hardly spoke. The atmosphere at home was full of tension, rather than the usual haze of Flit mosquito repellent. Then on Saturday morning, she announced, "Me, I done tire from all this resting. I beg, let us go to Tajudeen."

To me, that meant she'd forgiven me. Normally, we went to Tajudeen market at Christmas with our yearly bonuses. This time, we went with transport money alone. The market was not far by bus. It was indoors, three stories high and built around a quadrangle. There were stacks of imports and every kind of shopper came by: traders, professionals, students, young, old and rich even. We brushed shoulders along the corridors and searched for bargains. It wasn't unusual to bump into a friend or to duck from one because, for some, Tajudeen market was not exactly a place to be proud of. The stalls were cramped concrete lots. Fluorescent lamps lit them up and colors always appeared stark. Most of the shopkeepers were young men who looked like they would be area boys if they were not trading. They howled at women shoppers, "Baby, show me your particulars." Rose would answer, "Show me yours first."

Today, we walked arm in arm and refused to step aside, which was our *modus operandi* for getting through the market. People made a path for us along the corridors. "Let's try this one," she suggested at a stall we knew. My heartbeat quickened. The stall had shoes from Greece. They were colorful and supple. I had a weakness for shoes like that.

"Rambling Rose," someone said as soon as we walked in.

"Johnny," we both shouted.

It was Johnny Walker. We called him that because he looked like a bottle of whiskey and was forever perambulating. Rose flung herself at him.

"Don't touch me," he said, easing out of her arms.

"Why not?" she asked.

"You never ask about me," he said. "This is my only wife in Lagos."

He kissed my cheeks. Johnny smelled of musk cologne. I knew the smell would remain on my blouse for at least a week. If Johnny sat in a chair, it would stink of his cologne. Anything he touched would, including cups he'd used, and he took as long as a woman to get dressed.

"My dear Tolani," he said to me.

"Dear John," I said.

He was tall with freckles on his face. He was also a flirt, always asking when I would leave Sanwo for him.

"Rambling Rose," he said, hugging her finally. "Where you're rambling, heaven knows."

"What's your concern?" Rose asked.

When they were going out, Johnny irritated her by saying this. Rose took the words of the song personally. Who was Johnny to question her rambling? He was often wandering around himself, even on environmental sanitation days, when people were supposed to stay at home and clean up their surroundings. Her last curse on Johnny was that he would be detained indefinitely like those who dared to break the sanitation law. I walked over to a rack of shoes and picked up a purple stiletto with three-inch heels.

"You-sef," I heard Rose say. "What are you doing here? I thought you only wear snakes and crocodiles on your feet."

"My friend is the one buying," Johnny answered.

He pointed at a man who was seated on a bench before an array of men's sandals. The man's white silk shirt was open low enough to show a gold chain around his neck. He wore sunglasses, and there was a scar over the bow of his mouth.

"OC," Johnny called out to him. "These are my two favorite wives in Lagos."

The man nodded. He had a square-shaped face and thick sideburns.

"That is my friend," Johnny said to Rose. "He has just returned from the United States."

"Of America?" she asked.

I was not impressed. OC didn't look like an "Andrew" from America. They were usually fresh-faced. OC's face was drawn and his posture was hunched as though he'd spent time lifting heavy loads.

The stiletto in my hand was tempting me again. I visualized it with a purple cat suit I owned and even imagined myself dancing on Ladies Night at Phaze Two. Rose picked up a flat brown loafer from a separate rack.

"Johnny, since I'm your wife," she said, "will you buy this for me?"

Johnny dipped his hands in his pockets and pulled out the empty flaps.

"You know I don't carry money around."

"Why not?" Rose asked.

"Austerity measures."

"You miser!" she said. "You never want to pay for anything!"

The shopkeeper laughed. I walked over and lowered the loafer in Rose's hand. Johnny was quick to sulk, and the more he sulked, the louder Rose could become.

"Leave my brother alone," I said.

"No," she said. "He must pay today, today."

I eased the loafer out of her hand. "This ugly shoe? Please leave my brother alone. If he buys you a shoe, he will buy a better shoe than this."

Rose's stare didn't waver from Johnny's face. Every disappointment she'd ever had was in that stare. "They will bury you with your money, Johnny Walker," she grumbled. "You can't even buy somebody something, after all these years."

"Bring it here," OC said.

He was walking toward the shopkeeper with a pair of sandals. Rose eyed him.

"For what?" she asked.

She didn't seem impressed with him either.

"I will pay for it," he said.

She smiled. "Are you serious?"

"Yes," he insisted. "Let me have it."

"You see, Johnny?" she asked. "Hope you're learning how to treat a woman."

OC beckoned and she hurried over. He paid for her loafers. She thanked him as Johnny marched out of the stall with his pocket flaps still sticking out.

"No vex, my brother," I called after him and he didn't answer — me, his dear Tolani.

"I hope you're not staying with that man," Rose was saying to OC. "He doesn't like to spend money. He will give you water and *garri* to chop every day."

"I have a place of my own," OC said. "What is your name again?"

She exaggerated the "z" sound. Yorubas especially frustrated her when we called her "Roace."

"Rose Adamson," he repeated correctly. "It seems like you're a woman who knows what she wants."

Rose smiled. "Of course. Maybe I will come and see you, even sef. I'll ask Johnny how to..."

"Don't ask me anything," Johnny protested from the corridor.

OC laughed. "I'll be expecting you. He knows where to find me."

He was a bowlegged man, stocky, and left dipping his shoulders from side to side. Now, I wondered if I could ask the shopkeeper to set the purple stilettos aside for me. If I hurried, it was possible to go home, get some money, enough for a deposit, and return before the market closed.

"He's nice," Rose murmured.

"Hm?"

"That OC *bobo*," she said.

I was still preoccupied with the stilettos, but I glanced at OC. He patted Johnny's back to appease him. How would she know? Johnny for instance, was young, trim, funny, and could talk about politics until dawn. He was nothing like Rose's other boyfriends, who would not open their mouths for fear of revealing their dirty secrets. The trouble with Johnny was that he did not like spending his money. The first time he took Rose out, he'd asked her to pay half the bill. They'd come home not speaking. "What happened, Johnny?" I'd asked. "S-she's trying to b-bankrupt me," he'd said. He was so upset from having to pay the bill that he could barely explain.

I placed the purple stiletto back on the rack. OC was not nice; I sensed it then, and I hadn't even seen his eyes behind those dark sunglasses he was wearing. He sounded bogus with all that "woman who knows what she wants" business. "You don't know the man, Rose," I said. "You've just met him."

Her troubles started with the brown loafers, not because she'd lost her job. Bad things had happened to Rose before. She handled them by arguing, defending herself, drinking beer, or eating a bowl of pepper soup. Never did her solution come from unexpected generosity.

Her father, Boniface Adamson, was the only man to spoil her, she once told me. "Eh, you should see him, bringing me new church dresses and school shoes, giving me pocket money for Goody-Goody and puff-puff…"

She didn't even know where Daddy Adamson lived and she asked Sisi to stop insulting him during those visits. Sisi would control herself until Daddy Adamson left, then she would begin her tirade: "Him face like a horse, broken-down car, dirty shirt, mouth like *Oxford English Dictionary*…" Rose would cry, "Leave my daddy alone. He likes me."

She visited OC that same week and at first Johnny wouldn't say where OC lived. Then when he did, he kept pestering Rose about her relationship with OC.

"Can't you see?" she told me. "He's jealous because OC likes me."

My roommate and boyfriend were similar. They saw other people's envy instead of seeing their own flaws. I wondered what exactly had attracted her to OC and why he never came to our place and why Rose had to visit him each time. Week one, week two. She would come home and brag about how he'd bought her a bottle of Mateus or Liebfraumilch. OC didn't approve of women drinking beer or spirits apparently, and I got bored of hearing about his achievements.

"OC? He takes no nonsense from anybody. OC? He's a man in his own right. OC? He was successful in America. OC? He only came back home to buy a plot of land and build a house."

For someone who had had so many boyfriends, she was behaving like an impressionable teenager. OC didn't even want other men to look at her, according to her, and by week three, he had asked her not to speak to Johnny anymore. Johnny had asked too many personal questions. At the end of the month, OC paid her rent, and she began to come home with new shoes.

"I don't even like them," she said, flinging a pair on the floor one evening. The shoes fell by my feet. They were white with navy heels. I had a skirt and blouse to match perfectly, and I'd just returned from work.

"They're nice," I said.

"You can have them," she said.

"Not my size."

"Try them on at least."

"What's the point?"

My smile didn't reach my eyes. Rose had been sleeping most of the day. Four pairs of high-heeled shoes were between us, the kind of shoes that I liked.

She stretched. "Did anyone ask after me at work?"

"They all do. Godwin. Everybody."

"What did Godwin say?"

"He's praying for you."

She smiled. "Mr. Pastor. What about Ignatius?"

"You know him, he likes to boast that you are his countrywoman."

"What about Radio Nigeria?"

"Rose," I said, kicking off my shoes. "Won't you look for another job at this rate?"

I was lying. No one at work had asked after her.

"Why?" she asked.

"Because I've seen people stop work and never go back."

She pretended to shiver. "Me, work? So someone like Salako can harass me again? Over my dead body."

"All I'm saying is that you're getting too used to sitting at home. That's all I'm saying."

She sounded as if she had never worked a day in her life, and if OC left her, she would be as poor as she was the day before she met him. She threw another shoe on the floor. This one was turquoise with red trimming.

"I know you're wondering about the shoes," she said.

"I am not your keeper, Rose."

"He likes to give me gifts."

"That's very good."

She was studying my expression. "What is it?"

"Nothing," I said.

"My job is harder than you expected?"

"It's not that hard."

"Then why do you look so wrecked?"

Her tongue was like a blade.

"I'm not wrecked," I said.

She lay back on the sofa. "Me, I can't work again. OC says he will take care of me anyway. He says he wants to marry me."

I winced. "What?"

"He says he wants to marry me. He wants to buy me a diamond ring even."

"When did he say this?"

"Yesterday."

"After how many days?"

"I'm not counting."

"Less than one month, Rose."

"Why, is it paining you?"

Her shoes, her bragging, I was not sure. I had been waiting two years for Sanwo and his business deals. My smile was forced.

"Why would it pain me?"

She lifted her leg and checked the polish on her toenails. "OC is my concern, not yours. Whether he buys me gifts or not, whether he wants to marry me

74

or not."

Her nail varnish was bright orange, not the faded, chipped pink she normally hid in her loafers. I laughed. "You're not a small child. You can't marry someone you've known for less than a month. No one behaves like that unless they are looking for trouble."

She shrugged. "It's my trouble, not yours. Why are you so vexed?"

I didn't have an answer to that. Instead, I went to the kitchen to warm myself some of my yam pottage and found that she'd scooped out some of it and didn't even attempt to cover the hole with strips of smoked herring as she normally would.

"She says he wants to marry her," I said.

"We'll believe that on the day it happens," Sanwo said.

He was lying on my bed and stroking his chest hairs. I picked up my afro comb from the floor and placed it by my face powder on the table.

"She says he likes to take care of her and buy her gifts."

"He's a Bobby Shaftoe. He will shaft her before she realizes it."

Sanwo thought OC was a 4-1-9 man. The government claimed they were cracking down on 4-1-9 as part of their War Against Indiscipline, which was more of a joke than an insult; 4-1-9 was a criminal code for fraud.

"Can you imagine? Within three weeks of knowing her, he wants to marry her."

I dusted my table with my fingers as Sanwo sang off-key, "Bobby Shaftoe's gone to sea, silver buckles on his knee, he'll come back and marry..." I was in no mood for his evasive tactics. I interrupted: "I don't trust that man. He is doing something bad and Rose is not thinking straight."

"Leave the woman alone," Sanwo said.

I was pacing around my room and tidying up after him. He had used my afro comb and left it on the floor, eaten a bag of bread with some beans and set the empty plate on the table. In Sanwo's own place, I couldn't push a chair an inch without him pulling it back into position.

I faced him. "I don't want to stay here anymore. I'm ready to move out. Whatever he is doing to have so much money, I don't want to be involved."

"Move out where?"

"She doesn't work. She eats my food."

"She's always eaten your food."

"She's taking money from him. What if he stops paying her rent?"

I snatched his sock from my sheets and pushed it into his shoe.

He sat up. "Em, move where, by the way?"

"He doesn't come here. What is he hiding from? He stops her from seeing Johnny. What has Johnny ever done?"

"Nothing in his life, except to walk around smelling like a taxi's air freshener. But come, where do you want to move?"

I picked up his second sock and dangled it before him.

"What?" he asked.

"Can't you put something away for once?"

"Is it me or Rose we're talking about?"

Sanwo was a tidy person, unlike Rose. He was tired again, from work, but so was I, yet he was staring at me as if I had offended him. For as long as I knew him, he didn't think I was entitled to be angry, ever, and for all his high expectations of me, he himself was intolerant. He never gave Johnny a chance, eyed him from their first meeting; by their third, he was being rude. Johnny was busy describing his fantasy vacation, an island somewhere with reggae music, a beautiful woman, and room service. Sanwo kept cutting him short with questions: "Really? What island is this in Lagos, Tin Can Island or Apapa Wharf? Which beautiful woman? This same Rose? I see. So how will you pay for your room service? By the way, where do you work?"

He called Johnny the biggest bullshitter from north to south, but who was the bullshitter? Sanwo was one of the most uncompromising people I knew when it came to his principles of decency, yet the moment the subject of marriage came up, he couldn't decide. Suddenly, it was okay for him to live in sin. Suddenly, it was all right for me to be a corrupt woman. There was no need to withhold affection from him; I was so fed up, I no longer wanted to show him any.

"Listen," he said. "I've always told you Rose was crazy."

"Violet," I said. "Violet is the crazy one, not Rose, not like this."

"But they're obviously very unstable in their family. Wasn't their mother crazy too? How do you know it's not hereditary? It was a matter of time before Rose herself went off. Let her go out with whoever she wants and stay wherever she wants. She's right, it's not your concern, and this talk about moving..."

"I'm here on my own, most nights."

"While she's with this…?"

"OC."

"Is she with him today?"

I slapped the side of my head. "Are you listening? Do you hear a single word I'm saying? I say she spends most of her time with him. I'm saying that I stay here on my own. You know I don't like that. You know I've been wanting to leave this place. Two years now and I'm tired. I hate my work and tomorrow I still have to get on a bus."

My head hurt where I'd struck myself. A month before, my life was barely balanced and now it seemed to have tipped over and I was slipping into the black hole Rose had warned me about. Her bizarre behavior was contributing to that, as was Sanwo's normal disposition. He was just too satisfied with our present arrangement, too comfortable. Was it wrong to want a husband?

We heard the tap in the bathroom rattle and a

toilet flush next door. It meant that our water was flowing at last.

"This business deal of yours," I said. "Is your uncle backing you?"

"No," Sanwo said, shaking his head. "I don't want him involved. This time, I go in on my own. Once I make enough profit, I start working for myself."

"How will you raise the money?"

"Why do you think I'm running around so much?"

I rubbed my hands together. "Please, let me help. At least I can add my savings to what you have."

"I didn't come here to ask for money."

"Please. It will take you too long to raise the money. You said there was no risk involved. Isn't that what you said?"

The toilet flushed again, followed by a loud thumping noise outside. I stood up and walked to the window. It was Mrs. Durojaiye's youngest son, Ayo. He was jumping on the septic tank in our backyard. It was where the toilet waste in our block ended up and if it caved in, he could fall inside.

"Ayo," I called out.

He ducked. "Yes?"

"What are you doing there?"

"I'm playing."

His voice sounded like a girl's. He was wearing oversized khaki shorts and his eyes widened at the mention of his mother.

"Your mother will beat you if she catches you. Where is Philomena?"

"Inside," he said, dropping his chin.

"Isn't she supposed to be watching you?"

"I'm bored."

I pointed. "You'd better get down from there and tell Philomena to look after you, you hear me? Your mother is paying her a lot of money for that."

He jumped from the raised cement surface and ran off. I watched him until he'd disappeared behind the wet bedsheets hanging on the washing lines. His brothers had gone to stay with their father and really, there was nowhere for Ayo to play, but his mother had given her orders, no backyard play for him. A year had passed since his older brother had got cut while trying to scale the wall surrounding the property, for no apparent reason. Mrs. Durojaiye had beaten the boy as he bled. I'd had to beg her to take him to the teaching hospital for stitches.

Sanwo was still staring.

"You want the boy to get hurt?" I asked.

"The money," he said. "You can lend it to me. I'll accept anything you have. I can't take it when you're like this. How much do you want to give me?"

Principal and accumulated interest, I withdrew my savings the next morning and left twenty-one kobo to keep my account open.

I was walking away from the Cash and Teller department, minding my own business as usual, when I heard a voice from the banking hall.

"Tolani, my dear daughter, how are you these days?" Since my father had never appeared as a ghost, I knew the person had to be Colonel Daodu, and I was right. He was sitting under an oscillating fan, dressed in a black tunic and holding a walking stick. He waved. "I keep asking after you. They tell me you're busy. I wish I could come upstairs to visit, but, as you know, my situation prevents."

I was in trouble. I had not seen him in months. Why now?

"Morning, sir," I said.

Colonel Daodu was injured during the Civil War. I knew him because he came to our department on my first day of work, and Alhaji Umar asked me to help him up the stairs. I couldn't believe how heavy he was, and how tricky. One minute, his fingers were on my shoulder; the next, they were on my backside and I couldn't decide whether to pretend I hadn't noticed, or to let go of him and then pretend, if he tumbled down the stairs, that it was an accident. In the end, I'd escorted him up the stairs and down again after he'd finished his business with Alhaji Umar.

He gripped my hand. "How is active duty, my daughter?"

"Work is fine."

"You're stationed downstairs now?"

"Oh, yes."

"Rising fast in the ranks?"

"Definitely."

Colonel Daodu talked as if he were still in the army. The less I said, the better; otherwise, he might think I was encouraging him.

"Good," he said. "Because if you are not getting your promotions, I personally will complain to your superiors."

I smiled, although I was tempted to ask why he would do that and whether he thought anyone would listen to him. He would not let go of my hand, and he was looking at my cleavage.

"They are calling me in my department, sir," I said.

"They're working you hard?"

"Yes, I'd better go, otherwise…"

"I suppose you're still young. You can handle it."

Handle what? I thought, and I'd forgotten that his left eye twitched.

"Yes," I said.

"That's a pity," he said releasing my hand. "You never seem to have time for me when I come here. Well, good morning, my daughter."

I knew he was watching me as I walked away. Other people in the banking hall were sneaking peeks at him. Colonel Daodu was often in the newspapers criticizing the new regime. They were despots, he said. I thought he was just a little upset because he was feeling ignored. But for his war injuries, he would have been one of those in power. Now, all he had was a lot of money and no authority. The military men he criticized had tarnished his reputation. They claimed that he made his money through a girlfriend who smuggled Indian hemp after the Civil War and ended up dying in a Bangkok jail. She was another well-known socialite, but she was more popular in the seventies and had been imprisoned twice in England.

On my way back to my desk, I passed by Franka's. She'd been watching me from the moment Colonel Daodu called my name.

"It's good to have someone who takes an interest in you," she said.

"Isn't it?" I said.

Colonel Daodu never bothered me. Within minutes of getting to my desk, I'd forgotten about him. How many of us at the bank had to deal with old playboys like him? He probably had several young women who were willing to give him some attention, and if I had a true relation for every person who called me their daughter or sister at work, I would have the largest family in Nigeria. No, it was Mr. Salako I couldn't bear that afternoon. Mr. Snake of a Salako. He was the one that upset me.

After lunch, he had a phone call from one of his Big Man customers. The man gave both his titles first: Chief and Engineer. I confirmed his last name using his first title only, Chief.

"Engineer, Chief," the man barked. "Do you know who I am? Who is this? Where is Miss Adamson?"

"Sorry, sir," I said. "I'm new here. Please hold on."

Most times, the male callers were polite. Sometimes they assumed I was Rose and began to flirt with me. The women callers were nearly always rude, but at least I was well prepared for them.

I hurried to Mr. Salako's office. Mr. Salako grabbed his phone as soon as I told him who was on the line. He flattered the man, asked after his wives and children, laughed and rocked in his chair. I stood in his office with my head down as he gestured that I should remain. The smell of boiled eggs was strong, even from the door. I would eventually get used to him, I hoped. In time he might amuse me, and I didn't even have to breathe if I walked in and out of his office fast enough.

"Yes," he said, ending his conversation. "We will certainly take care of that. Goodbye, sir."

He replaced the receiver, and I waited for him to speak.

"I eh," he said. "I wanted you to eh, get my file in the cabinet."

He pointed to the gray cabinet adjacent to his desk.

"What file is this, sir?" I asked.

If there was one word I wished would disappear from the English dictionary, it was the word "sir." How many times a day did I have to lower myself by using it?

"Quarterly budgets," he said.

The cabinet was three drawers high, and I

found it strange because Mr. Salako could easily reach out and touch the cabinet. He had never asked me to get files in his office. I pulled the drawer out and searched the labels on the green file folders. They were in alphabetical order. I found the quarterly budgets. Mr. Salako got up from his seat and I immediately moved thinking he needed space to pass.

"S'cuse me," he said, in a singsong voice.

He walked between his desk and the cabinet. I tried to get out of his way, but we got stuck in the narrow space. I had my back to him. Mr. Salako's arms came round my waist.

"S'cuse me," he grunted.

I lifted my arms higher to free myself and he hugged me tighter. I lowered my arms. "There's no space, sir," I said. "Sir, there's no..."

Mr. Salako was rubbing his pelvis against me. I pushed him back so hard his desk moved.

"There's no space," I shouted.

"Filthy" was the first word that came to my mind followed by "fool." I was about to tell him off when his door opened and Franka stood in the doorway.

"Can't you knock?" Mr. Salako asked.

Her eyes were wide. "I thought you said 'come in,' sir."

Mr. Salako waddled back to his desk and sat in his chair. He was breathing heavily, and his trousers were buckled high. He adjusted his belt. I placed the file on top of the cabinet and straightened my blouse. Me? I thought.

"Sorry, sir," Franka said. "I'm here to tell you a messenger wishes to see you."

I had my back to her and lifted the file in my other hand.

"Messenger from where?" Mr. Salako asked.

"First Bank, sir."

"Tell him to wait."

I heard the door close. My hands were shaking. Me? I was still thinking. I couldn't describe what had happened, let alone prove it. I didn't even know how to react, but my instinct told me to dive across his desk, grab his tie and pull hard.

"Miss Ajao?" he said after a moment.

My voice wavered. "Yes?"

"Where is this file?"

He wiped his face with a handkerchief. I resisted the urge to slap him with the file and threw it on his desk. When I wouldn't move, he said, "I'm sure you have work to do now."

Quietly, quietly, I left his office. I even closed the door gently, as an obedient daughter would. How many times had I sworn that if a man touched me in that way, I would slap his face and that was just the beginning? Sanwo would praise me, "My girl! Her body belongs to me alone!" Then he would add, "You Nigerian women are all the same. You make a lot of noise and yet, when the time comes, you can't do nothing."

Had someone told me the worst to happen that month was Mr. Salako rubbing against me and pretending as if he never had, I would have said yes, definitely, that was the worst. Worse was what happened immediately after: Franka opening her big mouth to broadcast to the whole office what she'd witnessed, first with Colonel Daodu and then with Mr. Salako; Ignatius opening his own mouth to ask if what Franka had said was true. How I told him off! How dare he question me, I asked. He said he didn't want to get involved, he just wanted to know the facts. I said he was a gossip like Franka and that was why he was self-appointed settler of quarrels in the office. I didn't even bother to answer when Hakeem asked if it was true that Franka walked in and found Mr. Salako and I in *flagrante delicto* — because I didn't know what *flagrante delicto* was, initially. I stopped speaking to everyone at the bank and ate lunch on my own, developed stomach cramps from hearing Mr. Salako's voice laughing on the phone with his Big Man customers. Whenever he called my name, the cramps became stronger. After a while, the cramps were permanent. None of this was as bad as the moment Mr. Salako rubbed against me.

I didn't tell Rose about it because I thought she would be happy to hear I was having trouble with him. I couldn't say a word to Sanwo either. I thought he might ask, "How could you let that happen to you?" A question I first heard when I was thirteen, when a boy in my class at Baptist Missionary ran up and lifted my skirt. I reported him to our class teacher, and she gave him ten lashes of the cane. Afterwards, she conked my head and asked, "You yourself, in what way were you walking?"

Yoruba people believed in reincarnation. The Yoruba religion had a world for the living and another for spirits. There was a circle of life and other complex concepts regarding deity, royalty, and fate that I couldn't fully understand. For anyone to understand the Yoruba cosmos was a challenge without the wisdom and guidance of a *babalawo*, but ask any Yoruba who believed in the cosmos and most would refuse to accept that a person's past experiences had any effect on their present behavior.

"Oh, it's *oyinbo* people that say that nonsense," Sanwo said, if ever I talked to him about psychology. "My father beat me, my mother didn't love me," he called it. He believed people were responsible for their own choices and any psychological explanations were mere excuses. But why couldn't I confront Mr. Salako if I didn't think that I was at fault in some way: the sexy shoes I liked and the fashionable clothes I wore?

I might have come up with sensible answers if I'd had enough time to dwell. Perhaps that was the real blessing about living in Lagos: there was no time to dwell. I just had to carry on and be prepared for some other problem to come along, and like a joke, like a joke, another problem surely would.

My mother beat up my father when they were both ten years old. She was a spirited child. She became a patient woman, totally different from her childhood character, but I could draw a straight line from the girl to the woman. It was easy to see why she had changed, and there was a lesson for me to learn.

My father left town when he turned eleven years old. He was sent to another town to live with his father's friend, a drummer who schooled him in the art of the talking drum. He returned to Makoku as a man. My mother, at the time, was earning money for the work she did in her aunt's co-op as a cloth dyer. Customers were asking specially for her designs, but she was overdue for marriage. Her father had introduced her to a man he favored, but she kept refusing. She didn't want to marry.

That year, the ruler of Makoku, our *Oba*, died in his sleep. The town went through its period of mourning. His eldest son became the new *Oba* and inherited his father's court. The mourners had not finished crying when my father's father, too, died in his sleep. The townspeople said the old *Oba* had taken his favorite drummer to the other world. They said the new *Oba* would have to find a new drummer and my father was their favorite choice.

This new *Oba* was not a man the town feared. He was a youngster. There was talk that he did not want to be *Oba*, that he preferred to sit alone in his room and gaze into space. His mother knew the other *Oba*'s wives called her son a dimwit behind her back. She decided that to make them show him respect, she would have to find new wives for her son within the town by forcing unwed women into marriage. The new wives would dilute the power the old wives held and the townspeople would become fearful of her son.

For me, living in Lagos of the eighties, that situation was hard to imagine, a time and place when a royal family could have so much power over its people. The royal family in present-day Lagos answered to the military government like everyone else. Outside their circle, no one bothered with them. But my mother was talking about a time before military coups and independence. Traditional rulers had not yet been totally undermined by the colonials. All unmarried girls in Makoku Town were warned to watch where they went: the stream to fetch water, the next compound. If they ended up in the palace, no one would come to look for them.

It was a difficult time in Makoku when my mother met my father again. He teased her when he saw her walking along the path to her aunt's co-op.

"You're walking around unchaperoned?" he asked.

"Yes," I said.

"You're not afraid of being kidnapped and taken to the palace?" he asked.

"No," I said.

He adjusted his cap. "Weren't you the one who attacked me on this path when we were small?"

"I don't remember," I said.

"You called me a heathen, remember?"

"I don't remember any such thing."

"Your name is Arike. Your people are followers of Reverend Thomas."

"And so?"

"Reverend Thomas," he said, "the man who changed his father's name to please the priest who converted him and now he sings those sad songs in church every Sunday, glory this and glory that and holy, holy, holy. I hear he tells you Christians that drumming is evil."

"That is not true. Who said?"

He smiled. "Those who come down the hill to worship Shango behind Reverend Thomas's back. You can't get any of them to admit that they must choose between the oyinbo church and our shrines. Don't you find that strange?"

"It is strange that our new Oba is taking wives by force," I said. "And I have heard you will drum for him now that your father is buried. That is the strangest rumor of all."

We became friends. I was beginning to feel restless in my aunt's co-op. My apprenticeship was over and I was as skilled as any of the women. I had fresh ideas, but was not able to share them because I was young. Even though I was polite, I could not bear all that business about observing seniority. Showing respect wasted precious time. I began to see your father regularly. He was not one to say "don't say this" or "don't do that." I talked freely about the new Oba taking wives. Families had been arranging marriages for generations, I said. That too was wrong. Christians did not believe in men taking *more than one wife. Those who worshipped Shango were not hypocrites.* Shango *was like* Jesu Cristi, *except he was the god of thunder and lightning, a lesser god to Olodumare, who was the same the world over but known by different names like* "God" *and* "Jehovah" *because not everyone in the world was intelligent enough to speak Yoruba. Your father said that obviously* oyinbo *people had confused me with their simplistic interpretations of the Yoruba faith.*

   I also talked about my work. In the town center, far from the farming settlements, there were cloth dyers who worked in the marketplace. They worked on their own and not in co-ops. They used stencils made from tin cans instead of painting with feathers, candle wax instead of cassava starch, colorful imported dyes instead of indigo. They could finish a yard of cloth in a fraction of time the women in my aunt's co-op did, for a fraction of the cost. Customers could buy the cloth they wanted from the marketplace and give it to a dyer to work on. I feared that the day our town experienced the slightest hardship, our customers would favor the market dyers over us the traditional dyers. The market itself was a stopping place for lorries en route to Lagos. It was growing. It was an opportunity for a woman like me. Your father agreed. He confessed he didn't want to live in the farming settlements. He preferred to be in the town center, where his brother had a motorcycle business. He laughed when I asked if he would drum for the new Oba. *No, he said, the lorry drivers, the drunken lorry drivers in town would be his audience. He was a free thinker in that way.*

One day, I returned home to find my entire family gathered in our compound: my father, mother, uncles, aunts, Iya Alaro, and the elders included. I was in trouble. I knew it was a serious matter even before anyone said a word to me. My father was first to speak. He said an emissary had come from the palace to see him. The palace wanted me to report as a wife the next day. I told my father, "I will not go." He asked, "What? You disobey me twice? Taboo. Taboo, you hear me? I've been telling you for a long time, don't cause me any embarrassment. Otherwise, you will see what I will do to you. You refused to marry the man I chose for you and now you refuse the palace? What kind of daughter is this? This one wants to stay in our compound until she becomes old. Too proud, this one, yet she is not even that beautiful or graceful."

They all agreed I was too proud and not that beautiful or graceful. Then Iya Alaro spoke. "What is all this wahala *about? The girl is a good child. I spend more time with her than anyone here. She works hard. The new* Oba *should not be forcing women into marriage. It is wrong. We must take this matter to our district officer."*

Someone said, "That oyinbo *man? What does he care so long as he receives his revenues on time? He's just a messenger of the* Oba *of England. Money is all they are concerned about."*

"His deputy will listen to us," my aunt said.

The same person answered, "The deputy is one of us even though he tries to act like an oyinbo *just because he went to university in England. The deputy dare not interfere, particularly in matters involving women. He* knows that if he interferes, he will be well and truly cursed."

Iya Alaro shook her head. "You say this now, but when you see the district officer it is all yes sir, no sir."

"We fool him," someone else said. "He does not understand our ways and has never done us any good. He's always taking taxes and fining us. What does he know? Sickness will eventually get him, or the day will come when we will drive him back to England to meet his own Oba."

My aunt answered, "Well, our Oba collaborates with the district officer and this way of marrying women has to stop."

"But the royal house will curse us if she refuses," someone else said.

"Let them," my aunt replied. "I am not afraid."

That convinced them she was truly a witch. I stood there watching my family discuss my future. My life was ruined. Was I a child or woman, a daughter or wife? I vowed to myself that if I had to go to the palace as a wife, I would not speak, I would not bath. I would be the dirtiest woman. I would not eat. I would starve. My family would bring back my bones.

Iya Alaro called me aside for a talk before going home. "This is the way of our people," she said. "A woman your age can no longer be in her father's house. She must move on to her husband's house."

"But you're in your own house," I said.

"I had a husband," she said. "He died on me."

"But they say it was your fault. They say you caused it. They call you awful names and accuse you of having malicious powers…"

"Shut your mouth," she said sternly. "Why are you so disrespectful? You dare not repeat such gossip to me. Lies hide between words, like cowards, and the truth need not draw attention to itself. Do you think the life of a widow is easy? Do you think the life of a childless woman is so wonderful? Listen to what I'm saying. My matter has nothing to do with yours. You're getting old is what I'm telling you, and I see no reason why you can't marry that young drummer you keep running around with. Have some children at least, before it's too late."

I said, "But he's not a Christian."

My aunt answered, "None of us here are, if we're still scared of juju."

I never saw, because I was confined to my father's compound after the family meeting, but the story told is that my aunt Iya Alaro gathered the women of Makoku. She reminded them of the women of Abeokuta who had caused commotion for their Alake and his chiefs. Those who were reluctant to participate in a similar protest, she assured them that the new Oba would feel free to raise taxes as high as he wanted if they allowed him to behave as he pleased with women. The women were eventually joined by men: farmers, fishermen, hunters, Shango devotees, and so-called Christians. They all took the path now known as Market Road, carrying tree branches, and headed for the palace. They stopped within the courtyard and I imagined how they mocked the palace with chants.

They informed the new Oba that the town would no longer tolerate the practice of forcing women into marriage. It was the oyinbo district officer who eventually intervened, after seeking shelter in his bungalow for several days and ordering his deputy to send urgent telegrams to England. He knew full well about native uprisings and did not want one on his hands, especially after my aunt threatened to bare her backside to the Oba.

You see, we had our own ways of keeping our rulers in check, and they were quite effective, long before the oyinbos *came along. Our* Oba *reluctantly stopped the practice of taking brides by force, even though he raised taxes that year, the highest ever, to punish the township for disobedience. His rule did not last long, however. His mother was poisoned when she wouldn't stop telling him how to rule. He himself was driven into exile when he failed to make a sensible decision after her death. As for me, I quietly married your father before the whole world turned upside down. Imagine that trouble just for me? We moved to the town center; your father continued with his drumming; I started my cloth dyeing business. I did my best to behave. I knew the townspeople were watching me and waiting for me to take a wrong step. People are funny that way. Someone in power does something wrong to you and everyone treats you as if you are at fault. You yourself begin to feel you're at fault. And for what? No reason. No reason at all.*

I had to admit that my new job at Federal Community Bank was harder than I'd expected, so stressful that I looked forward to going home to an empty flat every evening. The Wednesday of the following week, I returned from work, blind to the people on our street who were chatting, buying food from hawkers, laughing for no just cause, and blaming the government for their woes. I noticed a new poster wrapped around a National Electric Power pole. Lateness to work was an act of indiscipline, it stated.

I'd reached the gates of our block of flats when I saw a bright light in our backyard. It seemed as if a star had fallen from the sky and landed there. I heard voices and knew that a crowd was gathered. Mama Chidi, one of the tenants of our block, who had four children and a baby she carried on her back, was standing by our gates. She was trembling. I thought we'd had armed robbers again.

"*Ewo*, it's bad, it's bad," she said, when she saw me.

"Armed robbers?" I asked.

They charged through our streets at least three times a year carrying fire torches and machetes. When they left, they killed at least one person. Mama Chidi bounced up and down. Her glasses became lopsided and her baby's head bobbed. I had to hold her still. I could feel her bones under my grip. There was no flesh on Mama Chidi, because she was looking after so many children, all under the age of eleven, and she always smelled of burned beans.

"The septic tank," she said. "He fell inside. It sucked him under. I'm waiting for his mother, to tell her myself."

I touched my chest. "Who?"

"Mrs. Durojaiye's youngest, Ayo. He drowned in the tank."

I threw my handbag on the ground and sat by her feet. I slapped my head. There wasn't a tear in my eyes. The septic tank had sucked Ayo in, Mama Chidi said. She was waiting to tell Mrs. Durojaiye and to hold her down until the poor woman recovered from shock.

The crowd in our backyard were other tenants. They were gathered around the septic tank, carrying kerosene and battery lanterns. When I saw them I became conscious of an awful stench, like a sewer. It was the waste in our tank. The cement surface had a huge hole. Mama Chidi's husband was dipping a long stick into it and seemed to be stirring the contents. "It's Tolani," I heard one or two tenants say. The heat from their lanterns made their faces shiny with sweat. Even their children were gaping at the hole. I stood by the pole of a washing line. I could go no further.

"We need a longer stick," someone said.

"This is the longest we could find," someone else answered.

"Go across the street to the tailor's. They have plenty of bamboo there."

"Don't! They will come rushing here!"

"Go across the street! Ask for bamboo! Don't tell them what it is for!"

Someone pushed a teenage boy in my direction, and he hurried off. I heard other people talking about Philomena, Mrs. Durojaiye's girl, who was meant to be watching little Ayo.

"She's run away."

"Wicked girl."

"What kind of heart does she have?"

"Abandoning the boy..."

She would be beaten and taken into police custody if ever she returned, they said. Philomena couldn't have been more than thirteen years old herself. She'd probably run home to her parents. From their talk, I gathered that Ayo's body was still inside the tank. I pictured him as I saw him when he was jumping on the surface in his khaki shorts. I must have been standing there a while when I heard Mrs. Durojaiye's voice.

"My son? My son?"

She stumbled round the corner. The terror in her eyes, had someone pushed her into a den for sacrifice, I would not have known the difference. Mama Chidi tackled her. Mrs. Durojaiye pushed Mama Chidi away. Mama Chidi caught her arm. Mrs. Durojaiye cried out. Mama Chidi's glasses fell off, but she continued to wrestle as two other women broke from the crowd to help. The men stood with their lanterns; their children watched. Mrs. Durojaiye flung her captors off, grasped the collar of her nurse's uniform and ripped it apart when she saw the broken surface of the tank. Her bra and girdle held her together underneath. She was breathing as if she were fighting for air. She slapped the woman who tried to cover her. I stood by the washing lines as they held her like a prisoner.

Mama Chidi was on one side of her and the other two women on her other side, begging her to be strong. Mrs. Durojaiye brought them all down as she began to cry, "Jesus of Nazareth. Lord, have mercy on me. Please. Have mercy..."

The teenage boy returned with the bamboo stick as the women dragged Mrs. Durojaiye away on the cement ground. I remained by the pole. Another man took over from stirring the inside of the septic tank and feeling around for Ayo's body. The smell grew stronger. More people filled our backyard as news of the drowning spread on our street. If a body were brought out, it would be a spectacle for them. I turned away from the crowd and walked out of the compound.

I was tired of these people; a birth, a death, they were there, ready to bear witness. They did not know the difference. They were grief mongers. The women who held Mrs. Durojaiye, why did they have to do that, hold her down and beg her to be strong? As she stumbled around the corner, dribbling from the mouth, the one thought I had was, Let her go. My bag was dragging on the ground.

"*Tss*, sister," someone said. "Don't lose your money, oh."

Omnipotent, omniscient, only sometimes. What kind of a god would allow that to happen to Ayo? I walked down our street without caring about the potholes. People were hurrying over to the scene, just to see. I passed a woman selling cigarettes by kerosene light. Her head-tie was pushed low over her forehead, and she shooed mosquitoes away with a small raffia fan. Had she not heard? The mosquito coil on her display box sent up smoke. I squeezed my stomach to ease the pain inside and realized I was walking with my arms wrapped around my waist.

Ayo was not yet ten years old.

The day my father's body was found, I came home from school. A group of women were holding my mother down in her room. They were the women of her former *esusu* group. They saved money together and my mother had for a while been in charge of taking and keeping their contributions. "Your father is gone," one of them said, before I had a chance to walk into my mother's room. She was my uncle's wife called Sister Kunbi. I could tell she expected me to be sad and instead she made me furious. "I know," I said to her. "He has gone to Lagos." She seemed offended that I wasn't crying. She reached for my shoulder. "This world is a marketplace," she said. "The other is home. Your father has gone home."

"This is my father's home," I said.

I marched toward my mother. My mother was lying on her bed. I saw tears in her eyes. "Mama mi," I said. "My teacher says I should cut my hair. She says it is growing too long."

I wore my hair cropped because it was against school rules to have afros. Whenever my hair grew longer than an inch, it curled like seashells. My mother was the one person I trusted to cut my hair.

"Mama mi," I kept saying, and my hands were trembling. "Please answer me. When will you cut my hair? My teacher says I should cut it." It was a complete lie.

I walked off the main street into a dark road. On this street, there were kerosene lanterns on every veranda. Behind the houses were palm trees. Some children were playing, others were helping their mothers sell. I walked past a group of teenage boys. Nothing pleased them more than to see a madwoman. If she were naked, better still. One boy shouted, "*Were*," as if reading my thoughts. The rest of his group giggled. I ignored their taunts and carried on. At the end of the road, I spotted another boy crouched behind a rusty oil drum, by a small rubbish dump. This one was a young boy. He rubbed his eyes as if he'd been crying. His eyes caught the light of the kerosene lanterns. His head was perfectly round and his nose was small and pointed.

"Ayo?" I said.

I veered off the center of the road and walked toward him.

"Ayo, is that you?"

My footsteps quickened. The boy ducked behind the oil drum. "Ayo," I shouted. The jeering boys fell silent. Everyone watched as I ran to the oil drum. No one but me could see the thin legs tucked behind it. I reached for the legs and knelt by the boy.

"Look at you," I said. "Where have you been?"

He smelled of human waste and orange peels. I rocked him.

It was Ayo. He had run away so his mother wouldn't kill him. He had been jumping on the septic tank when the surface gave way. One of his legs went in and he managed to scramble out. I lifted him and ran back to our street. I kept dropping him because his body was too long to carry. Eventually he ran by my side. I held his hand to guide him.

"Your mother will be overjoyed."

"She will beat me."

"No, she will be so overjoyed to see you. Run faster."

"She will beat me."

"She can't. She thinks you're dead."

"She will beat me until she kills me. She's warned me before."

"Your mother loves you. You don't know how much. Tonight is not like before. Come, let's hurry."

The spectators in our compound didn't even know it was Ayo when we walked through the gates of our block. They made a path for us because we both smelled bad. It was Mama Chidi who recognized Ayo first. She was coming down the stairs, on the way to check on her family. She jumped and her glasses almost fell off. I had to remind her about the baby on her back. She ushered Ayo and me up the stairs into his mother's flat saying, "Hallelu, hallelujah!"

Mrs. Durojaiye was sitting in her chair, surrounded by the women who were comforting her. The smell of the septic tank was in her flat. She was still wearing her torn nurse's uniform. Ayo walked through the doorway, and she collapsed on the floor when she saw him. Her hands were on her head. She was gibbering, and I couldn't understand what she was saying. The other women watched with their mouths open. Ayo crept into the circle we made around him. His mother was by his feet now. She held his legs and began to sob. At first Ayo was stiff, as if he was not used to such tenderness, but his mother's hold tightened, and he finally bent to place his head on her shoulders.

No one said a word for a while, and then Mama Chidi laughed. She laughed so hard she forgot the baby on her back, as usual. The other women shook their heads in awe. Ayo was alive, here, in this flat, in this block, on this street, in this part of Lagos. If I had brought in a dead body, if Mrs. Durojaiye were beating Ayo for straying, they would have known what to do, these grief mongers: beg or wail. But to see Mrs. Durojaiye cuddling Ayo, they were not used to that. Mrs. Durojaiye raised her face. "What happened to him?" she asked.

"Let him tell you himself," I said.

Her eyes were as red as tomatoes. I, too, was crying.

Rose returned late that night after we had our usual power cut. I came out of my room with a battery lantern when I heard the front door. It was past midnight, and I couldn't understand why she would risk making the journey from OC's place. She was wearing the jeans and black sequined t-shirt she normally saved for Phaze Two Disco.

"What happened here?" she said. "The whole place is stinking."

"You can't imagine," I said.

"Impossible," she said, after I told her about Ayo, and Mama Chidi, who was half-blind, even with her glasses. Mama Chidi saw the hole in our septic tank and assumed Ayo had fallen in. Philomena had probably run away when she couldn't find him, rather than face a beating from Mrs. Durojaiye. Rose sat next to me on the sofa, and we watched the battery lantern.

"Poor Mrs. Durojaiye," she said.

"The boy too," I said. "They both suffered."

"I don't think she will beat him again, any of her sons, after this."

"You should have seen her. Her uniform was torn, her girdle exposed."

"She definitely can't walk around eyeing anyone after that."

"Rose."

"What? It's true! She is always eyeing me, and for what? Look at us in this place, one problem after the other, one disaster after another. Instead of sticking together, we're fighting each other. I can't stand it. Me, I'm getting out."

I smiled. "To go where, Czechoslovakia?"

"They're no better than Africans over there. I'm going to OC's place, I mean. The whole place stinks. I'll come back when the tank has been mended."

"Why did you bother to come tonight?" I asked.

"I just decided."

"Any trouble?"

"No trouble."

I picked up my lantern. "My sister, I done tire. Make sure you lock the door."

As I lay on my mattress, I became aware of the aches in my body. I rubbed my shins and rolled my wrapper between my legs. I was hot and tired, too tired to sleep.

I was telling Sanwo the story of his uncle's wife, Mrs. Odunsi, the one he called a corrupt woman. She'd come to Federal Community Bank one morning to dress Mr. Salako down. Sanwo was too upset to listen. The smell in our compound had put him off and the news about Ayo seemed to have exhausted him more. He was holding my envelope of money. He'd just arrived from the domestic airport by taxi and was wearing a green striped shirt and red checked tie.

"She didn't even say please," I said. "She just faced Salako and told him, 'I'm not writing a letter, Mr. Salako, and I want my account reactivated right now.' Salako was running in and out of his office, summoning this person and that, and saying he wanted fast answers..."

I'd immediately recognized Mrs. Odunsi. She came to my desk wearing a black linen trouser suit. Her hair was pulled back in a bun. She tapped a shiny white nail on my desk. "Tell Mr. Salako I want to see him," she said. "Tell him it's Chief Mrs. Odunsi and I can't wait a second."

Skinny woman. Her hands were almost transparent because she'd been bleaching her skin for years. Her veins appeared green, and her knuckles were dark brown. She was used to people obeying her. I could tell. She squared her shoulders and didn't even bother to look at me as she spoke.

My life would be much easier being like her, I'd thought. Her buttocks were bony, but they were her source of power. She might even have slept with a former head of state. She was not really of high society; neither was Sanwo's uncle, Chief Odunsi, who was at least willing to admit that money was all a person needed to be of high society in Lagos. Chief Odunsi was humble about his background and apparently grateful to have a wife who overdressed and bleached her skin. He threw large parties, hired juju bands, and watched as she danced while other men sprayed her with naira and dollar notes. She slept with the high society men she encountered, behind her husband's back, to get him government contracts and also for revenge, because their wives looked down on her.

She also copied their ways and went as far as to send her children to a boarding school in England. Her children came back behaving as if they'd been cursed from birth. Her daughter sneaked out to parties. Her son was expelled from his school for taking drugs. What didn't I know about the woman?

Yet, the way she treated Mr. Salako impressed me.

"Tell her to come in," Mr. Salako said. "Of course, Chief Mrs. Odunsi. I know her very well."

As she walked into his office, she said, "Mr. Salako, I'm not staying. I've come about my account. I'm very angry with you. I sent one of my boys over with a check yesterday and your cashier sent him back. She said my account was dormant and she needed to see a letter of reactivation. What is this nonsense?"

"Well, eh, banking procedures," Mr. Salako said, rubbing his hands together.

The culprit was Franka, and she had behaved according to the bank's rules, but she was rude to Mrs. Odunsi's messenger. She later denied this, of course.

Sanwo looked bored when I finished the story. Normally, I didn't talk this much and for once, he was in no mood to hear about the exploits of Mrs. Odunsi.

I eyed the envelope in his hand. "You're not happy about the money?"

"I am," he said.

"You don't look happy."

"This business about the boy has upset me."

"At least he's alive."

"The smell is making me sick. You won't see me around here for a long time."

I wanted to punish him for saying that. At the end of a week I usually had news for him. I had not seen him in three weeks. He'd traveled up North on business. As he walked through my door, I'd jumped on him and didn't stop talking for one second.

"Rose too ran away," I said. "She couldn't stand the smell either. But me, I have nowhere to go. My own boyfriend doesn't live in a place that can accommodate more than one person. All he has is a room and a *shalanga* to share. Don't worry. Mrs. Durojaiye will soon pay for the repair and the smell will eventually go."

He frowned. "Mrs. Durojaiye has to pay? That is most unfair."

I thought of another way to offend him. "This money," I said. "It's my investment in your business, not a loan, by the way."

"I know," he said.

"Don't lose my money."

"Why would I do that?"

"The business, what is it exactly?"

"Well, my partner Shood..."

"Who?"

"Can't you remember him? Yes, Moshood, the same one. He knows a lot of army men. He imports dogs for them, to protect their homes. They want pedigrees: Doberman, Rottweiler, not the usual mongrels."

I could not believe what I was hearing. Moshood was the man Sanwo stayed with whenever he traveled up North, one of his old friends from the College of Tech. All I knew about Moshood was that he was always late for appointments and had a

Volkswagen Beetle with only one door.

"Dogs?" I said.

"It's profitable," Sanwo said, noticing my expression.

"You will definitely get a return on your investment. Double even."

I'd made a terrible mistake.

"I want my money back," I said. "I give you my life savings and you're telling me about Moshood and dogs? I thought you had a real business proposition and real business partner."

"If you don't trust me," he said handing the envelope over. "I never wanted your money in the first place. But I've told you, nothing can go wrong. These army men have a lot of money. Dogs are one of the things they buy. Moshood imports dogs from abroad. He doubles his money every month."

My hand dropped. "All right."

"No, keep your money if you want," he said.

He pushed the envelope toward me and I waved it away.

"I trust you. Just bring me back my profit."

A colleague of mine at Federal Community Bank made extra money by selling sanitary towels. Everyone teased him until his business grew. Trading was what people did, so why not with dogs?

Sanwo held his nose. "This smell is terrible. I can't even stand to swallow my spit."

I laughed. He could not bear the slightest discomfort.

"Your haircut makes you look like a bush rat."

"Chicks dig it."

"What chicks?"

I pushed him. He ducked. We play-wrestled — African romance, as he would say. He tackled me; I kicked him. My standoff was over. He'd bought me three ebony bangles and a Fulani beaded choker. As for the smell, the longer I was around it, the more I got used to it.

I heard Rose's voice before I reached our gate the following evening. She was shouting, and shouting was not unusual on our street. Street hawkers shouted to attract customers; mothers shouted at their children; drivers shouted at pedestrians; friends shouted at each other instead of talking. We were a nation of proud shouters, but this was particularly loud shouting. I wondered who Rose was shouting at, and as I approached our front door, I realized she was shouting out of anger. The other voice was Johnny's, trying to calm her down.

"Hello?" I said, opening the door.

"Tell him to get out," Rose said.

"Your friend is not well," Johnny said.

"What happened?" I asked.

He held his hand up. "She bit me."

Rose brushed him aside. "I want him out of this place."

I shut the door behind me. "Why?"

"I want him out, I said."

Johnny rubbed his finger. "Don't listen to her.

All I did was ask her to be careful of OC. I gave her a lift from his place. They had a big fight over there. You should have heard what he said to her."

"Who asked you to talk?" Rose said. "If you think I'm joking, keep standing there like a military tribunal. Let me walk into my bedroom and come out. Today, today, we will enter the same trousers."

She slammed her bedroom door so hard the front door shook. I turned to Johnny. Our flat smelled of his cologne. He was wearing a white shirt with no collar, and his khaki trousers were starched stiff. I dropped my bag on a side table.

"You two broke up a year ago and I'm still settling your fights?"

"Talk to her. The things OC said to her were terrible."

"What things?"

"I can't say."

"What things, Johnny? You'd better tell me now."

"He said she was lax."

"What?"

"He said she was lax. I can't repeat what he said word for word. I mean, a man cannot respect you if he insults you like that. Talk to her. I don't know him that well. I met him only four years ago. Since then he's been living in America and I can't vouch for what he was doing over there."

"You said he was your friend."

"Everyone is my friend."

I hissed. "You-sef, Johnny Walker."

Rose was no fool. She had to know OC was a

dubious fellow.

"Wetin concern me?" he said. "She is the one who doesn't want to listen."

Her bedroom door cracked open and Rose ran out shrieking, "Out before I kill you!"

She was holding a knife. Johnny managed to open the door and run out before she reached him. I grabbed her by the shoulders to stop her from pursuing him.

"What is this?"

"Why were you talking to him?"

"Can't somebody rest in this place? I walk in and you two are behaving like...like area boys."

"I told you to get him out of here!"

"Am I your house girl?"

She lifted her hand, and for a second I thought she would bring the knife down on me, but she dropped it. She began to mumble, "No one cares about Rose. Every man wants to use Rose. What did Johnny ever buy for me? He's standing here like a military tribunal."

My face was close enough to smell the beer on her breath. She was drunk again.

"Buy is not love," I said.

"What do you know?"

"As for OC, if he insults you like that, he does not like you. You hear me? I don't care what he gives you. I'm telling you now. It's a mistake to have anything to do with that man."

She pushed my hand away. "I'm not making any mistake, my friend. I know exactly what I am doing.

A mistake is when you walk around thinking the world will change for you."

I was angry enough to slap her, but I wanted my peace back. I was so tired of the shouting and wailing. "Rose," I said, trying to calm down. "We have to be careful. Too much is happening. When things go wrong like this, one after the other..."

She hissed. "Be careful of what? Bad spirits? They're flying around in the air? My sister, stop all that village talk."

I nodded. "Very good. I talk like a villager, and you are free to do what you want, you hear me? Go where you want, with anyone you want. Just remember, this is my place too and I pay my own rent. You give me *wahala* and I will give you *wahala* back."

She slammed her bedroom door again, and the front door shook. Later, she went back to OC's place, and I didn't say a word to her until she left.

As if I did not have enough to think about that week, as if I had time for any of his own nonsense, I came to work one morning, and Mr. Salako called me to his office. He asked me to get a file from his cabinet.

"I'm sorry, sir," I said. "I can't do that."

"Why not?" he asked.

The plaque on his table said LAMIDI SALAKO. Lamidi was a joker's name. Every Lamidi I knew growing up was an oaf.

"My leg," I said.

"What about it?" he asked.

"It's giving me trouble."

"How?"

"It's paining me."

"What happened?"

"I fell off a bus."

"You must take me for a fool. When did this happen?"

"Today."

"Show me."

Luckily, I had enough scars on my shins.

"Those are old scratches," he said.

"I still can't bend," I said. "And I can't get any files until my leg heals."

"Take a memo for me," he said.

I left his room, walking upright, and returned with a pad and pencil. Mr. Salako's plump fingers were pressed together prayer-style. He had piles of paper on his desk. He would not do a thing until his work had gathered a layer of dust.

"Yes?" I said.

"To Personnel," he said. "Re: Tolani Ajao. I wish to lodge a formal complaint about my secretary Miss Tolani Ajao. This morning I requested that she retrieve a file from my filing cabinet. She refused and became recalcitrant..."

I interrupted. "How do you spell that, sir?"

"What?"

"Recalcitrant."

"Look it up in a dictionary."

The man was a bigger oaf than I imagined.

"Recalcitrant," he continued. I'd given an

illogical reason for not retrieving his file. I had a lackadaisical attitude and was proving difficult to work with. This was my first and final warning.

"Thank you," I said, when he finished dictating.

"Make sure it's typed up," he said.

"I will," I said.

He cocked his head to one side. "I've been watching you, the way you walk around here. You think you're something, don't you? Is it because you had some connection to Tunde Twinkle? Is that it, your reason for being snobbish? I'm surprised. You ought to know that Tunde Twinkle himself was a commoner."

He bared his tiny, pointed teeth.

"Is this part of your memo?" I asked.

His head straightened. "You can, eh, write your response for the records."

Outside, I threw the pad and pencil into my drawer. Yes, I fell off a bus. I fell off a bus and damaged my leg, and it was affecting my ability to retrieve files. I would write that if Mr. Salako wanted, type it up and give it to any person who cared to read it in Personnel.

After I typed his report and my response, I was calmer and able to reason. I had no choice but to tell the truth, so I described how Mr. Salako had assaulted me the first time he'd asked me to retrieve files. I took both memos to Ignatius in Personnel, trusting that he would understand why I'd been so rude to him and perhaps even excuse my behavior, if not sympathize. He stood there, and read the memos for over fifteen minutes.

"I would like to know who typed this," he finally said.

"Me," I said.

"I notice there's a missing semicolon."

"I'll write it in," I said.

"And a misplaced predicate. Unfortunately, you might have to type it up again."

"Why?"

He raised a brow. "An employee cannot amend internal documents by hand. If everyone does that, we will not be able to tell originals from fakes."

"I will type it again if you want, Uncle."

"At any rate, I can't accept your memo as it stands."

"Why not?"

"Have you actually read this?"

"I said I typed it."

"Your allegations are…rather shocking."

I pretended to be surprised. "Of course. Of course, Uncle. I should have known you would be shocked to read them. It was shocking to me too."

The sad part was that he was enjoying the respect I was showing him.

"This is unprecedented," he said.

Again I acted surprised. "You mean this is the first time a report like this has ever been filed?"

"I don't know if I can file it," he said, shaking his head. "Mr. Salako is a married man."

I should have asked if that had ever hindered Mr. Salako.

"Mr. Salako himself asked me to write the

report. I'm sure he would like you to file it. You're free to confirm with him first."

If I was correct, my memo would be torn up immediately or disappear somewhere. I was frustrated with the system, but I wasn't trying to work within it; I was planning to destabilize it, the whole goddamn, as Sanwo would say.

"Do you realize the implications of what you're doing?" Ignatius asked.

"Oh, yes, Uncle, I'm very sure."

"All right," he said. "All right."

That was how I became the most difficult employee in the history of the office, and I made my face tough to boot, so people would know not to cross my path. I really didn't blame my colleagues. I blamed Salako alone. But I'd seen how my colleagues could make my life more complicated. A word from me could lead to he-said, she-said. I didn't want any of that.

One day, I went to buy groundnuts as usual at twelve o'clock. My colleagues Ignatius, Godwin, Hakeem, and Franka were there. Franka, who had been careful not to be alone with me, even in the women's toilet, asked, "What's wrong, Tolani? You don't speak to us anymore. We are all so worried about you."

Perhaps she thought enough time had passed since she'd spread the rumor about me, or perhaps she thought I'd forgotten. She obviously wasn't aware that I'd reached a point where she was in great danger of ending up in the gutter.

"Look at you," she said, breaking into a smile. "I thought you were angry with me. I thought, 'Tolani must be angry because of what I said about Rose. That must be the reason she's not speaking to me.'"

Franka had such a sweet smile actually, but I didn't respond as she continued to talk about me as if I weren't actually standing there.

"I mean, Rose was not easy to get along with. She was always fighting, but Tolani? I've always said when people ask, 'What is happening with Tolani? What is wrong with Tolani these days?' I've always said, 'Leave Tolani alone. Tolani is nice. She is working for Salako and it cannot be easy. After all, she's learning her new job and she's...'"

I could hold back no longer. "Shut up your dirty mouth, Franka."

It was exactly what Rose would say.

"Eh?" she said. "Me?"

"Yes," I said. "Keep your comments to yourself. You've done enough damage and I'm not going to let you insult me on top of it."

She patted her chest. "Me?"

"Don't say another word," I said, pointing. "Otherwise you will live to regret it."

Ignatius stepped out of the line. "Ah-ah? At least show her some respect, and this, fighting outside like a market woman..."

"You too mind your own business," I said.

No Uncle for him either.

He covered his mouth. "Me, an old man? What happened to you? You were always polite."

"Yes," I said. "You are old. Maybe that's why you didn't hear me properly."

He wasn't an old man. He was just older than everyone else. He was certainly old enough to know better.

"I'm glad you're all here," I said, "because I won't repeat myself after this. Do not speak to me. Do not question me. I owe no one an explanation. I've filed my report and, if you like, you can keep spreading your rumors from here to Timbuktu."

"Dat's right, dat's right," Hakeem said. "Leave 'er alone. Look at 'er dismissing Ignatius like a small boy. God only knows whom she is connected to. She might open her legs and get every one of us sacked. Don't mind 'er. She'll see. She's forgotten 'er predecessor, Rose…"

As usual, he was dropping his H's, and his hands were high up as if I'd stolen his money. The whole line, including staff from nearby offices, turned to gape at me. Some clapped their hands in disgust. I walked away feeling ashamed that I'd lost my temper.

The street was heavy with traffic. A driver finally allowed me to walk in front of his car. I had barely crossed over to the other side when I felt a tap on my shoulder.

"What?" I snapped.

It was Godwin. Really, I wasn't ready for

another battle. He handed a wrapper of ground-nuts to me.

"For you," he said.

"For what?"

I eyed his hairy wrist. We were by the pedestrian barricade, which was supposed to stop people from trespassing our bank's steps. Today, the buses, cars, and bicycles were as noisy as ever, with their engines, horns, and bells. I had to shout to hear myself. The bank guards watched us. Their Alsatians were asleep on the hot ground.

Godwin pressed the groundnuts into my hand. "You don't want to eat again?"

"What's your concern if I eat?"

"You want to fight me too?"

"No," I said after a moment.

He was a genuine born-again. No one in the bank had complaints about him, except that he was boring.

"Why are you bothered with Franka?" he asked. "You know she is an unhappy woman, and that's why she gossips. Her husband beats her almost every day."

"I'm very happy to hear that."

"You don't mean it."

"Yes, I do."

He smiled. "You should pray for your enemies, Tolani."

"Godwin," I said, "my father was a Shango worshipper. Right now, the way I feel, you might as well call me one."

"You don't mean that either. You're just carrying a heavy burden."

He freed my hand. Godwin's hand was softer than mine. He was one of those men: Christianity had made him womanly. I shielded my eyes from the sun and could see he was good-looking, even though his hair was almost an afro, and he was smiling like the man in the Macleans toothpaste advert.

"I'm here to encourage you," he said. "Put your trust in the Lord. He is forever faithful. Anytime you are ready, come to my church. I will introduce you to people who will help you."

"I'm not going to any revival, Godwin."

That was the second complaint people had about him. He was always inviting people to church.

He laughed. "My church family helped me when I challenged management over prayer meetings. Remember?"

I remembered that the Muslims took time off to pray during the day, and so the born-agains demanded their own time off. Godwin led them, in Jesus' name, and I also remembered that Mr. Salako stopped hiring anyone he suspected of being a born-again Christian, after he approved their prayer meetings. Rose told me the story from start to finish. Mr. Salako himself was a practicing Muslim, but he did not believe in praying during work hours, for Muslim or Christian employees. He called them lazy workers.

Godwin's church was a trick. His church family would come with their Macleans smiles. Tell-me-what-happened would end with forsake-all-others. Next thing, I would be baptized into their faith. But I was an Anglican, like my mother. I was already baptized and needed no other conversion.

"How much do I owe you?" I asked.

He was kind to have bought the groundnuts, and his salary was less than mine.

"Come to my church," he said. "That is my payment."

"Thank you, Godwin. You have a good heart."

He waved. "I salute you, my sister."

"I salute you," I said.

Why did I eventually become friendly with Godwin in that office? Not because I enjoyed hearing about Jesus during my lunch breaks, nor because I liked promising that I would attend one of his church services. It was because I couldn't fight everybody. I just couldn't, no matter the circumstances.

I began to tread softly, and it was exactly the same with my mother. People were funny, she said, because with age she had grown kinder. "Funny" was not the word I used to describe my colleagues at Federal Commercial Bank. "Treacherous" was the word I preferred. People in general. It was as though they waited for the opportunity to show just how deeply they hated each other. In my case it was office gossip; in my mother's, it was gossip over a motorcycle, a common motorcycle.

My Vespa. Yes. Motorcycles were rare in those days, not like now when you can get run over just by stepping out of your door. Your uncle, Brother Tade, owned the only motorcycle store in town. He offered one to your father, a Vespa, big and black and shiny, but your father said he preferred to trek around. I knew he was scared of falling and this amused me because many men were riding motorcycles in those days.

Let me see, this was before you were born. I was the collector of my esusu *group, and was responsible for taking contributions from the members and making a payout each month. We were all women in the group and we did not care for savings banks. We lived in the town center, some of us by the church, some by the school, and some by the marketplace. It took me hours to make my rounds for the collections and my cloth business suffered. Meanwhile, my fellow cloth dyers in the marketplace praised me for my efforts, calling me a good child,* omo dada, *because they knew how much business I was losing to them.*

One day, I went to Brother Tade's motorcycle store to take a contribution from his wife, Sister Kunbi. Sister Kunbi had just become a member of our group. Her own business was selling provisions like milk, sugar, and soap, even though she didn't need to sell anything because Brother Tade was wealthy. She was not at her stall that day. It was right next to Brother Tade's motorcycle store and Brother Tade was in.

"I've walked all this way," I told him. "I can't come

back. Will you give me your wife's contribution?"

He was smiling only because I was. Brother Tade was kind in that way. If you were charming and acted a little stupid, you could get anything out of him. Unfortunately Sister Kunbi had not learned that womanly trick. Only harsh words came out of her mouth and people said it was because Brother Tade, for all his cheerfulness, was strict with her. She could go no further than that stall of hers without his knowing where she was going and how soon she would be back. He loved her very much, you see, and kept her quite fat. If any man cared for me that way, I would have begged him not to. I preferred your father's way. He appreciated me enough to leave me alone and I could do almost anything I wanted.

Brother Tade said, "I will give you my wife's contribution. She has not gone far, but when she gets back, I will get my money back from her. That woman will soon be earning more than me at this rate."

We were both laughing, because everyone knew Brother Tade was generous and would not take money from his own wife.

"Brother Tade," I said. "How I wish your brother would get one of your motorcycles so I can ride around town."

"Ride?" he said.

"Yes," I said. "It is hard walking about. I watch people riding. I know I can ride better than any of them."

I didn't say men and I didn't talk about their falling either. If I did, Brother Tade would think I was trying to insult him. If he thought I was merely bragging, like a naïve child, he would be amused.

He laughed. "Of course. Why not? Try a Vespa. Maybe that will persuade my brother to get one, when he sees his wife riding."

Like that he gave me a Vespa. I struggled to get on with my wrapper. I was thinking, Who made such a vehicle? Do they not know that women wear wrappers? I sat on top, pushed with my feet as I'd seen men do. In no time I fell on the ground and my backside was in agony.

Brother Tade found that very funny. "I see you're a very good rider," he said. "I see you're the best rider in town."

I was smiling, but my heart was pumping fast. I held the Vespa handles and twisted them like goat ears. I pushed again with my feet. Now, the seat hurt my backside and I raised myself a little. The Vespa didn't move. In my anger, I'd forgotten to check my wrapper. It was tangled in the wheel. I fell again, same side.

Brother Tade laughed. "You're a very good rider. A very good rider indeed. The best rider in the world. My brother will certainly be humbled by your talents."

That was when I got the idea to buy a motorcycle, or perhaps I'd always thought of getting one, and only when he teased me did I think I should. I imagined what it would mean for my business, the precious time that it would save. I remembered the moment I got on the Vespa and my heart beat fast. I thought of the Vespa nonstop. I dreamed about the Vespa. I finally told your father, "You must get one of Brother Tade's motorcycles."

He said, "Absolutely not."

I said, "But all the men in town are getting one."

"So?"

"We alone are behind the times."

"I don't care to be current."

"But it's like having a goat."

He liked goats, you see. Any goat ended up in our compound. I couldn't bear them. They were always sitting on the grass patch under our mango tree and chewing. They left such a mess. I would actually give them away secretly, when they got too many, to friends, hoping that your father would not notice. He would come home and ask, "What about that goat?" "What goat?" I would answer, pretending not to know which. He would say, "The one with the white patch," or something like that. Then he would describe the goat from head to foot. I would say, "Oh! That goat? She wandered off. Such a shame…"

He asked, "How is a goat like a motorcycle?" I couldn't answer, but I kept pestering him about Vespas, from morning until night. Aren't Vespas beautiful? Aren't Vespas useful? Isn't it a blessing to have a Vespa? I knew that what your father hated most in the world was someone repeating themselves. He finally gave in one morning. "What is all this wahala about? Every day it's Vespa this and Vespa that," he said. "Take this. Go to my brother's store. Tell him I want the best."

The strange part was that he didn't even give me enough money to buy a wheel. In our own home, I was earning more money than he was from cloth dyeing. He was drumming for drunken lorry drivers. They were happy to fall on their knees and praise him whenever he entertained them. When it was time to reward him, they suddenly became sober — no money left. I took the little money he gave me anyway, and would have had to add my savings had Brother Tade not ended up giving me a Vespa for a quarter of the price. One of his boys rode it back while I walked. When I arrived home, I faced the Vespa in our compound.

It was that wretched Vespa and me. I, Arike, who was schooled by my aunt Iya Alaro to paint patterns with a feather. She still lived in the farming settlements and would have been shocked to see me when I tucked my wrapper between my legs like a man's trousers. I sat on the Vespa and pushed with my feet. Vroom! The goats in the compound got up and started running around in circles. Vroom! Fumes came out of the back of the Vespa. Vroom! The goats were colliding with each other. That made me so happy. Vroom! I went forward about three steps and stopped. I placed my feet on the ground before I could fall. I went forward again, about another step, and stopped. The goats were out of our compound. For that alone, getting rid of those goats, the Vespa was a blessing. I rode from one end of our compound to the other. By the time I got off, I was thinking, What are legs? Legs are completely useless. Only two of them, and you place one in front of the other. Unless you're running, they can't get you far.

I learned how to ride the Vespa around the compound. The trouble was, once I learned, how would I ride it outside the compound?

We lived on a slope. The road outside our house led to the marketplace. There were many houses down that road, more houses the further down you went, more *people around the marketplace than anywhere else in Makoku. The people, the slope, I didn't know what scared me most. If I didn't fall off the Vespa, the people might waylay me, drag me off, and beat me up for daring to ride. Not even my aunt Iya Alaro would come to my rescue this time. She believed there was women's business and men's business, and she was prepared to protect any woman so long as she kept to women's business. She didn't approve of women crossing over to the men's arena and causing confusion. Then the idea came to me: I would not be riding around town for my own sake. Really, I would be riding for Brother Tade's sake. Did I not have to thank him for selling me the Vespa for a quarter of the price? Did I not have to show him that, yes, I could ride a motorcycle after all, and tell him that yes, he was right, I was the best rider in town, and eventually, if I kept on riding around town, his brother would be humbled and want to ride a motorcycle? Those were Brother Tade's words, not mine. I was simply complying with my brother-in-law's wishes.*

I planned to keep practicing on the Vespa until Sunday when there were fewer people around town and the marketplace was closed. I would ride to Brother Tade's house early in the morning, just to tell him, "Thank you for what you have done for my husband."

I left the house before your father woke up that Sunday. The goats were already awake and they were lucky because I led the Vespa down the road. I was still nervous about the slope. I greeted the few people who had risen early, mostly women, and they watched me and wondered what I was doing and where I was going with a Vespa. I stopped walking as soon as the road leveled out, pushed my wrapper between my legs and got on that Vespa.

Vroom! You should have seen the old woman who was sitting on her chair with a chewing stick in her mouth. *Vroom!* Instead of spitting, she swallowed. *Vroom!* She slapped her chest. *Vroom!* She fell off her stool.

I sped down the road. The morning breeze was cool on my face. My sleeves were flapping in the wind. The pedestrians I passed were opening their mouths, pointing and bumping into each other. I did not stop until I reached Brother Tade's house. His store was closed and Sister Kunbi's stall was locked up. She was the one I met.

"How did you come?" she asked.

"I rode," I said.

"What do you mean you rode?"

"Brother Tade sold me a Vespa."

"What for?"

I realized she would not stop questioning me, so I explained why I came.

"You, the junior wife of the family, who hasn't even given birth," she said, "you rode a motorcycle here without your husband's consent? And I, the senior wife, cannot walk down the road without telling my husband where I'm going?"

"Don't be angry," I answered.

"Go home," she said. "I will relay your message to my husband."

She watched me ride off. Her hands were on her hips and I was thinking, she wouldn't get far on a motorcycle anyway. She was huge. One of her arms was equal to two of mine. I'd tried, but I could never quite get that fat.

Your father never went to church. He visited the babalawo *regularly though. Whenever I went to church, he said, "You're still going to your...?" and I answered, "So long as you are going to yours." People in our town visited both, and they did not find any inherent conflict in continuing that way, between two beliefs. Even three. One man I knew, on Sunday he was sprinkling holy water on his face and making the sign of the cross; midweek he was offering kola nuts at the shrine; and by Friday he was facing Mecca to say "Allah is great."*

I went to church later that morning, and by the time I returned, Brother Tade was in our house. He was talking with your father and their voices dropped when they saw me. I greeted them. Your father didn't even bother to look my way; Brother Tade didn't smile. You can imagine how worried I was. Immediately, I went to the next room and pretended I was preparing sweet pap. I heard them talking about me.

"She couldn't have," your father said. "Look at her face. My wife is innocent, like a child. She would never deceive me like that."

"She did," Brother Tade said. "And my wife says there were several sightings."

"That is serious," your father said.

"It shocked me," Brother Tade said. "People will say you have lost control of your home."

"I have not lost control of my home," your father said. "Who will say this?"

"The townspeople," Brother Tade said. "Remember how you married her? Remember how her aunt organized that protest and threatened to bare her back-

side to the Oba? She refused to marry into the royal family, she has no children, and now she's riding a motorcycle willy-nilly?"

I kicked a pot over by accident. I was in trouble. They must have realized I was listening. I was thinking that that was the end of my riding days. I would have to adjust to walking again. My life was ruined.

"Tell these people," your father said in a loud voice. "Tell them that it was I, Ajao, who gave my wife permission to ride a Vespa. I who gave her permission because I know that if she falls once or twice and breaks both her legs, and maybe that stubborn head of hers, she will learn her lesson."

He never mentioned the Vespa after that, and his silence made me uneasy, only for a short while. I enjoyed riding too much to have unnecessary regrets. I did fall once or twice, but that was because of my wrapper. I would have preferred to wear a man's trousers while I rode that Vespa. I never did. That would have been too much for the townspeople to tolerate. All I wanted was to continue riding and carrying on my businesses. Really. I wasn't a troublemaker. That was not in my nature. I was simply being practical.

Mrs. Durojaiye and I met on the stairway one night. I'd waited at work after hours to avoid the heavy traffic. She was walking down, and her flashlight was on full beam. She dimmed it when she saw me. Luckily, we had electricity that night, but there were no lightbulbs in our stairway or corridors, so we were almost in the dark.

"Tolani?" she said.

"Yes, ma," I said.

"Hope all is well."

"All is well, ma."

"Hm, how I wish I could say the same."

"Hope nothing?"

She was one stair above me, and the dim light made her face appear like an *Egungun* mask. She'd lost a lot of weight, and her cheeks were hollow.

"We've had so much trouble at the hospital. Too much trouble today."

"What happened?"

"You won't believe. We were having a peaceful protest, calling on the government to reconsider our demands, when we noticed a group in the crowd who did not belong to our union. We asked who they were. They were shouting insults and acting rowdy. Next thing we knew, another group arrived in a truck with cow dung. The two groups joined together and carried the cow dung in buckets. They ran through the hospital entrance, threw the cow dung on the floor, smeared it on the walls, the beds, the equipment. Everywhere."

"Ha?"

The people she was talking about had to be area boys. They waited for any protest so they could misbehave. Whatever life had done to them, they were ready to give back double. They had so much wickedness in their hearts from hardship. They stood on street corners and solicited clients: "*Tss,* you want marijuana or heroin? *Tss*, don't you have an enemy to dispose of?"

"Expensive medical equipment," Mrs. Durojaiye said. "Equipment we bought overseas, equipment we have not even used. Cow dung. The police arrived and they began to horsewhip people. Some fought back, some picked up stones to throw. The police tear-gassed us. Then they shot in the air. We lost two people. One bled to death, one was shot in the back of her head. She was a student nurse, peeking from the balcony of the hostels. Stray bullet struck her. Young girl. You cannot believe how much this has saddened me."

After her son escaped drowning, Mrs. Durojaiye talked freely, as if her tongue had become loose. I did not know what to say to her. One evening, she was mumbling to herself about her husband, when I asked after her sons who were staying with him. "He gambled," she said. "Lost all our money. Pools..."

In the same resigned manner, she continued about the nurse who was killed: "Worked in my ward. Going to see her people tomorrow. Had to take her body to the mortuary. Place is a mess. No electricity. Bodies all rotting. Poor girl's remains were sweating. It was terrible. Terrible. Ask Rose, I've just told her the whole story."

"You spoke to Rose?"

"Yes. She came to see me about my son. I told her Ayo is with his father for the rest of the strike. Barely a month and he's already begging to come back to me. He does not like staying there. Always complaining about his father's new wife. She rations food. I've told him he has to learn to cope like his brothers. Let their father take responsibility for a change. I can't do anything to help them right now. Ah, you cannot believe how tired I am. I work at night. Private clinic. Pay my bills and you know I still have to find money to fix the septic tank."

"Small by small, ma," I said.

She walked down the stairs as if in a trance. She'd been talking to herself all along.

There was a strong smell of simmering palm oil in the flat. Rose was in the kitchen, and she was wearing my Fruit of the Loom T-shirt. I really didn't care that she'd borrowed it without asking; I just wanted to be left alone. She laughed at my expression.

"My sister," she said. "You think say I no know how to cook or what?"

"I've just seen Mrs. Durojaiye," I said, shutting the door.

"I saw her too."

"She says you visited her?"

She clucked. "The woman done craze. Union strike, septic tank, somebody shot dead, dis, dat. I felt so sorry for her."

I threw my bag on the center table. Why did she visit Mrs. Durojaiye? Our sitting room looked unusually clean and from what I could smell, she wasn't making her usual pepper soup. She disappeared into the kitchen.

"What are you cooking?" I asked.

"*Banga* soup," she said.

"Since when did you make *banga* soup?"

"OC likes it."

There was a new fan on the side table.

"Is this his?" I asked.

"That one? I bought it myself."

"*Na wa.*"

The fan cooled my feet as I lay on the sofa. I lifted my face to the ceiling and watched the water stains. They were the color of pee stains. They never changed shape. They were like maps. Rose was making a noise in the kitchen, dropping spoons and slamming pots.

"You know what happened today?" she said. "I was coming here and as I waited on the main street by OC's place for a taxi, all the taxis were driving past. You know how they do. I was standing with my hand up. One man approached me. He slapped my chest. Just like that. I came here and checked myself quick, quick."

I shut my eyes. She was talking about *mago*. Every so often, the newspapers carried so-called true accounts about people in Lagos who went around slapping other people's chests. The stories claimed the slaps could make people's private parts disappear, or put them under a spell to make them hand their money over. They were like jokes, frauds, these *mago* people. Only a man like Mr. Salako would be afraid of them.

"You don't believe in that," I said.

"Well, I didn't want to risk it."

Mago didn't exist. She had nothing better to think about, or perhaps she was beginning to invent problems for herself like a rich madam. She tapped my shoulder.

"Here," she said.

It was good to have money to spend though. Her *banga* soup was actually tasty, and it had periwinkles. I ate it with semolina while the fan cooled me and was thinking that Rose was behaving as if she needed a favor. Why else would she cook for me?

"How is Sanwo?" she asked.

"Long time," I said.

"You quarreled?"

"He traveled up North for business."

"He travels too much, that *bobo*."

"Yes."

"How is your own work?"

Her beef was tough to chew, and she was asking too many questions.

"Fine," I said, with my mouth full.

"You don't like it?"

"My job?" I said. "It's all right."

"And Salako?"

I must have looked as if I'd swallowed a periwinkle shell.

"Don't worry," she said. "He suffered me too. It can't be easy working for him."

I shrugged. "I've just started."

"You seem fed up already. Is he being that difficult?"

I put my fork down. "He's written a memo to

Personnel about my work attitude and I've filed my own memo telling them exactly what he did to me."

"Eh, what happened?"

It was not the kind of talk that relieved me. I told her only because I no longer cared whether I shared my problem. Her reaction would make no difference.

"You see?" she said. "This is what I mean, and we will continue this way unless we change it."

"Change what?" I asked.

She leaned forward and grabbed my arm. "Tolani, listen. OC smuggled drugs to America. That is how he made his money over there. *Shh*, just hear what I'm saying. *Shh!* He has stopped doing that now. He looks for women like you and me. He will give us drugs to swallow and arrange for us to travel overseas. We get there and come back. That's all we need to do and we get paid, you hear?"

I dropped my plate on the side table so hard the *banga* soup jumped out of it.

"One journey," she said. "That's all. A thousand five hundred dollars. Are you listening?"

What was she saying for God's sake? Drug mules? Those women who were always getting caught? The government was executing them publicly at one point. Three of them had faced a firing squad, and then there were protests over their executions. The government had stopped executing them, but the women still appeared in the news-papers. They swallowed drugs, hid drugs in their private parts, and spent time in jail because of drugs. To me, they were like prostitutes. Was this the same Rose, this person who was considering smuggling?

"My sister," she said. "I'm not ashamed. Being poor is what I'm ashamed of. Being poor is what you should be ashamed of. See Violet? Everyone knows what Violet was doing in Rome. Now she's back home with her hair salon. No one can tell Violet she was not studying Italian in Italy. Our heads of state steal, our board of directors steals. Who asks where their money comes from? People praise them. They run after them and beg them to spread some of their wealth. I am tired of being poor. Every day is a struggle with this War Against Indiscipline and austerity measures. You sit in a compound stinking of shit. You walk down a street stinking of gutters. You're on a bus full of stinking people. You get to work and a man like Salako with his stinking..."

"Rose!" I said. "Salako or OC?"

"What about them?"

"Salako is an oaf! OC is a dangerous man!"

"OC did nothing to Rose. Rose Adamson made up her own mind."

I stood up. "No. I don't want to hear. I don't, and I am not poor."

"You are! You are just too proud to admit it!"

She was following me around, telling me I should consider what she'd said. I was the one person she could trust. The only person. I kept moving, as if she was trying to take possession of my mind, and could, if she came too close. I did not want her near me. She was free to do whatever she liked with her own body, I said, but I did not take risks with mine.

"What risks?" she asked.

"Death!"

Did I have to tell her? That was the one aspect of their work I couldn't understand, those mules. At least the prostitutes used condoms to save their lives. The thought of swallowing one made me want to gag.

"You think I want to die?" she asked.

"I don't care. It's my own life I'm concerned about."

"So, I want you to die?"

"I don't want to hear, I said!"

"I've thought about everything. Everything."

I pointed. "Do not tell me any nonsense here."

"But it's a fact. If everyone dies, no one will do it. We are not the first and we won't be the last."

"You," I said. "You are the one who wants to play with your life."

"In what way?"

"You swallow drugs, you play with your life."

"Not if you wrap the drugs well, well."

I almost laughed. "Why do people die? For no reason?"

"They are not careful."

"How can you be careful if you swallow drugs? How, for heaven's sake?"

"I'm telling you, I have the facts. I've found out all we need to know. You wrap the drugs properly, make sure they are tight. Don't eat or drink. People do it every day. How many deaths do you hear of? People don't die like that unless they are extremely careless, and do I look like someone who is careless enough to risk her life for money?"

She was desperate, I thought, so desperate, and she was not deceiving herself; she was trying to deceive me.

"Go back to OC," I said, pointing at the door, "and ask him that question."

"Just think about it," she said. "A thousand five hundred."

"No," I said, reaching for her arm. I pulled her toward the door. She had to leave immediately.

"A thousand, five hundred dollars," she said. "Clean. At least one good thing about austerity measures, our currency is so worthless that if you convert that amount to naira, it will be more than the small money the bank pays you, eh?"

"I said no!"

She wasn't even resisting as I dragged her; she was smiling. I opened the door. Had she lost all her pride or what? She was practically begging me.

"One journey," she said. "One year's salary. I'm telling you because I want to help you as a friend."

"Leave this place," I said. "Leave me alone in peace. You came here and found me in peace."

"Just reconsider," she said. "I'll be back soon. It's not as if I had to tell you, eh? I've made up my own mind. If you change yours, let me know, eh?"

"Don't come back here," I said. "You hear me?"

I pushed her into the corridor outside and

slammed the door, and then I locked it. I would have barricaded it if that were possible.

"Witch," I whispered.

I couldn't sleep that night. I kept picturing her waiting for me behind the door.

I prayed a lot after that and was looking forward to Sanwo's return. I did not believe in evil spirits or people who were capable of putting hexes on others. I believed in evil forces. When people lied, cheated, beat, insulted, they passed on bad will and created misfortune. Prayer could make me stronger.

Johnny actually came back to our flat after his near-stabbing, and I thought he was the bravest man on earth to attempt that. He said he'd come to find out how Rose and I were doing.

"How's that boyfriend of yours?" he asked, sounding casual, but his eyes were darting around as if he expected Rose to burst out from behind a door. He was wearing one of his traditional shirts with dog patterns that only reminded me of Sanwo's latest business venture.

"He's up North," I said.

"Up North again? Leaving a fine woman like you alone?"

"Johnny, please." I had no time.

He smiled. "It's true. He's never around. What is this? The man has to at least put a ring on your finger if he expects you to keep waiting for him."

"He will," I said.

"When?"

"Whenever possible."

"He's taking his time, my dear."

"It's a question of money."

He glanced at Rose's door again. "I hope he's not playing games. I hope he knows what he has. Rose will have a hard time finding another roommate like you when you're gone."

"She's never here anyway."

"When is she coming back?"

"I can't say. She's in and out of OC's place. Two days, one week."

"What will we do about that woman?"

"We? I blame you, Johnny."

"Why?"

"Because you introduced them and because she liked you and you let her down. You're too tight. Too tight with money."

Except with himself. He sat next to me, and I couldn't help but notice his black crocodile shoes. They didn't look like fakes.

"What work do you do?" I asked him.

"Things," he said.

"What things?"

"Import, export."

"Of what?"

He was forever dressed up and smelling of colognes. He didn't own a car and used public transport, but he had a decent apartment in Surulere and was guarded only about his source of income. Was he involved in drug trafficking? My intuition told me that he wasn't, but I could no longer be sure.

"I'm into sugar," he said.

"What about sugar?"

"Everyone knows about sugar."

All I knew was that the government controlled sugar, and there were multimillionaire importers who brought sugar into the country by the container-load. Employees at our bank received a monthly package of essential commodities, including sugar. How on earth sugar became essential was a mystery. It occurred to me that just about any substance, even a handful of dirt, could easily become costly if it were banned. It was the same with drugs.

"How are you involved in sugar?"

"I work for a middleman."

"In the middle of what?"

"Ah ah? What's going on with you, Tolani? You're like granite these days. Since when did you become so hard? At least one could talk to you before without fear of an assault."

"Just answer me."

"I don't divulge my personal business."

"I'm asking what you do," I insisted.

"Do I ask you your business?"

"No."

I had to admit I was badgering him like a lawyer. Fear had turned me into the hard woman I'd initially pretended to be. I couldn't bring myself to ask if he was a trafficker. I'd always assumed

Johnny was secretive about his work because he was worried that he might have to spend his money on others, if word got out that he was making any. I watched him closely to see if he was lying.

"This OC," I said, "you're sure you don't know him well?"

"Very sure."

"What does he do?"

"You're asking me? How would I know?"

He opened his palms like Jesus, which only made me more suspicious.

"You brought him into my life," I reminded him.

"Honestly," he said. "I don't know what he does. Do you?"

"I'm asking you," I said.

"You must be asking for a reason."

"What reason?"

"You tell me. Has Rose said anything to you?"

"Like what?"

He laughed. "Are you hiding something from me?"

"You're the one I'm asking," I said, poking the air with my forefinger.

"I don't know," he said. "I really don't. OC and I are acquaintances. We have mutual friends. I heard he was back from the States. I went to his place to welcome him home. He said he needed sandals because of the heat. He couldn't find them to buy in the winter season or something. I took him to Tajudeen market. That's all."

It was hopeless. I imagined that this was how

military men approached each other about their coup plans, talking back and forth without revealing anything that would incriminate themselves. The trouble was, the moment Rose shared her secret with me, I became part of her scheme and couldn't open up to anyone.

"What's wrong?" Johnny asked.

"Nothing," I said.

I had no choice but to rely on the little I knew. He couldn't be a trafficker; he'd never been abroad. He couldn't be a recruiter, either; everyone recognized his face, and someone would have talked. Rose herself would definitely have found out. She used to go through his belongings, searching for cash.

"Would you like a drink?" I asked.

"You have beer?"

"I might."

I went to the kitchen. A cockroach darted across the doorway and hid between two cardboard boxes, as if it were scared that I would interrogate it.

"Sorry to probe you," I said, "but people get drawn into all sorts in this city."

"That's because we've lost our connection to the land," Johnny said.

Apart from perambulating, he also pontificated occasionally and was always quoting one line or another, from lyrics, to support his assertions. I found a bottle of Star beer in the cupboard under the sink. It was warm.

"We come to Lagos in search of money," he

explained. "We get caught up in the quest. We take and take and give nothing back. The land becomes a fertile ground for corruption."

His belief was similar to my father's, and my father would also say the solution was for people to return to their hometowns and pick up hoes. I found that highly idealistic.

"Maybe we should all be farmers again," I said, returning to the sitting room.

"Fishermen," Johnny said. "Hunters and cloth weavers."

I handed him the Star beer. "Could you go back to your hometown as you are?"

He shook his head. "The pace is too slow. Could you?"

"No," I said. "What would I live on?"

"People don't need much to survive in rural areas."

"I do."

Why deny it? I needed money, plenty, plenty.

"That's because you're used to city life," Johnny said. "The trappings. In rural areas, they have no use for any of that."

"You think?"

I'd made a mistake by offering him a beer. I was in for an afternoon of listening to his views.

"Of course," he said, lifting the bottle to his lips. "People in the interior, they are down-to-earth. Uncomplicated. Let me tell you how they live."

Indeed. No one can say for certain what life is like anywhere in the world unless they actually live there. One thing I can vouch for, complications will arise so long as money and people are involved.

There were days I regretted leaving the farming settlement for the town center. I missed the quiet atmosphere of my aunt's co-op. I was working on my own in the noisy marketplace. There was a section for cloth dyers right next to the basket weavers. We were meant to collaborate with each other, even though we ran our separate trades, but the basket weavers would accuse us of encroaching on their territory. My fellow cloth dyers would complain that the basket weavers were constantly leaving a mess in the marketplace. The two sides would bicker; this would lead to a formal petition to our local council, who would then appoint an ombudsman. The ombudsman would hold meeting after meeting. It was quite frustrating. I had no idea that town life would be so trying.

My colleagues must have noticed that I was not interested in their weaver-dyer skirmishes. Perhaps this was what bothered them about me, enough for them to begin to turn some of their attention to me. I was quite successful, you see, especially because of my esusu *business, yet I had not given birth to a child. The others brought their babies to the marketplace, and every day they asked, "When are you going to have yours?"*

When was I going to become a mother, they meant, as if that had any bearing on their lives. One woman in particular upset me. She would ask, "What are you making all this money for, if it's not to spend it on your offspring?" I wouldn't have minded if she wasn't the same person who had borrowed a little something, as she called it, from me, and never bothered to pay it back.

Still, I ignored her and the rest of them. I was consumed with creating innovative designs and trying untested methods of cloth dyeing. That was how I began to attract more and more customers. They came like bees to honey and if they were willing to pay, I upped my price. I was excellent at haggling. No one could tell from my expression what I was thinking. My customers left my stall feeling satisfied, even when they'd paid high premiums for my cloth. Because my designs were unique, they showed them off wherever they went and brought more new customers my way.

I made a lot of money. I enjoyed having money, so much that I even used to sniff my bundles. There was no denying, and I was grateful for my success because I knew that, in life, people worked like cattle and they died destitute. My colleagues, not surprisingly, began to pressure me more and more about having children. Every day they would ask, "When are you going to have yours?" I thought, How strange, unless I was God, how did they expect me to answer that question?

Of course I was worried. Of course having money to spend and save was not enough to satisfy me. To top it all, I was going home to face the same kind of inquisition from family members. Some were truly concerned, like my aunt Iya Alaro, who on her deathbed said to me before she passed away, "Arike, so I never did see your child after all," and I wept so hard because I'd disappointed her. Others, like Sister Kunbi, would give me advice like, "If you would only sit down for one minute and stop riding that motorcycle around, you might not have a problem conceiving." She would make such statements at family meetings that had nothing to do with me in the first place; then everyone would forget the issue at hand and focus on me.

After one of these humiliating episodes, Brother Tade sent for me. He said he wanted to talk to me about the Vespa. I rode it to his house, since it was the object in question.

"Why did you ride that Vespa here?" he asked.

I was about to explain.

"No, no!" he said. "I don't want to hear it! That's the trouble with you, Arike, you've never known when to stop. My brother should have put his foot down long ago and now look at where he is today. I'm on my fifth. He hasn't even produced his first issue."

I listened in silence.

"What a shame," Brother Tade said. "I'm actually tired of the matter, but let me tell you a bit about that man you married. He was mollycoddled as a boy because he was sickly and nearly died. I believe that was where our mother went wrong with him. It was a good thing that our father decided to send him off to a guardian. That helped my brother to grow up a little. He is an exceptionally talented man, but he's basically a dreamer and that is why he allows you to ride a motorcycle. I was never spoiled like him. I got whipped consistently. You hear me? I learned discipline and in turn, I became a disciplinarian. See? None of my children can get away with misbehaving, and as for my wife, Kunbi, she'd *better not be disobedient, no matter how much I care for her. She knows her limits with me. Ask her. One false move and I will drive her out of the house. Now, I must admit she's said hurtful things to you that I don't personally approve of, but that's her way. I can't apologize for what comes out of her mouth at family meetings, but I can assure you of this, she has only your best interest at heart, and it's time that someone told you straight to your face. This matter is more than a personal one. It has become a family embarrassment."*

"Brother Tade," I had to ask. "I don't understand. Which matter?"

"You have no child," he said. "You're riding around town on a motorcycle. You're out of control. Everyone is talking."

"I cannot help that," I said.

He waved his hand. "Don't! Don't! This is not my brother you're dealing with here and you cannot manipulate me! It's difficult enough having to take charge of his household for him. He himself knows the gravity of the situation. He knows how long he has tried to test his virility each time he travels, to no avail."

What was he telling me? That my husband had women in other parts of the country? I was terribly offended and said, "That's what men do."

There was nothing I could do to stop him from womanizing, but couldn't he at least marry one of them to help me around the house? If a woman had enough energy to sleep with another woman's husband, then she ought to have enough energy to contribute to the chores in his household. It was only fair.

"If I were him," Brother Tade said. "I would not allow my wife to be in your situation. Pitied and mocked. That is my point. I would perform my duties, make sure you were with child. I'd certainly be mortified that you earn more than me, but he doesn't seem to care. He has you working from morning until night and he tells me you're dedicated to your craft. He does not value you enough, as far as I'm concerned, and I feel responsible because I practically handed you that Vespa. Is that not true?"

"That is true," I admitted.

"No matter. I can take responsibility for my actions. I know how to correct a wrong when the time comes, and I'm afraid this has gone on long enough. I'm not going to indulge you any longer, Arike. I'm ordering you now, as the head of this family, to stop riding. Forthwith. Don't let me hear you've been spotted on one of your little trips and don't let me have to call for you again about this. You hear me?"

The most painful part was that I had to look extra humble so as not to incur more of his wrath.

"I hear you," I said. "Don't be angry."

I rode home anyway. Did he expect me to drag the Vespa all the way or what? That was my very last ride though, so I took my time. Meandered. I was thinking, so that was all I was born for, to give birth? That meant that I was a failure in life. When I reached the compound, I leaned the Vespa against the mango tree and retired it. I could have wept. The world was an awful place. Your father came out of the house before I had a chance to recover. I deliberately had on my bargaining expression, to make my face unreadable.

"Hope nothing?" he said.

I shrugged.

"Did you not see my brother?" he asked.

I delayed my response.

"Answer me," he said.

"Yes," I said.

"Have you...reached an agreement?" he asked.

"Yes," I said.

He followed me to the house. I was looking for a particular palm frond and found it on the veranda floor.

"So," he said, "what else did you discuss with my brother?"

There was a time I would have told your father word for word, but I'd had such high expectations of him only to discover that he was just like any other man. He had enough money to chase women, but did not have enough to fully support every woman he wanted.

"Family matters," I said. "Nothing more."

"So," he said. "It's in your hands then."

He returned to the house. It was barely afternoon and I grabbed that palm frond from the veranda floor and swept that compound clean. I made half-moon patterns in the soil, cleared my tire marks away and walked backward so my footprints would disappear.

I decided to take a note to Sanwo's place that week. Without him around, I was like a stray dog in Lagos, alone and sniffing at other people's stinking mess. The note I wrote was a quick one: THIS IS A MILITARY ORDER. REPORT TO ME AS

SOON AS YOU TOUCH BASE. I WILL NOT
TOLERATE ANY DISOBEDIENCE.

I didn't want him to worry. Sanwo lived on
Victoria Island in the boys' quarters of his uncle's
house. He had one room; his uncle's cook and driver
slept in a second room. The driver was a bachelor,
and the cook had a wife and four children who lived
far from the island. The three men shared a shower
and latrine. Sanwo complained about the habits of
the other two, how they left soap remnants on the
shower floor, messed up the latrine and never
cleaned it. I'd seen worse latrines and showers. Their
shower wall was at least whitish, sort of, and the floor
was scrubbed with disinfectant. What if the walls
were as black as a cooking pot? I asked him. What if
he stepped on the floor and immediately fell because
of mold? Sanwo was not satisfied. He said the walls
ought to be repainted and the latrine replaced with a
proper toilet. He complained and complained, used
his own money to buy a light blue paint for the walls;
he drew up a cleaning roster and made rules, like no
peeing on latrine floor, no throwing cigarette butts,
no dumping of rubbish, no burning of leaves, no
hanging of laundry, except in the designated area of
the premises. The rules went on for about two pages
and he made the other men sign them.

They fought over the rules. The cook was the
oldest, almost fifty years old, and so he demanded
to be treated with respect. The driver was in his
twenties. All he knew was chicks, Sanwo said. He
was always patting the breast pocket of his shirt and

asking, "Who took my cig'rette? Where is my cig'rette?" His fingernails were yellow and his lips were black from smoking. He was extremely rude to Sanwo and once called him a commoner.

I did not like visiting him there; there was too much politics over their living arrangements. Victoria Island itself was hard to get to. I had to take a danfo van, then a bus, and then another bus. The island was a ghetto, I'd told Sanwo, just like the one I lived in, except that it was a high-class ghetto. Houses were hidden behind walls, because everyone was scared of armed robbers. They didn't have broken glass pieces on top of their walls, but they hired watchmen from the North, who manned their gates. Their grounds were huge, with trees and flowers. On the streets were rubbish dumps, piles of bricks and sticks, gutters full of slime, and the usual potholes and hawkers.

Sanwo said I just didn't want to see the good in Victoria Island. They had mansions with swimming pools and electricity generators, expatriate shops and restaurants. I quoted from one of Johnny's favorite songs: "Time will tell. You think you're in heaven, but you're living in hell." Victoria Island would need a border to protect it from the ruin that was spreading throughout the city.

The gates of his uncle's house were made of bronze and had the face of a roaring lion. When the gates opened, cars drove straight into the lion's mouth. The watchman let me in through the side entrance used by servants. I walked down the pavement leading to the boys' quarters. The main house was the color of white sugar and had a wide balcony and tinted windows. On the ground floor was a terra cotta veranda full of potted plants. Mrs. Odunsi was standing there with her back to me. Her posture was so stiff she made me nervous. She was carrying a green watering can. Sanwo had said she gardened for relaxation and was a member of a horticultural society, although, he claimed, any flower she touched ended up wilting. Her trousers were too tight, and her ponytail almost reached her back.

"Afternoon," I said, when I was close enough to her.

"Good afternoon," she said, without turning.

Her voice was deep for a woman's. I continued down the pavement. The front of the boys' quarters was as white as the main house. It was well maintained because people could see that part of the quarters from the gate. I turned the corner, and the paint had the same smoky gray film of the block of flats in which I lived. I could smell palm oil fumes. The other men were away on Sundays, so I assumed the fumes came from the next house. I slipped my note under Sanwo's door.

As I stood up, I noticed his curtains were apart and saw a quick movement through the mosquito netting, as though someone had ducked.

"Sanwo?" I called.

I waited a moment. When I heard nothing, I turned the doorknob. The door opened. Sanwo was standing behind his chair.

I smiled out of relief. "I didn't know you were back."

"Be careful," he said.

"Why?" I asked.

He gestured that I should shut the door.

"What is it?" I asked.

"That woman. I don't want her to know I'm around."

"But she's in front of her house watering plants. You're avoiding her?"

He had not shaved and his haircut was out of shape. He had taken a bath. I could smell his soap. I shut the door.

"What's happening?" I said. "Didn't you see me standing by your window?"

"I thought you were her."

I smiled. "I don't sound like her. I definitely don't look like her. When did you come back?"

"Two days ago."

"Why didn't you contact me?"

"I don't have a phone."

"When has that ever stopped you?"

His door creaked open because I had not closed it properly. I was trying to make sense of his behavior. He'd bothered to bath but not to shave. His bed was made. His collection of Bollywood videos was in a neat stack. From the position he was standing in, I knew he'd seen me outside.

"Is it me you're hiding from?" I asked.

"Of course not."

"Why are you hiding from me, Sanwo?"

"I'm not hiding from you."

"When did you get back?"

"I told you."

"You've been out of your room to sweep the veranda. Suddenly you're avoiding Mrs. Odunsi?"

"I don't want her to know I'm back. She'll ask what I was doing up North."

I walked toward him. "Did you stay with Moshood?"

"Who else?"

I imagined a Northern woman with kohl around her eyes. "Or was it a Miriam you were with?"

"What are you saying?"

"This beard you're growing. Your new haircut. Do you have a girlfriend there?"

"You must be joking."

I crossed my arms. There could be another explanation. Sanwo could not tell a convincing lie. He sat in a chair, and a thought came to my mind.

"Where is my money?"

His lips barely moved. He picked at his beard.

"Where's my money?" I repeated.

He reached for me and I stepped back. I knew him too well.

"I want my money," I said.

"Please," he said, "let me tell you what happened first."

"Show me my money first."

"I can't."

"Why not?"

"I don't have it. That is what I want to say. I lost it. Moshood and I, we got there, they brought the cages out. No dogs. The cages were empty. The man who sold us the dogs disappeared. I would have gone after him, but Moshood said we couldn't. We didn't have the proper documentation and..."

He was rambling. I imagined Moshood and the empty cages. The story was incredible.

"I've been so ashamed," he said. "I've been thinking about what you said. How you warned me not to lose your money. I'm sorry. Honestly. I'm going to get it back. Don't be angry."

I wasn't. Truly. It was like a third bucket of cold water over me. I was not flinching and I believed he was telling the truth.

"4-1-9," he said.

"It happened to you," I said. "Not to Moshood. Can't you see? He was the one who duped you. They were working together, he and this other man. That was why he stopped you from going after him. They planned it together."

At first, Sanwo seemed puzzled, and then he seemed to understand. Proper documentation indeed. He knew all sorts of economic theories, but nothing practical. I could not help him anymore. It would have been better if he had stolen my money, or spent it on some other woman.

"I will get it back," he said. "As God is my witness."

"As God is my witness," I said. "This is the last

time you're seeing my face."

I couldn't even bear to look at his; I was ashamed that he could have been that naïve. He followed me out, telling me he was going to return my money and didn't care if I never saw him again. I trampled on the lawn. Sanwo had warned me about that. Mrs. Odunsi required visitors to use the pavement. As we approached the main house he began to whisper again, "She will see us. Be careful…"

I shouted loud enough to bring the building down, "I do not care! I do not care if she sees me or not! You lost my money! You lost my money! Tell me something, do you hate me?"

"How can you ask me that?"

"Then why do you hurt me as if you hate me?"

I thought my ears might pop, but I wanted him to hear me clearly. Mrs. Odunsi, too, heard. She stepped off her veranda as I reached the lion gates.

"Who is that woman?" she asked.

"No one," Sanwo answered.

"Why is she raising her voice in my house?"

"No reason," Sanwo answered.

"What happened back there?"

"Nothing."

"Did you take her money?"

"I took nothing."

"When did you get back?"

"Two days ago."

"And you stayed in my quarters without telling me? Come here."

Her voice was like a schoolteacher's, but it made

no difference to me that she'd spoken to him in that way. My respect for him was gone, but as I walked down the street, I was saying, "Look at you."

My father told me once, "You are not special. There are many like you in this world. Do not consider your good fortune a blessing or their bad fortune a curse. It could easily be the other way around."

I went straight to my mother to tell her what he had said. She asked what I'd done to deserve such a dressing down. I'd called two boys in my school hooligans. Their mother had died, and though their aunts made sure they ate, bathed, and went to school, they still couldn't learn their tables. Simple tables: four times two, four times three, four times four, and so on. We laughed at them in class and sang that silly song to tease them: "Dullards, all you know how to do is eat fish eyes..." The older brother had failed a year. The younger brother was a year older than the rest of us. They both got ringworm and our teacher made sure they shaved their heads. We called them baldheads and ran away from them. They began to chase after us, threatening, "We'll give you ringworm," and caused such a commotion in the classroom. Our teacher caned them, the headmaster of Baptist Missionary School caned them, and the more they were caned, the more pranks they played. They stole pencils, danced behind the teacher's back, and fought other students, usually girls.

The younger brother was the boy who lifted my skirt and ran. My mother said, "You are right. They are hooligans. That is not your fault. That is not your concern. Just keep away from them. In your life you will meet people who are not quite right and you will try to help them if you follow your father's way of thinking. He will give you many reasons why you should not look down on other people, and I can tell you one good reason why you should. If you sleep in the dirt, you will eventually begin to smell like it."

I knew her answer had nothing to do with my question.

As I found my way from Sanwo's place that afternoon, I thought about my father. He, too, was careless with money. How many times had I heard that from my mother, and instead of having enough sense to learn from her, I'd trusted Sanwo with my entire savings. Was I just destined to repeat my mother's mistakes?

Myself or my fate, myself or my fate. I thought I might lose my mind from trying to determine why I was practically penniless. It took me over three hours to get back home, and then there was that old family rumor that I was not my father's child coming back to me, staying put, and going nowhere convenient. It followed me long after I'd reached my flat. Was there any truth to what I'd overheard? How would I know if there wasn't? What if my mother was keeping such a secret from me? I could no longer trust the ground I stepped on; even the air I breathed was suspect. Had I not seen? People were separated by honesty and connected through deceit.

I began to have doubts about my father. I was not special, he had said. A real parent would have been more inclined to tell a lie. A real parent, like my mother, would tell their young child, "You are the most important person in the world to me," whether or not it was true. But then, my mother had made the same statement as my father, many times before, in her own way, especially if I behaved spoiled. She'd ask, "You think you have two heads?" I always saw her question as a rebuke and never took her seriously because her anger could last no longer than five minutes, but my father did not speak as though he was angry with me that day. He spoke as if he was stating a fact. I was not special.

Perhaps that was why his words stayed with me, or perhaps it was his way of living, the way he accepted all people. Anyone. They could be *obas* or they could be rubbish people, as my mother called the uninvited guests who ended up staying in our house.

Sleeping on my floor, eating my food. I housed and fed them all. What kind of man would allow his wife to ride a motorcycle when only men were allowed to? The kind of man who would allow anyone into his home and call them a friend.

Let me see…this was after you were born. Make no mistake, I didn't mind your father's fame and fortune once he joined Tunde Twinkle's band. I heard you boasting to our neighbors' children, "My father is the best drummer" or *"My father is on a music record."* I, too, had my own way of showing off. At the marketplace when other cloth dyers asked, *"How is business?"* I answered, *"Not so good these days, but we cannot complain."*

Some didn't even wait for me to turn my back before they hissed and said, *"Look at her. So smug. Just because her husband is doing well."*

These were the same women who had called me a good child when I was trekking up and down town and collecting contributions for our esusu group and losing business to them; the same women who had resented my success when I was making the rounds on my Vespa. How I laughed when they heard your father drumming and forgot their grudges against me. He had a way of stirring a person's spirit. He would beat a rhythm, stop, and start again. Even the most reluctant dancer danced and danced, as if she were in a trance, until her wrapper almost fell off.

Your father was earning a lot as a member of Tunde Twinkle's band. He was traveling a lot too, and when he returned, he was spending a lot. I worried about his generosity. There were people who became friendly with us because they had heard how easily he parted with money. I had to protect him from them. That was my main concern, my only concern, until I realized that I was cooking for these people and your father didn't seem to care about what was happening to me. In one day, I could cook for almost twenty people. He never asked how the food was prepared, where the food came from, or how much it cost. The people came and ate as if they were celebrating. After a while their thanks weren't enough to pacify me. I became sour-faced, although no one bothered to notice. *I could frown if I wanted; the drummer was all they cared about.*

Our house became a meeting point. We had people who ended up staying for days. We even had two oyinbo men, one after the other. This was just after the Civil War. The first oyinbo man I met one afternoon when I came home from the market. He was sitting under the mango tree and his hair was as long as a woman's, down to his shoulders. "This one is an oyinbo?" I said. He looked like a pauper. His trousers were covered in dust. I called my neighbor's daughter, Funke, who knew how to read and write English, but this oyinbo could speak English no better than Funke. His name was Alex. He'd come from Belgium.

"Far from here?" I asked.

"Very," he said. He'd crossed an ocean.

"Where is it near?" I asked. "Tell me one big place."

"Germany," he said.

"I know that place," I said, "from when I was small and the Congolese soldiers marched through the farming settlements and we sang about Hitler, and my mother sold tobacco to them, and they behaved badly, and they were going to Burma, and they didn't know when they were coming back."

We called them "Boma Boys." Alex was surprised by my story. He said, "The Belgians are in charge in the Congo, you know."

I asked, "So how come you're not over there being in charge?"

He said he came to meet Tunde Twinkle. He was a student of "ethnomusicology."

"Really," I said.

I could have been a student myself. I was highly intelligent and knew that when students add an -ology to a word, the word sounded more important. I asked why he was studying such a subject. He said he wanted to be a doctor. I said, "Help me cure my back."

He said he wasn't that kind of doctor. Oyinbos, you never knew with them. This Alex said Tunde Twinkle sent him to see your father. He was studying music from Austria, "waltz," and our juju music. They were call-and-response music, he said. A universal concept that everyone understood.

"That's very good," I said.

He brought out a record from his load and played it on our gramophone. All I heard was a noise like a cat crying. I could hear no drums. I asked if the bandleader was famous. Alex said yes, the bandleader was very famous. His name was "Strauss."

I asked Funke to leave when I got tired of listening to the music. I offered Alex roasted corn and he sat under the mango tree, chewing. Your father came home with you and you started crying once you set eyes on Alex. "Egungun! Masquerader!"

"It's just an oyinbo," I said, but you wouldn't stop. You thought it was a mask that Alex was wearing. I almost fell from your grip on my legs. I told your father who Alex was and why he came. Your father took one look at him and walked straight into the house. You were still crying, "Egungun, it's scary, it's scary." Alex was standing under the tree with his mouth open. What a welcome for a stranger. I carried you on my hip and went *after your father.*

"It's you he came to look for," I said.

"I don't care," your father said.

"He's been waiting long," I said. "Why not talk to him at least?"

"I don't speak English," your father said.

"Neither does he," I said. "Yet he calls himself a student. Ethno something or the other. What am I to do with him?"

Your father was nice to everyone except oyinbos. *I grew up seeing* oyinbos *every week, in my church. They spoke Yoruba and they were more dignified than Alex, but they were* oyinbos *all the same. I did not hate them or like them.*

Your father said, "Tunde Twinkle has already told me about him. He said the man would stay a while. He said the man is writing theories. He said it's a pity because oyinbos *write theories about things they can't understand, and by the time they finish, you can't understand either, even if they're writing about you."*

Like that your father refused to speak to Alex, and like that I was left to talk to Alex, through Funke. Alex stayed a week, sleeping on our floor. I gave him bananas and pineapples. He liked them. He tried fried yam and liked that. He liked fried fish, too. He asked many times about your father. "When will he speak to me?"

I kept answering, "I don't know."

He said, "But I have to speak to him. He is such a genius with the talking drum."

Soon I was saying, "Listen, he's very tired, you know." Alex continued to ask, so I finally I told him to his face, "Look here, he doesn't like oyinbos. He says you are all full of mischief. He says any African who follows you will end up lost."

Alex looked sad, so I told him a lie. "Don't worry. I like oyinbos."

He asked too many questions. Why did I prefer the town if I grew up in the farming settlements? He said the surrounding bush was beautiful.

"What is beautiful about the bush?" I said. "Bush is bush. Half of it is abandoned and the other half has been felled."

"Nevertheless I'd like to explore it," he said.

"Do so at your peril," I said.

He asked about my family. "My father is dead," I said. "My mother is dead. My aunt, who taught me how to dye cloth, died in the year before my daughter was born. My brothers, three of them are dead."

He said it was sad that so many in my family were gone. I agreed. "Such is life," I said. "The generations come and go in cycles. At least I have a child." He asked why I only had one child. "One is what I have by the grace of God," I said. He said there were women in his country that wanted no children. "They must be very lazy," I said.

I'd seen oyinbo women, priests' wives mostly, and they were always sick with fever. If they had a light load to carry, they handed the load to their husbands. They couldn't take the heat. Sometimes they fainted, and after they woke up, they wanted water to drink. I'd heard them speak with squeaky voices, skew! skew! Only one I remembered that had a booming voice, and she was married to an Itsekiri man, and she commanded her choir and didn't tolerate any yawning during practice. The rest, I really couldn't trust them to handle a serious situation.

Alex had a wife and two children. He showed me a photograph of his family, his wife, a girl and a boy, with the same stringy hair and pointed face. They were ugly. "They look happy," I said. He wanted to know about the Vespa in the compound. I told him it was mine. I used to ride before I had my child, when I was taking esusu contributions. Now, our esusu group had hired a woman to collect our contributions and we paid her for her services and she rode a motorcycle. I was the first woman in town to ride one. Thankfully, times had changed. It was rare but not impossible to see a woman riding.

You would think Alex would be satisfied, but all he did was ask more questions. He asked about our country's independence and the Civil War. He wanted to know if we were affected in Makoku. I said, "No, our town is always protected from bad fortune, even from epidemics. Maybe that is why most people here have time for pettiness." He said even in times of war and sickness people find time for pettiness, and I saw in his eyes that he understood me. "Our Civil War saddened me," I said. "To think that the oyinbos left and we began to fight each other like that. It was not right. Only children behave that way when their parents leave the house."

He wanted to know about the old method of cloth dyeing: how to make indigo from elu leaves; how to mold and fire pots; how to prepare cassava tubers into starch. He even asked about my patterns. Poor Funke got tired of translating. "He's asking all sorts," she complained. "I can't keep up." As for me, I was shocked how long it took to explain the old method of dyeing. If it took so long to explain, I was glad that I'd stopped using it. Then I wondered why no one came from overseas to study what I knew, or to write theories about me. I was envious of your father. Whatever my hands were capable of, music was the one work that people all over the world seemed to appreciate the most.

Alex ended up writing notes though, even about my esusu group, and how we saved money together. On the morning he left, he came with me to the marketplace to buy cloth and almost caused a riot. "This one calls himself an oyinbo?" the other women said. Ragged to his feet, yet he walked around as if he were our landlord. It shocked me. Soon they were calling him as if they knew him very well, "Alex! Alex! Come over here!" They were trying to steal my new customer from me. I fought them off. "Leave him alone!" I said. "I saw him first!"

Really, he was like a goat, but nicer. The first oyinbo I ever spoke to at length. We were picking up his hairs from our floor long after he left. He later sent me a book with photographs of my designs in it. I'd sold them to him at such high premiums I couldn't believe he'd pay for them, but that book of his made him rich. Yes. It was translated into several languages and sold all over the world. Your father said, "You see? Your precious Alex exploited you." I said, "Ah, but I exploited him first," and in the final analysis I, too, was now famous.

Then another oyinbo man came to visit. This one had a round face and afro hair. I arrived home to find *him taking photographs of your father. He was calling your father "My brother" and calling me "Ma'am." He said he was a journalist from America. He did not stay or eat though. I told your father, "At least Alex stayed. At least Alex ate. At least Alex took notes about me."*

Your father said, "You think everyone has time to follow women up and down? Alex had nothing better to do. He and his theories. He was trying to explain what he couldn't. I have spiritual powers. When I beat messages people take heed. At least this man understands."

"I don't care for this oyinbo," I said. "I don't care for him at all. He's impolite. He doesn't eat my food."

"He's not oyinbo," your father said. "Can't you see his skin?"

It was true. This oyinbo was black, blacker than me to be honest, and quite a pretty man if you studied his face.

That was how famous we both were. I was in a book in Belgium and your father ended up in a newspaper in America far away. We were the center of attraction in Makoku, and at least the oyinbos were exciting to meet. The people from our town who came to visit, I knew them all. There was nothing new they could tell me. Half of them were related to your father or me. The pleasant ones brought gifts and left with prayers. "May God bless you with more children," and such. The difficult ones, like Sister Kunbi, brought gifts, left with prayers and went home to criticize us: "Why are they so lavish? I didn't care for her fish," and such. She was so resentful of us, she even went as far as to convince Brother Tade to sell his business and leave town. Makoku was too small a town for them, she said, and therefore, they packed up and moved to Abeokuta. I thought, finally. Finally.

The other visitors, the rubbish people, as I called them, these were the people who came because they wanted to be around your father, or anyone who was well known. Theirs was to eat free food and take gifts, and of these people, one became a big problem in my life.

He was born Taofik. He was the third son of Adigun the hunter, Adigun the hunter who disappeared into the forest for months and returned to the farming settlements to tell children stories of two-headed beasts. Total fibs. This Taofik had no real job. From an early age, all he did was provide women and palm wine to the lorry drivers who passed through town. He was married to a young woman, pretty like so and deaf. She smiled a lot and only Taofik could understand what she was saying, yet he favored another woman, an older woman with legs like a chicken. I couldn't understand. Taofik knew this older woman lay with men for money, yet Taofik was her shadow. To me, he was a lout to follow such a woman and abandon his pretty wife. He drank a lot of palm wine and, God rest his soul, died when he fell off a palm tree in a stupor. It was terrible. But I had no way of telling that such a fate would befall him. All I knew was Taofik was always in our house. I woke up, he was there. I left for the market and came back, he was there drinking, and when he drank too much, he ran around our compound making noises like a train, "Fakafikifakafi-woo woo!" For that your father never called him Taofik. He called him "Faka-fiki."

That was not funny. Taofik was not responsible and

to encourage him was wrong. One morning, I realized he had not gone home in almost two weeks, so I went into the room in which he slept and found him with his bare feet facing me. I shook him and asked him to turn his feet away. He knew that was rude.

"Don't be angry, my lady," he said, alert, as if he was never sleeping.

"You're still sleeping?" I asked. "Are you tired or what?"

"I'm not tired," he said.

He was always rubbing his red eyes, that man. One thing I learned about drunks, through him, was that they always apologized. As for his calling me "My lady," it was because he called your father "My lord." He took off his cap and prostrated to greet us. He over-praised us, hailed us the richest people in the world, which was another thing I learned about drunks — they exaggerated. I asked your father why Taofik was living in our house for so long. "Leave him alone," your father said. "He is my close friend," ore mi atata ni.

I tolerated him for another week. Perhaps the man had troubles I knew nothing about. Your father would not tell me anyway. Taofik must have thought I'd accepted him as part of my household. By the end of the week, his chicken-legged woman was visiting him at our house.

I asked her to leave. "I know what you do," I told her. "You defile young men. You usurp married men for money. I don't want you around here."

She looked me up and down. "Who do I usurp? Did I usurp your husband? Men come to me of their own free will, and anyway, you can't look down on me like that. After all, we are both women."

I didn't confirm. She was trying to make my mouth dance, that woman, but there are certain people you don't lower yourself to. I told Taofik, "I give you until the end of today. I want you out of here by nightfall. She must leave meanwhile."

He started his usual talk, "My lady, you know how much I respect you…"

I told him, "None of that nonsense. You heard me. Everyone go to your respective homes. This can't go on."

God only knows why I felt guilty enough to give him a little something, you know, once the woman had left, to help him find his way. It was just a feeling I had, that he was in need. I went to the mattress under which I kept my money. I could have kept it in a savings bank, but I did not trust savings banks. I could have hidden it elsewhere, but there was nowhere safer than the place I slept. I lifted the mattress and the floor underneath looked as if I'd swept it clean. I started wailing, "My money, my money."

My contribution for a whole month's savings was gone. Taofik ran into the room and saw me kneeling by the mattress.

"What, my lady?" he asked.

"My money," I said. "The bundle I kept here. It's gone."

"But it's not gone," he said. "My lord gave me the money. I needed it for my friend. She's sick. She needs money for treatment."

"Sick with what?" I asked.

"I don't know," he said. "But it's terminal, and she might go crazy, she says."

I pointed at the door. "This same woman, who came to my house to abuse me, suddenly she's dying?"

"Yes," he said. "She can't even walk properly. That's why she needs immediate treatment. It itches her, but she came here to thank me nevertheless."

"Itches?" I asked.

I was quite naïve and furious. How could an itch cause death? It made no sense to me.

"Yonder," he said. "That is all I need to say."

The way he moved his hands, I immediately knew she had a venereal disease.

"Get out," I said. "She knows how her sickness befell her. As for you and your red eyes, I want you out of here too. As for your lord who brings a person like you to my house, he will tell me why he thinks he can take my month's work and give it to a drunk and a prostitute."

Words are like eggs. You drop them and you cannot put them back together again. This was the final thing I learned about drunks: even though they apologized and over-praised people, they secretly wanted respect like everyone else. Taofik went behind my back and told your father what I'd said. That was the beginning of a real division in our house. Whatever quarrels your father and I had had before were minor. He grumbled, I complained, he turned his face away. He never bothered me. This time, he faced me and narrowed his eyes.

"You ask no one to leave this house," he said. "If I say Faka-fiki can stay here, he can stay."

Taofik was standing behind him, as though he was innocent, smiling even.

"What is amusing you?" I asked.

"Don't be angry, my lady," he said, standing straight. "No need for a fracas."

I turned to your father, "I want my money back. I don't care what happened, who asked for what, who took what, who gave what to whom. That man has a house and a wife. Now that chicken-legged woman is visiting him here, saying she's dying, taking my money and insulting me. I want him out of this house and I want my money back. Back to the beginning as if none of this ever happened."

Your father smacked his chest. "You will do as I say."

"That will be difficult," I said. "How do you know they did not plan this together to trick you? It's not as if they are pastor and wife."

"Are you talking to me?" your father said. "Is it me you are talking to in that manner? I'm warning you, Arike, for the last time, do not insult my friends!"

"What friends?" I asked. "When did they become your friends? He with his train noises and she with her chicken legs. You know what she said to me? She said we are both women, she and I. Me, Arike." I slapped my chest.

"Don't you dare do that in my presence," he said.

"What?" I asked.

"But you are," he said.

"Eh?"

"You are both women, are you not?"

I was shocked. "Are you questioning my virtue?"

"I'm saying who sent you? I didn't send you. Haven't you learned your lesson? She told you the truth. Yes. This is my house. You've taken liberties for too long."

I clapped. "Me? Liberties? All those years I worked hard to make sure we ate, and now you've stumbled on good fortune, you want me to be quiet as you throw it away? I cook for people I don't know. People who don't care for me. Look at my hands. Like an old woman's. You want me dead? You pity everybody in this town except for me."

"Arike, it's time you know your place!"

"I know my place," I shouted. "I've given you your due respect as a man."

"Do not raise your voice to me, or else…"

"Or else what?" I asked.

I was not afraid. I'd suffered to please him and he could not even take my side against Taofik; this Taofik who was now shaking his head and pacing, as though I was addressing him personally.

"Ah, my lord," he said. "Drive her out of the house. Drive her out. It appears this woman needs to be thoroughly lashed. Thoroughly. Administer the whip, my lord, and then follow up with a general beating occasionally to make sure her head remains correct."

I forgot about dealing with the matter in a sensible manner. I chased Taofik out of our compound. I warned him that if he or that chicken-legged woman put a step in my house again, they would see what they'd bargained for. He ran out and told the whole street, the whole town, that I'd gone mad. I'd said such terrible words he could not repeat; I'd insulted them all, even insulted my husband. What didn't I hear about myself after that? How I refused to marry the royal family, how I rode a motorcycle, and how, because of my riding, I only had one

177

child. How I was proud. Your father was the one they praised. They said he was a generous man, spoiled me and never took another wife, even though I'd given him only one child.

As for Taofik, to be honest, I could not be angry with him for long. At one point he was peeing on himself like a baby and sleeping on the streets. Little boys in town were baring their backsides to him. If he saw me walking on one side of the road, he immediately crossed over to the other side.

One day, I pursued him. "Taofik," I said. "You can't greet again?"

"Oh," he said, jumping. "I didn't see you standing there."

I didn't give him a chance. "Do you see how wicked you are?"

"It's not so," he said, raising his arms. "My lady, I beg you in the name of God. It's them. The people in this town. It has shocked me. They're so full of malice. I asked them to stop speaking badly of you, but they won't listen. Don't pay them any mind."

"It doesn't matter," I said. "I don't expect anyone to have good words to say about me, even though I've welcomed most of you in my home in the past. I'm not quarreling with anyone over mere gossip. But this, you come to my house, you eat freely, you sleep freely, you take my money, then you turn around and ask my husband to administer the whip?"

He prostrated. "I'm sorry, my lady, that was said in jest. Don't be angry. No need for a fracas."

"Get up," I said. "I want you to understand, my

husband will not beat me. He's not capable, and even if he were, I will not wait around to be beaten. I've been more than tolerant, and this has led to disorder in my life. I used to be afraid to offend. Not anymore. I've seen that nothing I do will be right by people. I don't care now, and if anyone crosses my path, anyone at all, they can be sure that I will not tiptoe around them. I will trample all over them. Let it be known. I, Arike, say so."

It was the truth. How long I'd spent getting away with so much, because people thought your father supported me. Now that they knew there was a disagreement in our home, I could get away with nothing. They would say of me, "But she is wicked, that woman," o ma buru. *I had to defend myself. It was as though my anger left me with that declaration to Taofik. I crossed the road and continued my journey. I can't remember where I was going, but I remember clearly that I wasn't capable of being deterred anymore.*

Godwin agreed that I deserved a vacation. "You look drained," he said.

"I do?"

"As if you've been ill," he said.

"I'm not ill."

I did not want the latest office gossip to be Tolani-is-mysteriously-ill. I was exhausted from my break up with Sanwo, heavy around my heart. The rest of my body hurt as if I'd been beaten up. There was no justification for the physical pain, and I was trying to defy it. Heartache was humiliating.

Godwin smiled. "You keep talking about taking a vacation."

He rubbed groundnuts between his fingers, and the shells fell on his desk. This surprised me; I'd expected him to be a neat eater. His desk was normally tidy, with his "in" tray on one side and his "out" tray next to it. His Bic biros and pencils were in a big blue commemorative plastic cup. On the cup was a photograph of an old man wearing an *agbada* and cap. The man was Godwin's grandfather. The print on the cup said he was born in 1895 and had died in 1983.

"You're tired of your new job?" he asked.

"Yes," I said.

That was all I wanted to share with him. Even though we ate lunch together, usually at his desk, and talked about our families and hometowns, we were not so close that I could reveal what was really happening in my life. Where would I begin anyway? Rose's drugs, Sanwo's 4-1-9, or my fears about being a bastard child? I'd guarded that secret for years, as closely as if I were bound to it by a covenant. Now, on the one hand, I wanted to escape Lagos; on the other was the possibility that, in my hometown, I would discover that I was not my father's daughter. Godwin's worst story was about his Christian fellowship. Two members had warned him about a certain Jezebel in the office. He thought the Jezebel they referred to was me. Godwin, the least talked about employee, was now the object of his fellowship's concern. I told him that anyone who looked at me and considered me a Jezebel needed extra prayers, so it was convenient that they were in a prayer fellowship.

"I'm tired of everything," I said.

"I hope it's not really about man and woman matter," he said.

"What do you know about man and woman matter, eh?"

"In my heyday..."

"What heyday? You're still a young man, Godwin."

"Let me finish. I was an expert love counselor, is what I'm saying, with a lot of experience, but I've left that life behind now."

"Ah, yes," I said. "You gave up your life of sin."

I didn't believe him; there was no other life for him. Godwin was too nice a *bobo*.

He leaned forward. "I'll have you know that I was president of the social club at my polytechnic."

"You?"

"Yes, and if you'd seen me then, how fine I was, you would definitely have been one of those who fell in love with me."

I almost choked. "I beg you, Godwin, I'm not in the mood."

He frowned. "Why does everyone see me as boring? I'm not boring. Just because I am a Christian doesn't mean I didn't once have an exciting life."

"Tell me about this life then."

"Well," he said straightening his tie. "I got into

polytechnic at the age of sixteen, because I was brilliant."

"Oh yes?"

"Yes, I was, but I had girls everywhere for the first time in my life. I went crazy. For my initiation into the social club, I had to drink ten bottles of beer and then base two chicks one after the other."

"Wow." Already I was bored.

"I passed out by bottle two," he said.

"Really…"

"I was lost by the end of that semester. I became a big boozer, then I picked up cigarettes and chicks. The hottest chicks. They loved me because I looked innocent. I would go to their dorms at night. They sneaked me in, you see. I stayed with them while they talked about other guys, how badly they were treated. They cried on my shoulder. I based them all."

"Hm, that was bad of you, Godwin."

He was bragging, and I still did not believe one word. Perhaps he got one girl that way; a girl who couldn't have been very intelligent.

"Who was your girlfriend at the poly?" I asked.

"I had almost fifty."

"Godwin, I beg you. Okay, after your dedication to God then."

"I was engaged."

"It's a lie."

"True."

"What happened?"

"She died…no, in fact, she was killed. Yes, she

bled to death in my arms. I was the one driving. Lagos-Ibadan Expressway, our tire punctured. Her sister was in the back seat. My girlfriend, her leg was severed. We carried her to a hospital. They had no blood for transfusions. I just held her until she passed away."

He brushed the groundnut shells to one side of the table. When he finished, he was smiling.

"Sorry," I said. I'd expected a romantic story, not a horrific one.

"My sister," he said. "Don't look at me like that. You want me to cry?"

"I didn't know this happened to you. My father, too, was killed in an accident."

"Don't feel bad for me. I'm saved now."

Saved. What did that mean?

He laughed. "Our lunch break is over. Aren't you going to ask Salako about your vacation?"

Frowning, laughing, crying, smiling, there was no normal way to react to the news that people died unnecessary deaths, avoidable deaths, ridiculous deaths. African deaths.

I went to Mr. Salako's office after we'd cleaned up Godwin's table. Mr. Salako's office smelled exactly like a pigsty — or perhaps it seemed worse because I was eager to go back to my hometown for a vacation.

"Ee-yes?" he said, as I walked in.

"I've come to ask for time off," I said.

I held my breath. He had that expression I had become used to. His eyes were almost closed and he was raising his chin as if he was someone important. I had worked for him long enough to know that Mr. Salako had practically had to beg the board of directors to get his position. He was wrong about tribalism. He himself knew that, as a Yoruba man, he was at some disadvantage in our bank. If he was Igbo, he could beg all his life, he would have no chance of being promoted, not since the Igbos seceded to form Biafra. They were still being punished for that. Our chairman, meanwhile, handed Alhaji Umar his position, and Alhaji Umar worked no harder than Mr. Salako. At least Mr. Salako had an excuse for slacking: he directed most of his energy toward licking the boots of his superiors.

"Time off for what?" he asked.

"Vacation. I was due for one before I transferred to your department."

"Why didn't you take one then?"

"My new duties."

"But that does not preclude you from taking time that has accumulated to you."

"I-I did not have time."

I had not imagined he would try to argue with me.

"But you said you were due for a vacation. Was that not what you just said? You used the word 'due,' now you're saying you did not have time."

"I meant that I had time, but once I got here, I did not have...time."

He leaned back in his chair. "That does not make sense. Either you have time or you don't have time. Which one is it?"

"Both, sir."

I regretted calling him "sir."

He laughed. "That is a contradiction. Do you understand what a contradiction means?"

"I understand what a contradiction means. I'm asking for vacation time. One week only, please."

"That will not be possible, Miss Ajao."

"Why not?"

He tapped his desk. "Because you've been here less than six months."

"But you said..."

"I said you've been here less than six months."

"But..."

"Are you hard of hearing? I said you have not been working for me long enough to take a vacation!"

I had to control myself. If I didn't, the first Salako on earth would not have been spared my insults. I was also scared that he could stop me from going home. I steadied my voice.

"I am entitled to my leave, even if I move departments."

"I too am entitled," he said, "to grant you leave or not. It is at my discretion."

"Please, Mr. Salako."

"No. You have done nothing to deserve leave. Nothing at all."

I had tears. "Mr. Salako, you are not being fair."

"What?"

"I'm sure, you have a daughter my age."

"What has that got to do with you?"

"Would you be happy if someone at work chased your daughter?"

He smacked his desk. "What? What?"

"I mean," I said, "is it because I turned you down that you won't let me go on vacation?"

Mr. Salako sat up and pressed his plump palms together. "Miss Ajao, my daughter will not comport herself the way you do around here. Yes, and if she does, she will not come crying to me as a result. Rather, she will face the consequences. Let this be the last time you mention her in a work-related matter, and let this be the last time you imply my behavior toward you was in any way inappropriate. Understand me? I've queried you once before, and as a rule I do not query my staff more than once. You are an intelligent girl, despite your lapses in judgment, and don't think I'm not aware of the bogus report you filed against me."

"Mr. Salako, you assaulted me. You did, Mr. Salako."

He was silent for a moment and then he said, "I am suspending you, Miss Ajao. For insubordination. From today. For two weeks. That will give you time to adjust your attitude, and if you ever contravene the rules of this office again..."

"Sir..." I wanted to apologize; I would have begged him.

"In any regard," he said. "I will make sure you leave this job. Understand?"

The way his cheeks trembled, anyone would have thought that it was I who was guilty of grabbing him by the waist and pressing myself against him. How I wished I had that kind of anger in me. Anger to spare.

There was a blind minstrel in Lagos. He was a man of my father's generation and walked around with his tambourine and chanted proverbs. I saw him that evening, as I walked to the bus stop. He was small in stature with a bushy white beard. He shook his tambourine and his gray eyes danced.

How did he hear, taste, smell, and touch the changes in the city through the decades? From independence to the Civil War, through military and civilian rule; before oil money, after oil money; dirt roads to highways, fresh air to soot, free land to tenements. Lagos had the worst of city life, yet people from the interior were laughed at, as though we were privileged to enjoy the mess and decline. The fact was, my father said, no one could claim the land in Lagos. It was a foundation of cement and tar, and if anyone made their roots here, nothing would grow.

On my way to the bus stop, I passed a mad woman. She was naked, and her pubic hair was red with dust. I saw one of those prophets who claimed to be able to predict the future. He wore a white cassock, and his thick dreadlocks reached to his waist. He stopped a girl who was carrying a tray of mangoes on her head and put his hand on her shoulder, and then on her back. "Make you no touch me, oh," the girl said and hissed.

At the bus stop, an army officer with his stomach protruding over his belt parted the crowd to board a bus. "Single-file line," he repeated and lifted his horsewhip to warn those who protested. Two men fought over who would get on the bus after him.

"Why you dey look me like dat?"

"You-sef, why you dey look me like dat?"

"Fool."

"Who are you? Who are you?"

"Nothing good will come to you!"

The army officer leaned over halfway up the stairs and lashed out at them.

"Sharrap! Both of you! Form a single-file line now. Otherwise, you will trek home today."

To be blind was best. After a while, a person stopped seeing any good, any hope. As people shuffled into a line, I did not move. I eyed the army officer. He'd taken a whole front seat on the bus and was waiting for the rest of us to comply. I heard the usual grumbles: "You see?" "Are you satisfied now?" "Fighting over nothing like small children."

"Those who give orders," I said in a voice loud enough for the others to hear. "Question them. You can't just obey without thinking."

"Sister, who's not thinking?" someone behind said. "You see a soldier with a *koboko* in his hand, ready to whip us. Are you all right?"

"*Tss*, tell her to shut up," a woman said.

"Question them," I said. "Whom do they answer to?"

"Oh, I hate people like this," the woman said. "What is wrong with her? Move your skinny self, sister."

"Sister, he will flog us like dogs," the first person said.

"You're already dogs to him," I said.

"Hm? Perhaps she thinks she's a philosopher."

A philosopher himself: he sounded well-educated, and there was envy in his voice.

"Sister, who you dey call a dog? You with your hair all over the place like scattered showers! Move before I move you to one side, oh!"

"*Abi* she's deaf?"

"Maybe she done craze."

"Sister, 'dress oh!"

"Yes, address yourself to the corner and continue to *tanda* for dat side with your body like *bonga* fish."

"*Tss*, keep shut. Don't start another fight."

"I beg, what is your concern in de matter?"

The grumbling began again: I was not obeying orders; they wanted to get on the bus. What if the officer got angry and flogged us with his *koboko*?

I didn't have to look at any of their faces. I knew they had red eyes, shiny skin, and their lips pouted from hardship. To me, they were strange, almost evil, to act as though I was the cause of their problems. And to what end? To silence the one who dared to speak out? I wanted the officer to see me. I kept glaring at him. His eyes were to the left of me, then to the right. They almost landed on me when I felt a tug on my arm. This voice came from an older woman. "My dear," she said. "I don't know what is wrong with you today, but disobey and question as much as you like when you get home. Over here, there are elders like me and children waiting to board this bus. You hear? You don't have two heads. Now, come on."

She prodded me up the bus stairs. As I boarded, my only thought was that every involvement I had, every association I had, had turned to chaos, and it was time to examine the first person I knew, my mother. I found a seat at the back and remembered how I'd met her at home on the day my father died. She was crying that day, and the women of the compound were consoling her. Sister Kunbi, that huge woman, stood in the doorway barring me. "Your father has gone," she said. "I know," I said. "He has gone to Lagos." She lived in Abeokuta and I'd heard my mother talk about her, how mean-spirited she was. "This world is a marketplace," she said. "The other is home. Your father has gone home." "This is my father's house," I said and marched past her. Then I heard her whisper, "Your father's house? As if the whole world doesn't know who your real father is. You insolent child."

I went to see Violet. I wanted to find out if she knew OC's exact address. Violet's hair salon, Simpatico, was not far from the bus stop at Tafawa Balewa Square. It was on the way to Ikoyi, on a small road where artisans and craftsmen exhibited their works like miniature wooden villages, canoes, painted drums, and rag dolls. Today, most of their wood-carvings were under plastic wraps and only a few paintings were hanging. I walked past their row of shacks and past a block of apartments. I reached Simpatico hair salon.

Simpatico was half of a duplex. The other half was a boutique called Afrique-Chique, and the owner was a designer who used *adire* to make clothes. Her fabrics were without symbols and patterns. I wondered if she actually knew what she was doing. She had not been trained to dye cloth the traditional way. Some of her fabrics looked as if the rain had fallen on her dye and created patterns by accident, but I liked her clothes: skirt suits, pantsuits, and blouses. The shop window was dusty and an old man was wiping it clean. The small car park that bordered the street was already full. I walked between a silver Peugeot and a black Mercedes belonging to customers of Simpatico.

For a mother to hate her daughter was strange. I remembered how Rose told me about her mother, Sisi, who pushed Violet out of her way, even if Violet wasn't standing near her. Sisi would cross a room to push Violet and say, "Get out. You're always looking."

Always looking. That was Sisi's way of insulting Violet.

"But she was," Rose said. "When she was small, with her big eyes like this. She walks into a place and she's studying everything around. Little devil."

Violet's big eyes were a sign of her materialism, Rose said, but as she told me more and more, I saw what had really happened in their family. Violet was beautiful. Violet looked exactly like Sisi. Violet was slimmer than Sisi, and Violet was beginning to get attention from men who visited Sisi. Violet liked money, yes, but who didn't? Violet was shy, I was sure. She was barely thirteen when her mother instructed her, "Smile for your uncle, dance for your uncle."

She was the woman her mother had forced her to become. Now, she flashed her eyes, shimmied around and threw her head back to laugh as if she believed that whoever you were, whatever you owned, and however much you knew, you wanted to have sex with her.

I'd heard her say, "I'll take her husband away from her if she's not careful," or "Don't mind him. Put him in a room with me and he'll be jumping out of his trousers." She talked about ugly people with such contempt that I was sure she was joking: "Why is her neck long like that, like a giraffe?" "Did you see his mouth? Or does he want to suck out all the air in the room or something?" She was thoroughly nasty and it was hard to like her, yet I could not dislike her. She hugged me and called me "darling." She asked me to beg Rose to forgive her whenever they fell out. She looked at me with her big eyes and I saw empty shells.

While she was in Italy, she was with a ring of Nigerian prostitutes. She claimed she was attending night school and doing cleaning work on the side, and that was how she met one Italian doctor, Fidele. He came from a rich family, and the whole family was waiting for their mother to die so they could inherit. Fidele was the family disgrace, the only professional of the lot because he had rebelled and pursued a medical career. His family thought that was so middle-class of him, so nine-to-five-ish. Fidele was thrice divorced, and they knew about his bad habits with his African cleaning woman. All he ever did was complain about his family, Rose said, even though he was in his fifties and had lost most of his hair and wore a gray wig. Violet finally told him off and started talking about her own family in Nigeria. "I did not know," Fidele said. "Forgive me. For the first time I'm seeing you as…a real person."

Violet ended up having a daughter, Ibimina, by him. Fidele's mother disowned him when she found out. No way would an African monkey inherit from her estate, she swore on her sickbed, and Fidele continued to complain about his family politics, so Violet packed her load and came back home with Ibimina. For that alone I praised her. She had pride, although Fidele financed her move and paid for her hair salon. Violet's Italian visa had been expired for five years. Fidele came to visit her in Lagos anyway, only once, and Violet booked him into a French hotel on Victoria Island, to prove that Africans were sophisticated. She had forgotten her people. They saw an old *oyinbo* man with one of their women and drew fast conclusions. A group of taxi drivers stoned them, shouting, "*Ashawo*." Prostitute. Violet ran into the lobby of the hotel. Fidele's wig fell off. When they reached their hotel room, Rose was waiting there, with Ibimina.

"I actually felt sorry for Vio that night," Rose said. "She was breastfeeding and Ibimina had a temperature. Vio was crying like no man's gaga."

The next morning it was Alitalia immediately. Fidele fled.

Rose said she was sure Violet had had a baby by Fidele because of her vanity. "She thought her baby would be beautiful, but unfortunately God backfired her plans and delivered her a rat."

Ibimina was cute, as far as I was concerned. Her nose was long and pointed. Her chin was tiny like her father's and her teeth stuck out because she sucked her thumb. Really, she was like a cuddly rat, and I could not resist her. But there was no way, looking at her sweet six-year-old face, that anyone could think she was going to be beautiful.

It was as though Violet decided to pretend anyway. She bought the child the prettiest dresses. Whenever Ibimina ran through the hair salon, she praised her, "*Bella! Bellissima!*" The hairdressers, too, praised Ibimina. "*Bella! Bellissima!*" I thought Bellissima was her middle name, Bella for short, but the hairdressers just loved to imitate Violet. She was their queen, and walking into Simpatico, I felt as if I was walking into a mental asylum — perhaps that was because of my mood.

Violet was standing behind a hairdresser talking to a customer. The hairdresser was sewing fake hair into the customer's cornrows. She manipulated the wefts, using a needle and thread. The fake hair covered the customer's head, so I didn't know what she looked like. Violet hugged me as usual and asked me to wait while she finished her conversation with her customer. I watched the hairdresser's hand movements in the mirror as they continued talking.

"For me, it's Ferre," Violet was saying. "Ferre is the king. No one can touch Ferre."

"Ferre?" the customer said. "He's for old women."

"No, no," Violet said. "That's Chanel."

"Chanel, for grandmothers. Me, I like Chanel for bags only, or Fendi or Gucci."

"Louis Vuitton does nice ones."

"Ugh, Vuitton, so naff."

"Shoes then," Violet said.

The customer's voice sounded more English than Nigerian, as if her nose was blocked with mucus. "Shoes?" she said. "It depends. I'm into Manolos for dressing up because they're unique; Nigerians haven't yet discovered them. I know everyone's into Ferragamos these days, but I can't stand them. I'm telling you, they're just too common, and if I see another Nigerian girl on Bond Street, trying to squeeze her fat feet into a pair of Ferragamos…"

"Oh, *mamma mia*, don't kill me," Violet said and patted her chest.

"It's true, and they're made especially for

narrow feet, you know. For European aristocrats, not for any bush Nigerian."

"Oh, *mamma mia*, you're so wicked."

"It's true. Shod like a princess. That's their motto."

"What about jeans?"

"Hm..." The customer with the fake hair was actually thinking hard.

"Armani?" Violet asked.

"Calvins," the customer said.

"Calvins? Serious?"

"Oh, definitely Calvins. Armani jeans are so untrendy. I like mine cheap and cheerful. American, you know, 501s especially, because my arse is flat. They're not exactly cut for your average African arse."

"Oh, *mamma mia!*"

Violet excused herself, and we went to her back room. I sat in the customer's chair facing her. She took a lump of pounded yam out of her top drawer. It was wrapped in cellophane. The *efo* stew was in a blue plastic plate on her desk.

"Sorry," she said. "That girl talks too much. I'm so hungry, I have to eat right now. My 'Ghana High' is getting cold."

She unwrapped the pounded yam. "Ghana High" was her meal from a group of women who had a cooking co-op by the Ghana High Commission nearby. Violet ate with her fingers, tearing off the pounded yam and dipping it into the *efo* stew. She talked as she ate.

"So how are you, darling?"

"I'm fine."

"You came to do your hair?"

"I'm looking for Rose."

She screwed up her nose. "Rose? Isn't she living with you?"

"She hasn't been home. She is with her boyfriend, and I don't know his address."

Violet chewed on a piece of fried meat. She was squinting. "She has a new boyfriend?"

I nodded, noting that her face was bare of makeup as usual, because Violet thought a woman's beauty should be natural.

"He's messing up as usual?" she asked.

"No."

"That's good. For once." She lifted a piece of meat that looked like fried tripe and studied it. "I don't know where Rose is, but if you see her first, tell her to be very careful. She comes to my house to beg for money, eats my food, and says I'm trying to poison her. Why would I try to poison her? I have no time for that."

She spoke as if killing her sister was an option, if she wasn't busy. She threw the tripe into her mouth.

"Talk to her," she said, chewing. "I don't think that girl's head is correct. She herself knows she never pays back loans, and I'm too tied down with my business for her usual nonsense. You see the girl I was with outside? Her sister is getting married. It's a big wedding. They're flying the dress and cake in from London. I'm doing the hair."

So, no one sewed or baked in our country, I wanted to say.

"She drives the big Mercedes outside, as you're seeing her. Their father is..." He was in the government. "Half the country's money is in his bank account, and I hear the bride is six months pregnant..." She choked and patted her chest. "What's wrong with you today? Why are you so quiet? You look haggard. Have you lost or what?"

"No," I said.

"You've definitely lost."

She meant lost weight. Violet usually said this to me and to Rose she would ask, "Have you put on?" to annoy her.

"You should stay and do your hair," she said. "Maybe I can layer it for you."

"No, thank you," I said.

"Why? I can do it well, well. This your ponytail is too thin. Do you have alopecia or something?"

"No."

"Alopecia areata," she said, studying my hairline. Violet was offended by ill health, in particular ill health that could lead to ugliness. She made no secret of the fact that she approved of me because of my looks. "Tolani may not be pretty, as such," she'd once told Rose. "But she definitely has something."

"I don't have it," I said, meaning alopecia.

"You don't want to add an attachment?"

"No."

"What about a fall? We have falls for sale."

"It's all right."

I smiled so that she would not be offended. Violet was being kind, in her own way, and she didn't like to be turned down. Her hair was cut into what she called a classic bob. She patted it down. In her salon, the hairdressers specialized in fake hair. The long ponytails, they called "Sade," after the singer, and their braids were called "Bob Marley."

She finished off her *efo* stew by using a lump of pounded yam to clean her plate. She flexed her jaws and spat out bones. The way she ate, she could easily have been raised in a hamlet, yet if she held a champagne flute, anyone would believe Violet came out of her mother's womb sipping Moët. It was one of the things Rose held against her: she was not genuine.

We walked back to the hair salon after she washed her hands. The hairdressers were working and at the same time singing a song on the radio. "Holiday, celebration, come together in every nation..." The disc jockey was saying, "She's sexy. She's cool. She's Madonna."

Violet's salon was painted red and white. On the walls were mirrors, and the fixtures were black. The place smelled of burned hair, pomade, and chemical relaxer. On the floor were strands of straightened hair that the hairdressers had swept into piles. They were mostly teenage girls, these hairdressers. If they shampooed hair, they wet their customers' faces. They could roll hair, but not cut. They could finger wave, but not blow-dry. They could braid, and like Violet, they had evil thoughts about their customers.

Rose called them "open-eyed" because they also envied their customers' clothes. Their customers were mostly young women who walked in wearing jeans, designer belts, and sunglasses. The older women wore linen skirts and colorful *agbadas*. They were the elite of Lagos, calling Violet every five seconds because her hairdressers were so incompetent: "Vio, come and check my hair." "Vio, get someone to do my feet." Vio this, Vio that, as if Violet was their house girl.

I finally saw the face of the customer with the fake hair. She stood up and a hairdresser brushed the hair back. Violet told her the "Diana Ross" looked wonderful. The customer held up an empty Coca-Cola bottle and asked, "Um, does someone want to take this to the Coca-Cola woman outside? You get to keep the um, redemption thingummy."

She was looking at me. The redemption money for an empty bottle of Coca-Cola was a few kobos. Couldn't she find a beggar to give? Children of the elite were rather dumb. Out of common sense, why wouldn't they care about what was happening? They saw others looking hungry, poor, frightened, and all they cared about were foreign clothes. The whole country could be in flames, and they would be trying to get on the next flight out, packing their Ferragamo and Fendi into their Louis Vuitton bags, yet they couldn't sleep peacefully at night for fear of armed robbers. Wasn't that enough to think about?

The Diana Ross customer laughed and brushed stray hairs off her clothes. She was in her late teens and wore blue contact lenses. Her denim shorts were frayed. Her hair stuck out. Her nails were also fake and painted a light gold. She didn't look like Diana Ross at all. She resembled a witch.

Violet came to the door when she finished talking to her.

"Are you vexed?" she asked.

"No," I said.

"Don't mind the girl. She's young. If I see Rose, what shall I tell her?"

"Tell her I'm reconsidering, please."

"Okay, darling," she said.

Her hairdressers were singing to Michael Jackson now: "Thriller." Violet joined them. She didn't know or care what I was reconsidering.

Rose wanted to know. She came home and found me sitting in the dark with a battery lantern. We were in the middle of another power cut. She'd sprayed the room with enough repellent to suffocate us, because she was no longer used to mosquito bites. The mist was settling, and she rubbed her nose to stop herself from sneezing.

"It's a long story," I said. "Just listen and I don't want you to tell me what to do because I already know."

"I won't," she promised.

"Salako has suspended me from work."

"Eh!"

"Just wait. I haven't finished. He has also

threatened to sack me. I think it is a matter of time before he does. Meanwhile, Sanwo has lost my savings."

"What! How?"

"He was duped."

"How?"

"Just listen."

She put her hands on her hips. "You gave a man your money? Why did you give the *bobo* your money? You didn't give me money when I was desperate."

"Rose, just listen. The next thing is..."

I had to pretend I was talking about someone else to get the words out; otherwise, I would not have been able to. I was betraying my mother, father, my entire family, those who had come before me and those who would follow.

"I'm not sure about my father. I mean, I do not know if he really is my father. I found out the day he died. Someone told me. I pretended not to hear. I was in shock. I cannot describe it. It is like finding out the moon is the sun. You know? As if day is night, and my mother had taught me wrong from the day I was born."

I was trembling and felt no older than a ten-year-old.

Rose frowned. "Your mother didn't tell you?"

"She should have."

"Hm, maybe she thought it would be too painful."

"Can't I at least question her, Rose? Shouldn't I know? I mean, if you don't know where you came from, you know nothing. I have a right to know and..."

"And?"

"I think my father's brother is my real father, Brother Tade. You know that if a woman is infertile she can't hide it. If a man is sterile, no one has to know. Understand? The wife finds someone else to father her child, and keeps the whole thing a secret."

Rose shook her head. "I can't believe your mother wouldn't tell you."

"And she and I are like this." I put my hands together.

"She didn't talk about your father?"

"She did. Small talk. She liked to tell stories, nothing really serious. There were gaps in her stories. You know how mothers talk with gaps? She never talked about when I was born, only before and after. I know she had a lot of trouble because she had one child. Never from my father."

"Did they ever fight?"

"My parents? Maybe they grumbled at each other. They were both strong-minded. Why?"

"Sisi will tell you the size of your father's penis if she's angry enough. Hey, I can't believe this. I've always been jealous about your mother. Now see. This one done pass me. Traditional African sperm donation. Hm. I wish every man Sisi met had been rendered impotent beforehand."

She embarrassed me, but she had defended my mother so I defended hers. "Not every woman has to be a mother."

"Why did Sisi have children then?"

"She had no choice, I'm sure."

"Six? She could have stopped at Lucky. Look at Somebody. We still have to clean Somebody's mouth. No choice? I beg you, my sister. I never abuse Sisi, but let us not talk about Sisi today. That woman has put me off having children for life."

"Rose, it is the way it is. See me, I'd almost convinced myself that I must marry. Where did I learn that?"

"It's rubbish. How many motherless children do we have around? Yet we continue to see childbirth as the ultimate. You must born *pikin*, you must born *pikin* by force. That's what I've always said: we Nigerians, we follow blindly. Meanwhile, the whole system is a mess because not everyone agrees, and when we follow without thinking, we all enter the same black hole."

I smiled. "What black hole is this?"

"The black hole of the African existence."

"Other continents don't have the same problem?"

Rose confused her mother with her motherland. She sneezed and wiped her nose with the back of her hand. "I don't care. So long as when I come back from overseas, OC gives me my money."

"How will we travel?"

"From here to London and back," she said.

"I'm scared," I admitted.

She waved a hand. "Don't start. I've just stopped myself from panicking. I almost went mad.

OC was calling me mentally unstable and threatening to cut me out. Why do you think I've been boozing like this? My stomach was running like a tap for a week. I had to put my fears aside. The women who are successful, they don't get scared."

"What if we go and die?"

"My friend, you can die going to work by bus in this place."

She was right. "But why do people take these drugs for God's sake?"

"I don't know. Me, I booze."

"Are we…encouraging them?"

"How? They are mostly rich *oyinbos*. Their parents have money, or they are musicians. People like that. They do it to be cool."

I remembered the disc jockey praising Madonna for being cool.

Rose shook her head. "Only God knows whether they will feel so cool when they know their drugs have been up an African woman's yansh."

"Or when the drugs finally hook them."

"That is the hidden price. It spoils your head totally."

"Kills," I said.

"True, but look, common Panadol if you take more than you should to ease your pain, you will die."

What else was there to expect from us? More stories of bad fortune? That Rose wanted to save Somebody's life, or that I wanted to save my mother; that sort of sad story to justify why I finally said yes? The prospect of misfortune was more than enough threat, and it was around us, killing people, turning them into prostitutes, making them sick, hungry, crazy, and I was not special. The time was right to put other people's opinions aside. Who cared about mine when I was born? I was not close to Brother Tade. I knew him as my father's brother who laughed a lot and asked about my studies. He lived in Abeokuta where he owned a mechanic business. I did not look like him. My face was exactly like my mother's. My silences were like the man I thought was my father.

A secret, if you succeeded in keeping one, was nonexistent. If you carried a secret to your deathbed, it never happened. Wasn't that what I'd learned? A terrible act wasn't wrong; being caught made it a crime, and people were caught when they made mistakes. A mistake was thinking I could get a new job in a recession. A mistake was expecting to recover my lost money from Sanwo.

If anyone claimed that they smuggled drugs because they were poor, they were lying. Poor people begged. They were all over the streets: lepers, cripples, and the blind. They walked around barefoot and put out their hands to pray, mostly to Allah, for alms. Kobo coins. Pittance. So what would a jury say to women like Rose and me? "Why couldn't you beg?" We were not poor enough, is what that question amounted to. We wanted shelter and expected two meals a day and had enough pride to wear clothes that were not dirty and tattered.

One trip couldn't buy me a house; it could fund a trading consignment large enough to start a business and to pay my rent. The truth was that most smugglers were women like Rose and me. We had seen enough to know that it was possible for a woman to walk into a place and people might almost help her to wipe her ass just because she had money. We'd accepted that this would never happen to us. We were prepared to cope until the day we died: thirty, forty, fifty years. Then, hard living became harder for some reason or the other, and we became broke, and there was no means of recovering, and no one to depend on, and then someone offered us a way out.

Smugglers also claimed to be ignorant — or innocent — when they were caught. A boyfriend or some other benefactor bought them a ticket and handed them a suitcase already stashed with drugs. This was not the case with us. Rose and I knew the facts. Most smugglers were not caught; otherwise, the trade could not survive. The barons could not buy their big homes, and the launderers could not make their spreads either. Women who got caught made mistakes: Jane Does, of no fixed abode. They spent time in jails at home and overseas for their mistakes. They paid with their lives. They definitely were not women who sat around contemplating sins or wondering where the drugs came from and where the drugs were going — Pakistan, Amsterdam. They were not scared.

"Forget being scared," Rose said. "That will

guarantee you end up in Holloway Prison as…what
do the English call it again? Her Majestic's Guest?"

*A woman who can't stop complaining must eventually ask
herself this question: "What exactly am I complaining
for?" Truly, and I don't mean this in a duplicitous way. I
mean "What is the purpose of complaining?" Not the
reason for. There is always a reason to complain, but if there
is no purpose — nothing to gain from complaining — then
there is no use complaining, as far as I'm concerned. It is
time for some action.*

*I saw the way your father was depleting our
resources. I went straight back to work double time and
hid what I earned from him. He'd say to me, "You're
always in the market nowadays." I'd say, "Business is
rather bad." He'd say, "But there has been an upswing
recently. Hasn't there been an upswing recently?"*

*I wouldn't confirm. How would he know an
upswing from a downturn? A man who didn't even
know when he was broke. He gave his tailor some cloth
to sew a new* agbada, *asked for elaborate embroidery
around the neckline. God only knows where he was
going in that outfit. The tailor gave him a handwritten
bill. As usual, my husband couldn't haggle. He accepted
the bill without question, came home and handed it to
me.*

*I looked at the scrunched up piece of scrap paper.
"What am I to do with this?" I asked. I couldn't read,
but I could count the zeros, and there were two of them.
Too many.*

"Settle it," he said.

"But we're broke," I said.

"How?" he asked.

I had to laugh. He actually wanted to know, and that agbada of his stayed in his tailor's place for over a year gathering dust. For the first time he talked bad about the tailor, said his sewing was always crooked, and his bills were never straight.

He was a giant as a drummer, your father. Perhaps that was why he gave away so much, because he feared that, as a man, he'd never measured up.

In the marketplace, some of the other adire dyers were giving me furtive looks because I was working so hard. My designs threatened them. Some accepted that I was the best because I put in a lot of effort, and some could not. One of them dared to accost me. She said, "You this woman, you're just producing your fabrics like a machine these days. Won't you ever rest?"

"What else can I do?" I said with a smile.

That started a lot of muttering. But there was this one dyer who was new in the marketplace, she called me over and said, "Don't pay them any mind, Sister Arike. Let me tell you, I've traversed this country and it's the same all over. We women, we sabotage each other instead of working together."

She'd come from the East, which made her stick out. She was a Yoruba woman like us, but she'd married an Igbo man and that was not done. She was such a strange one. She didn't even look Yoruba; she was as dark and thin as a Tiv woman, with delicate features, yet she'd had several children by several men. Apparently, she couldn't last long in their homes. The slightest wrongdoing and she was off. Her previous husband was tight with money, she said, and the one before had failed to satisfy her.

I asked, "And men don't?"

"We don't come together," she said. "We should. We can't and then, when the time comes, we wonder why we're lagging behind the men."

"In what way do we lag?" She needed to come to my house.

"I've told you," she said. "I've traversed this country and it's the same all over. We women, we sabotage each other: mothers against daughters, sisters against sisters, friends against friends. If there is no unity between us, how can there ever be progress? It's a spiral that will never end, and I don't need the gift of prophecy to say this. I have eyes, ears, and a mouth to talk, God willing. I've seen you, Sister Arike. You're doing well. You are taking the right steps. One should not rely on a man for anything, to provide or to pamper, not even to procreate. Is that not true?"

I didn't say a word. I just moved away from her and went back to my work.

It wasn't a month before she left us. The rumor was that she'd found herself a new man, an Ondo. First an Igbo man and now this? Of all Yorubas to go with! Ondo people ate dogs!

She was an itinerant woman of sorts, moving from one man's house to the other. I heard that she abandoned her children with their fathers as soon as they were old enough for school, but took time to visit them. Whenever *their fathers called her an abomination, she told her children she'd fallen under a spell and that was the reason she'd left.*

As I said, she was a strange one, but her analysis that day in the marketplace was close to the truth, too close for comfort, and I was relieved when she left. What I would have liked to ask her was this, and sincerely, not in a duplicitous way, I was genuinely curious to know: compared to the men in her life, was she better or worse?

I saw Johnny. It was the same week I started swallowing, and I'd been vomiting all morning. I had to leave the flat to clear my head. My mouth tasted of palm oil. I couldn't swallow my condom; it was the size of my thumb and as hard as a bone. What used to be my throat was now a pipe, my intestines were a drain, and my stomach had become an empty portmanteau. It was as though every possible emotion had charged at me and left me flattened. I didn't have the will or the ability to care about myself anymore, even to feel sorry for myself, and it was just as well, because the physical challenges I had to face were all that mattered now.

Rose and I were to swallow condoms of cocaine. OC said pushing them up our vaginas or packing them in our luggage was out of the question; the risk was too high. He would give us further instructions when the time was right, take us to the airport, hand us tickets and spending money. Our passports and visas would be arranged meanwhile. We would assume new identities. We were both cashiers, working for a foreign trading company and going overseas for the first time. On vacation. We were to practice by swallowing condoms filled with *garri*. Margarine, groundnut oil, or palm oil would help us get the condoms down. Tablets for constipation would also help. If we succeeded, OC would consider us for the journey. If we spoke a word about his plan, we would both disappear. We were tough enough to follow through; Lagos had made us that tough.

We had to watch what we ate, how often we moved our bowels, and avoid being constipated. For Rose, this was difficult. She did not eat regularly. Swallowing made her vomit, but she got her condom down slightly before it came up. Mine wouldn't go past the back of my tongue, and still I vomited. I vomited when I tried to swallow, vomited after I'd spat up. I kept heaving. I finally lay on my mattress, exhausted, and watched the water stains on the ceiling. My tears ran into my ears and blocked them. I sat up and went to the bathroom to wash my face with cold water. I tried again. First I rinsed the pellet, and then I oiled it with palm oil and slipped it into my mouth.

There was an invisible wall covering my throat. I counted downward, and the wall remained. I counted upward, pinched my nose. The wall in my throat collapsed. I spewed from the roof of my mouth. The smell of palm oil and the sight of the pellet-shaped condom nauseated me. I covered my head over the toilet bowl.

I had to hide the condom in a shoe and pretend I'd never seen it, so I could breathe properly again. I brushed my teeth to remove the orange stains of oil and retched, drank water and threw up yet again. I became sleepy, and then the smell of the septic tank began to turn my stomach. I left the compound.

After Rose succeeded in getting her condom down, she threw it up. She decided to go to OC's, to try to persuade him to change his mind about how we would carry the drugs. Rose thought he might change his mind. I was waiting to hear his decision, but she did not return that afternoon as she had promised.

When I saw Johnny, I was walking past a shoe shop in Tajudeen market. It was Saturday and the place was as busy as ever. In a way, I came to remind myself of what I could buy if I made the journey. I never stopped to look at one shoe though. At one point, I slowed because of a crowd, and noticed a gaunt man waving at me.

"John..."

He was almost half his size, and dried up. I hoped he would not smell vomit on me. We approached each other by slipping between people.

"My dear Tolani," he said.

"Johnny? What happened to you?"

I held his hand. He was bending over.

He smiled. "I've been sick, my dear."

"Malaria?"

"They don't know."

"Have you been to hospital?"

"Me? For where? I can't afford that. I go to the clinic at my work."

I still didn't know where Johnny worked. "Are you getting better?"

The crowd began to move. We stayed in the same spot. I hoped it was the fluorescent lights that were making him look so washed out.

"How body, my dear?" he asked.

"I'm here," I said, because I couldn't give an honest answer. "No money to spend as usual."

"Austerity measures," he murmured.

"You have to take it easy," I said.

"I am," he said with another smile.

"What are you doing here then?"

I was trying to sound stern, but didn't have much energy myself. He brought out a plastic package from his pocket and held it up.

"Tablets," he said. They were small and white.

"Are they imported?" I asked.

"Yes."

The imported medicines were less likely to be fake. The crowd dispersed. Johnny put a hand on my shoulder. I was surprised; he wasn't wearing cologne.

"How is my Rose?" he asked.

"She's there."

"Still with that OC?"

I could not meet his eye. "Yes."

"Me, I'm keeping away from those two. Their *roforofo* is too much for me. How is your own boyfriend? What is his name again?"

"We broke up."

Johnny tilted his head to one side, as if I'd told him that Sanwo had died. He was studying my expression and I could have wept. I mimicked Johnny's expression and he laughed.

"My dear Tolani. I'm sorry to hear that."

He leaned on me. I rubbed his back. He was still trying to be his normal flirtatious self.

"Dear John," I said.

I wanted to order him to go to a hospital, but I knew the doctors would misdiagnose him, or write off his sickness to general body weakness, and then they would take his money.

"Tell Rambling Rose I say hello," he said. "Tell her she's the only woman I ever loved and she's a silly so-so-so-and-so for following that OC. You hear me?"

"Get well, Johnny."

"Pray for me."

He walked away without saying goodbye, and I thought of the night he'd sat with Rose and me and boozed. I myself boozed that night, which was unusual. Gulder beer. We had just come back from a party, and Rose was drunk on Liebfraumilch and angry because we had teased her for not knowing our national pledge. She said she did not care and would never pledge to a country like Nigeria anyway. We never should have been given our independence, she said, and we were a bunch of ignorant Africans who needed the British to come back and whip our asses. I was furious with her. I blamed the military. I also blamed the elite. They were the usurpers of the land.

At first, Johnny was peering into his glass as if he could see naked women dancing inside. Then he watched Rose and me, when it looked as if we were about to fight. He told us both to calm down. "The proletariat," he said.

"Pro-what?" Rose said. "Who asked you to talk? Your face like tea without milk."

That was the exact color of Johnny's skin, weak tea without milk, and his freckles were like tea leaves. But Johnny continued to speak sensibly for a drunk man. "We the masses," he said. "We the common man. We the people. We deserve the government that we have."

Our country, our continent, could be everything we dreamed, with enough food, water, health, education, and peace, he said, if only we used the power we had.

Johnny Walker was a graduate of agricultural science. His favorite songs were by Bob Marley and by another Bob he called Dylan. I promised myself that I would go to church as soon as possible, just to pray for him. That was the last time I saw him.

Rose came back before I returned from Tajudeen market. She was sleeping when I arrived and snoring loud. I ironed my clothes for the next day and ate sweet bread and beans. Each mouthful I took was small, so I could keep them down. I tidied my bedroom and noticed a fork between my mattress and the wall. I was sure Sanwo had dropped it there. I slipped my hand between the gap and pulled it out. The fork was covered in dust. I took it to the kitchen and washed it.

Thankfully, we had electricity that night, so I was able to watch the television; first the news and then one local drama without paying attention to either program. I wanted the television on just for the sound. A government War Against Indiscipline advert came on as Rose walked in from her bedroom.

"How now," I said.

She was wearing a brown wrapper and a pink hairnet on her head. She rubbed her arms. "Too much noise. Too much..."

The jingle of the advert was irritatingly loud. Lateness to work, the lyrics went, jumping bus queues, these were acts of indiscipline. Rose was muttering to herself like an old woman. She dragged her feet to the kitchen and then to the bathroom where she began to cough. She was particular about personal hygiene, and for her, the mucus in her throat was filth.

"Did you speak to OC?" I called out.

I had become used to being on my own and looked forward to the days she left for OC's place. Her hacking stopped, but she didn't answer. She had a hangover. If Rose was quiet and complaining about noise, this was the usual explanation. She came out of the bathroom chewing.

"What's in your mouth?" I asked.

"Ginger."

Her expression reminded me of Violet's. They looked nothing like each other until they frowned. They had the same deep crease between their eyes. I heard a thumping sound from our water pipes.

"Are we still swallowing?" I asked.

She nodded. "We have to."

The government War Against Indiscipline advert ended. A Joy soap advert began. The jingle went, "Hey, Joy Girl..."

"He won't let us do it the other way?" I asked.

"Won't. The risk. He says we are a liability. He normally uses women who've had children. At least they know the score."

"What is that?"

She looked up.

"Hm?"

"The score," I said.

"They know what they need to do. We're too indecisive, he said. He wants us to get it down our throats or forget about it. I decided to try ginger. Pregnant women chew it for morning sick..."

Her mouth was full. She returned to the bathroom to spit. I heard her say, "Jesus." Then she came out smacking her lips.

"When will they fix this septic tank, eh?" she said, flopping into a chair.

The Joy soap advert came to an end and another foreign program came on. This one was about a detective called Columbo. I'd seen the episode twice before.

"I saw Johnny," I said.

Rose eyed me. "Where?"

"Tajudeen market. He was there buying medicine."

"He's sick?"

"He's lost weight, Rose."

"Malaria?"

"They don't know. You should have seen him."

She stretched her leg. "Really?"

"He looked bad. It was no joke."

She hissed. "Please, don't mention Johnny around here again. He is a waste of spit."

She made me so angry. "He said I should greet you."

"For what reason?"

"He said OC cannot care for you."

"Who asked his opinion? Did I tell him I cared for OC?"

"He also said you were the only woman he ever loved."

Rose wiped her face with a hand. The gesture was not convincing.

"Johnny can't do anything for me," she muttered. "Don't talk to me about him again."

"I was just delivering his message," I said.

She continued to chew her stick of ginger as if she didn't care.

I dreamed about Johnny that night. He was striding across our street, looking so handsome in a starched white linen shirt. He was on his way to church. I smelled his cologne, strong, and woke up crying. The dream scared me badly.

How time passed after that. Each day seemed to be chasing after the next. I was trying to swallow. I was alone most evenings because Rose was at OC's place. She was still bringing up condoms after getting them down her throat. I was unable to get one past the back of my mouth. I'd stopped vomiting, but my tongue would not budge with the weight of a condom on it, not with palm oil, groundnut oil, margarine, water, or Coca-Cola; not lying down, with my eyes shut, or pretending my mouth was filled with toffee, but I kept trying.

On the Sunday before I was to return to work, I went to Godwin's church. I really didn't want to. Johnny was the one I decided to go for, to pray for. Godwin was happy to see me though.

"This is a miracle," he said.

"Verily," I said, smiling.

"I was so worried when I heard you were suspended."

"Don't worry about that. I'm back to work on Monday."

"I'm happy you're here. Your boss needs extra prayers."

"How long is your service?"

"Two hours," he said. I was just teasing him, and he was used to my rudeness. He was still smiling like the man in the Macleans toothpaste advert. Surely, he would faint if he knew the kind of woman he was going to worship with.

The church was as big as a palace, with white pillars. There were so many cars outside in the car park: Volkswagens, Benzes, and Peugeots. It was like going to happy hour at Phaze Two. Inside the church, the floor was marble and wood; the pulpit was red velvet, the exact color of my skirt suit. The pastor was wearing a black suit, well-fitted. His bald head shone like his shoes. He walked up and down calling God "Gahd." His accent was American, and he was Nigerian.

The born-again churches were new and becoming popular; I wasn't sure why. The main difference in their services were the hymns and clapping, and what this pastor called ten percent. "My Gahd is not a poor Gahd!" he said. "My Gaahhd...is a Gahd of abundance!"

He spoke as if God was in a back room, and he'd come to the pulpit to repeat to the congregation exactly what God had said. He was that certain of his message, and his sermon continued in the same fashion: money, money, money. Ten percent of this and that. Tithes. It was there in the Bible, a covenant, and those who did not give were sinners. The church had a prophecy to fulfill through money. Money was power. It was God's promise that the congregation be enriched and empowered. Those who received God's promise must fulfill His prophecy, in order for missions and other works to turn around the devilishness in the world. It was devilish to say that people should not give money to the church and to say that poverty made people wholesome. It was also devilish talk to criticize God's anointed who preached prosperity, and it was time for the congregation to cast out the demon of poverty and let God come into their lives and expand their coastlines.

"Can I get a hallelujah?" he asked.

Members of the congregation responded by shouting, "Hallelujah!" "In Jesus's name!" "My portion!"

The priest's ensuing prayer was more like a war cry: "May the evildoers that walk the face of this earth be consumed in the flames of hellfire! May the soldiers of Satan be devoured by serpents, Father Lord..." in a bottomless pit, he said, and the purveyors of witchcraft be pierced by arrows, through their hearts, and the demonic forces that perverted the sacred covenant of marriage fall prey to sickness and disease. May this and that be dashed and crushed and destroyed, all in the name of Jesus.

One woman with a hat as wide as an umbrella collapsed at the mention of the word "marriage." She was one of dozens. They were single women in search of husbands. We were almost by the door, and I kept peeking at those who were walking in and out of the church. Why did they bend and tiptoe that way? I'd done that before, and people noticed me anyway.

The congregation soon began to sing. A

middle-aged woman in a light blue up-and-down skipped from one end of the church to the other during "Count Your Blessings," and then she sobbed throughout "It Is Well With My Soul." The man she was with pretended not to see her. I knew he was the cause of her woes. Many of the men rocked from side to side like Godwin, as if they were afraid to let loose. The better their clothes, the nearer people were to the pulpit. The pastor ordered the congregation to speak in tongues after a while. He stretched out his fingers: "I command you, in Jesus's name! *Bombala yatima shati wati!*"

The noise became loud enough for me to cover my ears. Open mouths surrounded me. Godwin was saying, "*Shambala wato fatayata...*" I shut my eyes thinking, wasn't tongues a gift? Didn't tongues happen when the Holy Spirit gripped a person? How could a pastor command and suddenly a whole church was gripped and gifted?

Again, I couldn't understand. We gave our ten percent. Mine was not up to one percent, but I prayed for my mother and for Johnny's health, and next came a part of the service I was not prepared for, when the choir started another hymn. This hymn I had not heard before and the music was so moving.

Preciously, tenderly Jesus is calling
Calling for you and for me.

The congregation swayed as the choir led them. The singing was so low and full of grief, it carried me high and I almost became dizzy from my sins.

Calling all sinners come home
Come home
Come home

People began to leave their seats and walk up to the pulpit. I tapped Godwin's shoulder. He stepped aside because he thought I was going to the pulpit for a blessing. I followed the man next to him, right to the end of the pew and walked in the opposite direction, out of the church.

The service was a 4-1-9. If the pastor couldn't confuse his congregation with his message about money, or scare the hell out of them, or pressure them into speaking in fake tongues, he lured them with the promise of salvation. Who didn't need salvation? Who didn't want to be delivered? Everyone needed deliverance once in a while, and for a moment I was almost caught. I blamed Godwin for inviting me to such a church, a con church. Didn't he know? Couldn't he see, or was he aware and acting as some sort of shepherd hand anyway? He found me in the car park.

"I'm sorry," I said. "I have to go home."

"Don't be afraid," he said.

I was breathless. I wiped the sweat from my eyes. The sun was too hot. I pointed at the church. More people were on their way to receive blessings from the pastor. They'd formed a line to the pulpit. I could have cried for every one of them.

"They're brainwashing them," I said.

"What?" Godwin said.

"Inside there. They're brainwashing people.

They're twisting their minds. It's..."

Juju, I thought. The hymn had brought warmth from my stomach and spread it up. I continued to walk. Godwin followed me between cars.

"You're overcome," he said.

"I don't want anything to do with your church."

"You're running away from His love."

"Who is He? I do not know this Gahd."

Godwin grabbed my arm. I struggled to free myself as if he was about to drag me back in. "I'm not going back there. Your Gahd is not my God."

"That is blasphemy," he said.

"They say He loves you. They say He is your..."

"Portion. He is my portion."

"What does that mean?"

"My destiny."

I was even more furious. "Are you hearing me? I mean your Gahd is not poor! And they're taking money from people inside. To give to Him!"

"Mine is not to question."

"You have to question, Godwin. You must. God gave you brains to. Look at you. You had a woman you wanted to marry. She bled to death. The hospital you took her to had nothing. What was your Gahd doing? What was He looking at when that happened to you? Hadn't you given your life to Him?"

Godwin reached for me, and I slapped his hand down.

"That's another thing," I said. "You need a girlfriend. When was the last time you had a girlfriend, Godwin?"

He blinked, as if he was not sure about my sanity. A lot of people looked at me like that these days.

"When?" I said. "Since your girlfriend died seven years ago? Is that how you expect to be saved?"

I was breathing deeply now. Godwin seemed frightened when I held his hands. I placed them on my chest. At first he tried to make fists but they were weak.

"Y-you bitch," he said.

That shocked me, but I was glad Godwin called me a bitch because that was exactly how I'd behaved. At least, for once, he was sincere. He went back to his church, and I went home thanking God for sending me there to receive the blessing that overcame me: pure strength. I did not recognize it at first because it came out as anger. Yes, from being duped in a church. Christians expected blessings to come from a pat on the head, water sprinkled on their faces. Why not some other way? And how could a person receive a message if they were expecting them in another man's language, another man's books? In complete riddles. How could I receive a message properly if it didn't come in exactly the way I spoke, from an image exactly like mine, a Nigerian woman just as broke? It was no wonder we suffered and our children suffered; we were praying to the wrong gods. My father was right, and the realization made me laugh. I felt light-footed, as if the Holy Spirit overcame me.

Miraculously, Rose was home. I threw my shoes in

the corner, and the sound made her jump. Our sitting room smelled of ginger. She was chewing again.

"When did you come back?" I asked.

"Must you scare somebody?"

I laughed. "I'm so happy! I went to church!"

"You've found God or what?"

She had that look on her face, not quite scorn, but I couldn't care less.

I patted my chest. "I received a message in a stealing pastor's church. My spirit will not allow me to be a smuggler. I've tried and I cannot swallow. I've been thinking, 'Why can't I do this? Why?' My tongue won't move. What is that telling me? That I must have been crazy, very crazy to think of doing such a thing. Hiding drugs in my stomach, getting on a plane to go to another country to shit it out."

Rose chewed as she spoke. "What spirit? You've gone mad, my friend, from poverty. You look as if you're possessed. You've been walking around like that for weeks and now you come here talking about spirits."

I nodded. "Yes, it's easy to abuse. You think I can't abuse you, too? Isn't that what you like more than receiving gifts? Receiving insults? Why are you back here? Did OC say something else to you this time? Did he beat you on top of it? When will you go back to him? This man who tells you that you are not good enough to smuggle drugs."

I thought Rose might spit at me. I'd found it hard to say the words, but I wanted her to know I was no fool. She could not treat me like one.

She got up and went to the bathroom. She didn't make a sound. I heard the tap and the usual thumping of pipes. When she returned, she was wiping her mouth. "God save you that I'm weak today," she said.

"You've been trying to fight me since you lost your job."

"If any man beats me I will pulverize him."

"Shut up, Rose. Who cares about him? It's you I'm talking about."

She rubbed her eyes until she seemed to agree.

"Okay," she said. "Okay. What is your problem with me? Say it. Say it."

"Did you sleep with Salako?" I had to ask.

"What difference will it make? Did you yourself sleep with him?"

"No."

"Ehen! But today you're not sure of your job!"

She unzipped her denim shorts and I knew she was in pain once she winced.

"What's wrong?" I asked.

"My stomach," she groaned.

"What have you done again?"

"It's inside me. Are you satisfied? I swallowed it and kept it down. So what do you want to say about my own spirit?"

I moved toward her as she prodded her midriff. Retaliation had only given me a sense of shame.

"No," she said, waving me away.

"But you say it pains."

"Just leave me. I want it to stay down."

"My sister, don't go."

"Why not?"

"It's not worth it."

"I have to."

"We'll find work. You'll see."

She widened her eyes. "Doing what? Do you know what that bloody bastard called me? He said I was a nobody. He said that if I lost my job, I would be lucky to find myself living in a gutter."

"Why did he say that?"

"That's between me and him."

I hissed. "He's an oaf. He called me a commoner and I didn't mind him."

"Because you have people."

"Which people?"

"Your mother."

"She's all I have!"

"Well, I have no one. No one. And don't you sometimes wonder if we were from somewhere else, looking at ourselves as strangers, how would we find our lives? Whatever happens to us, we accept it as normal. We even laugh about it, as if it is funny. I mean, what a life. What a life, eh? You're right. Imagine earning money by swallowing drugs and shitting them out."

She was laughing and I raised my hand in resignation. I could not stop her.

"You're on your own," I said.

In my bedroom, I undressed. I was ready to fight, but not with Rose. If anything, I had to start off by facing the cause of our troubles. Perhaps he thought he had got away with what he'd done, but he was wrong. He would not easily forget my name when I finished with him, Mr. Lamidi Salako.

On my way to work that Monday, a woman with elephantiasis hitched her wrapper high enough for everyone to see her leg. It was thick and black. She dragged it in the dust and cried out like a muezzin. Pedestrians moved out of her way. One man wouldn't; he looked like an office clerk. He was wearing a brown polyester suit with a matching tie. When he saw how the woman charged toward him, ready to mow down anyone in her path, he quickly stepped aside.

I carried a worn plastic bag that morning. It had taken me hours to decide on the contents. Inside the bag was half a calabash, limestone, and chicken feathers. They were especially for Mr. Salako. He came to work earlier than most other people in the bank, so he could carry out his fraudulent activities. I hoped to catch him in his office before the others arrived. One knock was all I needed before I heard his voice, full of guilt.

"Ee-yes? Just a minute, please..."

"Lamidi Salako!" I said, striding into his office.

Mr. Salako scattered the papers he had been handling.

"What is the meaning of this?"

I raised the calabash high. "You have offended my dead father. His head is about to avenge. I have been to the *babalawo*..."

His mouth fell open as I walked toward him.

"They have given me a potion," I said, placing the calabash on his desk.

Mr. Salako peered at the contents. The limestones were arranged in a circle and the feathers were on top.

"What is this?" he asked.

"I am taking my vacation from next week, Mr. Salako. If you sack me, your own job will be in jeopardy, your life at home will spoil. Your first son's head will turn, your daughter will sleep with ten men and become pregnant. The rest of your children, those in school will not finish, those who have finished will roam the streets..."

"Are you sick?" he said. "Get out of here before I throw you out."

My heart was beating fast. He did not look scared. I picked up the calabash as planned and blew the chicken feathers into his face. He stood up so quickly his chair fell backward.

"*Ye!* She's trying to blind me! I can't see! I can't see again! *Aje! Aje!*" Witch.

He was waving the feathers away, cleaning them from his face and clothes. I'd found them in the rubbish dump outside the block of flats in which I lived. The limestones and calabash came from my kitchen. As he stumbled, I grabbed the calabash from his desk and left his office.

Moments later I heard the key in his lock. It was the sign I'd hoped for. He was afraid. My heart was still beating fast. I'd taken the risk that Mr. Salako might come out with a termination notice for me.

My colleagues started arriving at work. As usual, we dragged the words of our national pledge as we recited it together:

I pledge to Nigeria, my country
To be faithful, loyal and honest
To serve Nigeria with all my strength
To defend her unity and uphold her honor and glory
So help me God.

Mr. Salako didn't emerge from his office to officiate as he normally did. At eight o'clock, I went to his door to listen. Not a sound. I thought he might be dead from a heart attack. It was possible for a man like him. I was rubbing my hands together in deep prayer when I heard a sound. Someone was shifting around inside his office. I returned to my desk to wait.

Morning came to an end, and Mr. Salako never left his office. I was beginning to think my plan might have worked better than I'd hoped, when Franka came to my desk. She glanced at her watch.

"Is he in?"

"Who?" I asked.

"Your boss."

She hissed like a snake and then pursed her lips. Franka was a lot slimmer these days. Her clothes were not as drab as they usually were, and she wore pink rouge on her cheeks. She was selling gold bangles from Saudi Arabia. She carried them around and offered them to every woman but me.

"He's very busy," I said.

"I have to see him."

She stamped her foot. I didn't want her to see Mr. Salako. Not yet.

"He's busy," I said again.

"Listen, he personally told me to come here."

I was tempted to ask when, but I stopped myself. If Mr. Salako was going to sack me, it couldn't happen in front of Franka, and I was sure she could smell my anxiety. Franka was like an animal, watching and sniffing.

"I'll go and get him."

I knocked on Mr. Salako's door. "It's Tolani. Franka is here to see you. She says..."

Franka interrupted. "It's pertaining to our meeting yesterday, sir!"

She pulled her collar in place. I waited for Mr. Salako's reply. My heart was beating on my eardrums now.

"I'm tied up," he said. "Tell her I will see her tomorrow. Thank you very much, Miss Ajao."

That was the confirmation I needed. He really was petrified. Now, I crossed my arms and faced Franka. "You hear that? He's tied up."

She eyed me. "Since when did you become his microphone?"

"I'm his secretary."

"I don't need anyone's permission to talk him hitherto."

Really, for a forty-year-old woman, Franka's mind had not developed. I came down to her level.

"And you," I said. "Since when did you use words like 'hitherto'? Or have you been getting private lessons from Mr. Salako?"

She covered her mouth. "Who...what are you referring to?"

Just as fast she tried to compose herself, but it was too late. I clapped my hands.

"Franka, don't tell me, you and Mr. Salako are in *flagrante delicto*?"

She pointed. "Don't insult me! I'm not your age-mate!"

She hurried off, adjusting her collar. I sat in my chair and immediately felt sleepy. I'd hardly slept thinking about how to scare Mr. Salako. Whether or not Franka was his new girlfriend was of no interest to me. How he would react was all I cared about.

Other people came to look for him that morning. Before lunch, I'd turned them away at least twice.

"What's he still doing?" one rude messenger asked.

"He's deliberating," I said.

"Again?" the messenger asked.

My boss was known to be a lazy man, and I vowed that if eventually I lost my job, I would never take a job as a secretary again, even if it were the last job in Lagos. The work was too much like a marriage: the same person day after day, looking at his face, never getting used to his habits and having to defer to him because he was my superior.

The one person I did want to see that Monday was Godwin. At lunchtime, I went to his desk and without trying to look humble, I told him, "I'm sorry."

Godwin arranged pens and pencils. He took his time before he spoke.

"I was the only one in this office who would talk to you, yet you turned around and bit me."

His nostrils flared. He was still angry. Was it possible that once a woman refused to behave herself, she could end up fighting the whole world? Godwin finished arranging his pens and pencils.

"So you pitied me," I said.

"I'm talking now!" he said.

He didn't talk, he just glared at me. I could have told him that he too owed me an apology, for enjoying the gossip about me and chasing me in Jesus's name.

I picked up the last pencil and dropped it into his grandfather's cup. "I've said I'm sorry."

He turned his face away. "I misjudged you. The woman I end up with will not take advantage of people's vulnerability."

"I'm going on vacation next week, Godwin."

"It is washed," he said.

In the blood of the lamb, he meant. I left thinking even Jesus himself had to wonder. It would be glorious if he did return, just to Nigeria, for a brief moment to say, "Look here, leave me out of this." God Himself had to be watching over us and wondering, "What on earth is going on down there?"

I withdrew the rest of my salary later that afternoon and was feeling calmer before the end of the day. Mr. Salako had not yet come out of his office, and I suspected he wanted me to leave before he did. I'd laughed at him, but if someone asked me to touch a calabash of juju, I would not. Life was full of enough unexpected misfortune. Why invite more? Violet had told me about beautiful hotels in Italy without thirteenth floors. It was the same rationale.

On my way to the bus stop, I passed a group of women selling roasted corn under a breadfruit tree. I stopped to buy a cob from a woman who had a baby strapped to her back. I passed four Queen's College girls in blue pinafores. They laughed and walked fast, trying to keep up with each other. I heard two men discussing women. "Statuesque," one of the men said. "The first one is black and skinny, the second is yellow and fat. I can't decide. I love them both. You think say I fit marry both of them?"

"For where?" his friend said. "Short man devil like you?"

They slapped hands and then held hands. I ate my corn slowly as other pedestrians brushed past me. It would make no difference to rush. The warm kernels popped under my teeth. The air was cool for the end of the dry season, and the sky was the exact color of washed-out indigo mixed with the tangerine of the sun. Sweet dusk.

My plan that week was to rest, pack my portmanteau and on Friday, take the next bus to Makoku from the depot at Tafawa Balewa Square. Rose had decided she was going to OC's early on Wednesday morning. She was ready for her journey overseas but would not give me details. The more I knew, the more she and I would be in danger, but as we both packed for our separate trips, I told her she could drop out of the deal, even that late.

"Why would I do that?" she asked.

"Nothing is impossible," I said.

"Unless I make a mistake," she said. "I'll be back the next day."

"Let OC carry his own nonsense," I said.

I'd never mentioned the word "cocaine" before, and now I'd stopped mentioning the word "drugs"; this way, my guilt was erasable. To Rose, getting caught was "making a mistake," as if she had some control.

"It's me who wants to carry the nonsense," she said.

"Maybe I should report you to the authorities to stop you."

She laughed. "Authorities who are behind it? I beg you. I will report you too. Your leg was deep inside before you pulled it out. Don't worry, I have no fear anymore. At least I'm going to England, not

America. In England, they're more civilized. You plead guilty and they will give you a short sentence. I hear in America, they lock you up where prison guards can rape you."

"I hear in Bangkok, they throw you in dungeons."

"Those ones? They're no better than us."

I was trying to assure her that there were worse places in the world to smuggle drugs. English prisons were packed with Nigerian women who had made mistakes. Making a mistake was not a consideration for Rose. The money was her first and only consideration, but in some countries, mistakes were for life.

"As for the Arabs," I said.

"Forget them," she said. "They behead you."

She didn't have much to pack, but she stayed long after she'd finished, and then she took the rest of her ginger and slipped it in her pocket. I sensed she was reluctant to go to OC's place and asked why.

"The man is temperamental," she said.

Now, I could have laughed, but I was too sad for her; I had seen OC only once.

Rose couldn't believe what I'd done to Mr. Salako. "You're wilder than me," she said, yet she had slept with a man like OC, a thug, the worst kind, and he had the power of a parent over her.

"Rose," I said. "I don't understand. This is the man you can't walk away from?"

"After my journey," she said. "I will. Let me first go where people are civilized, and for once on a plane that doesn't shake."

She walked up and down wriggling. It was nervous talk. She could not eat. She was preparing her stomach. Later, as we walked down our street in search of a taxi, she said, "I take God beg you, my sister. Sorry I misbehaved, eh? My whole life has been one disappointment after another. Sometimes, I don't know how to react. No vex, eh?"

She patted my shoulder and I couldn't answer. What would I say anyway? "Hope you deliver the drugs properly?" "Make sure you enjoy yourself in England?" No. I escorted her knowing that hardship was bearable until there was a way out, and this was hers, not mine.

That night I dreamed about a place I knew was my hometown. I was standing in a field, and it smelled of burning firewood. I heard drums in the distance and saw an old woman with tattoos on her arms. Iya Alaro. Her palms were stained with indigo dye. She was kneading clay with her bare feet. Around her neck were coral beads. Did the spirits forgive? I hoped so. Iya Alaro died in the year before I was born and my father believed her spirit had returned in me. In my dream, I asked Iya Alaro, "Where is my father?" I knew the drumming was coming from him. I desperately wanted to see him.

"It's not your time to meet your father," she said.

"Who is my father?" I asked.

"Ask your mother," she said. "She will tell you when you get home."

On Thursday morning, I was more than ready for Friday. By afternoon, I'd unpacked and packed my portmanteau three times. I swept the balcony and dusted the tables in the sitting room. In the kitchen, I scrubbed soot from the bottom of my pot. After that, I could not face another moment of cleaning, so I left the flat. I decided to visit Mama Chidi, instead of Mrs. Durojaiye.

Mrs. Durojaiye slept during the day, now that she worked at night, and she was not a person I could relax with anyway. These days, she was more like the strict woman she used to be. One morning, while I was still swallowing, she took one look at me and asked, "Are you pregnant?" I was so shocked. "I'm just asking," she said. "You look as if you've swallowed a cockroach." I told her no.

She was still involved with the strike. Her union had protested the killing of the student nurse. The government had offered the union no apology, and I hoped their pay demands would eventually be met, if nothing else.

Mama Chidi was not someone I visited often. Whenever I walked through her door, she started running up and down, asking what I wanted to eat or drink. I knew she had nothing to offer. She knew she had nothing to offer, but if I said, "No thank you," she apologized over and over. In short, visiting Mama Chidi made me feel as if I was a nuisance.

She read anything she could get her tiny hands on, newspapers and tattered books. Her favorite pastime was doing crosswords. If she saw a crossword, she begged the owner to rip out the page and giggled like a girl, saying, "Thank you! God bless you!"

Mama Chidi was a Catholic and didn't believe in contraception, hence her seven children. She and her husband were exhausted from taking care of them. "You've done well, Mama Chidi," I'd heard him say to her. To me, he behaved as if someone else was responsible for the births in their family. He had a shrill voice and after work, he walked around the compound with his cloth knotted from his shoulder, looking like a small chief. Papa Chidi, we called him. His eyes were as bad as Mama Chidi's, but he was longsighted while she was shortsighted. He cleaned and cooked, and didn't end up burning food as she did.

One morning, Rose and I watched from the balcony as their family arrived from Mass in the rain. Papa Chidi was ushering his children through the gates. "Hurry up," he said in his shrill voice. Mama Chidi held a newspaper over her head. I was thinking how lucky she was, at least, to have a husband who helped her. Rose whispered, "I'm not sure about that man." I asked what she meant. She said, "I'm not sure that he's a real man." I said, "With so many children? Of course he's a real man, and his wife is a strong woman to take it." Mama Chidi was pregnant again and her stomach was two paces ahead of her. I was so sure she would have been an academic anywhere else in the world. Here in Lagos, she was a housewife who loved reading so much she forgot reality and burned her meals.

Rose was a total tribalist. She did not trust Mama Chidi's family because they were Igbo people. "They never forgive," she said about the Igbos. "They can't forget about Biafra. They will sell their own people for money. Oh yes, and they listen to country music."

That was because, she explained, when the Igbos seceded to form Biafra, they forced minorities from Eastern Nigeria to join their camp, invaded their towns and villages and kidnapped men. Lucky and Hope's father was conscripted into the Biafran army to fight against the federal troops. He never came back, so when Lucky ended up marrying an Igbo woman after the war, Sisi rolled around the floor crying, "How could you do this to me?"

As far as I was concerned, Sisi was up to her usual antics. It was true that we sometimes heard lyrics like "Country roads take me home" and "You picked a fine time to leave me Lucille" from Mama Chidi's flat, and it was a pity that Lucky and Hope's father disappeared, but who knew if he was conscripted or if he ran away? It was also a pity about Mama Chidi. She told me a story about the war, how she hid in a Catholic church during an air raid. A bomb dropped on the church. The roof collapsed killing thirty-two people, babies included. How could she forget that, or forgive?

I knocked on Mama Chidi's door. "Ah?" she said, adjusting her glasses. "I did not know you were coming. We're just back from Mass."

She was wearing a scarf that almost covered her eyebrows. Her baby was on her back, so I patted him to stop her from running off.

"You should have told me," she said, ushering me in. "I prepared some food."

"I'm too full. I've just eaten."

"We had so much to eat here. Papa Chidi is resting."

As I expected, her flat smelled of burned beans, and her older children were playing a game of Ludo. Her toddler slept on a wrapper spread out on the floor. Chidi, the ten-year-old, watched over him. Chidi already cooked and washed baby's nappies. She fed her brothers and sisters who couldn't yet feed themselves. I'd never seen her play, except with her siblings, and in her spare time, she did her homework. Her parents never raised their voices let alone their hands to Chidi, but of the children in our block, Mrs. Durojaiye's boys included, I pitied Chidi the most, even though she was always cheerful. The girl was too responsible for her age, far too well-behaved.

Mama Chidi had a newspaper on her dining table and kept glancing at it. I'd forgotten that she loved reading so much that she sometimes didn't want visitors to disturb her.

"I'm going home on vacation," I said.

She smiled. "Eh! That's good!"

"Tomorrow, to stay for a week."

"Oh, that's good. How I wish I could go home,

but these children. It's difficult to travel with them. Safe journey, Tolani. Make sure you rest well, oh."

"Rose too is away, so our place will be empty."

"That is a real pity."

She was trying to be polite. She didn't like Rose, and I knew her mind was back to her newspaper. She adjusted her glasses.

"I just came to say goodbye," I said.

"Ah, goodbye, that's very nice of you, Tolani."

"You were reading?"

She shook her head. "No...actually, yes, yes, only my newspaper." She lifted the newspaper and I saw palm oil stains on it. "Have you read it? There's a story about drug smugglers."

I hoped my face appeared blurred through her lenses. I tried to keep calm. This was a coincidence. Drug smugglers were often in the papers.

"What about them?" I asked.

"They're interviewing two of them. They caught them at our airport. They say they're innocent and I don't believe that."

I couldn't look at the newspaper. I expected to see Rose.

"Why don't you believe them?" I asked.

Mama Chidi pushed her glasses back. "They're criminals! Both of them! They put marijuana in their luggage, now they're saying they don't know how — who put — the marijuana got there? This one says she got the suitcase from her boyfriend who disappeared. They found the marijuana in her lining. This other one says somebody gave her a bag to carry, and told her it was filled with gold. Who will believe that? They are liars! Both of them!" She clucked. "Ah, let me not be angry. It's too soon after Mass."

I myself wished she would not be angry. Mama Chidi couldn't tell a story without becoming excited. She spoke so fast and muddled her words, wagged her forefinger and trembled. Her glasses became lopsided.

"But you don't know why they did it," I said.

"They're looking for easy money!" she said. "That's why they did it! You smuggle marijuana and you will bear the consequences. If not, who wouldn't do it? You think I wouldn't do it? You think you wouldn't? Everybody in this place would do it. Mrs. Durojaiye, who is more — has suffered more than her? Her husband gambled her money, drove her out of the house, die-vorced her, married another woman. Government won't pay her salary, nurses went on strike, son broke the septic tank and now she has to pay. Her friends had to do a collection for her."

"For Mrs. Durojaiye?"

"Yes, and you know how proud that woman is."

"Her friends took a collection for her? I never heard that."

"Who would publicize it? I wouldn't publicize people begging on my behalf. She's a proud woman and her friends did a collection for her, is all I know. But don't tell anyone. It's not in my character to spread rumors. In fact, I don't know why I said that, God forgive me. Anyway, you must know that the woman is doing private work now. She is there from night till morning. She's left her sons with that woman who tries to starve them. What do these two smugglers want to tell me? That they've suffered more than Mrs. Durojaiye? And they're both mothers. Can you imagine?"

"No," I said.

"Giving us a bad name, all over the world. They see a Nigerian woman today at customs and they want to check her. They ask her to naked herself. They take her children into protective custodial — custody and put on surgical gloves to..."

"Please," I said, imagining Mrs. Durojaiye in that position.

"Inspect her privates, and for what? She's traveling on her hard earned money. Because of women like these. See now, one of them has just perished from swallowing drugs. See?"

"When?"

She pointed at the newspaper. "It's here. Raheem or something. Sidi Raheem. Yes. The bags burst inside her. She perished on a plane yesterday night."

The headline read: *Epidemic of Drug Mules* and the photograph underneath was of the two marijuana smugglers. Their eyes were blocked out. Neither woman was Rose.

"You know her?" Mama Chidi asked, noticing my expression.

"No," I said, "but it is sad."

I read the Raheem story with nervous eyes. The woman had convulsed and later died at Gatwick

Airport when a balloon of cocaine burst inside. She was forty-seven.

"Cocaine," I said.

"Yes. That is the very latest. Cocaine and heroin. It's as easy as that for them to smuggle until they're caught, then they don't know what they're doing. Look at them. Guilty. All of them. They know what they're doing."

"Yes," I said, thinking of myself.

Mama Chidi slapped the newspaper. "I wish they'd shown us their full faces, so we can see what is inside their souls."

I pretended to be interested in her sitting room. Every piece of furniture was broken. The tables had re-nailed legs, the rugs and chair had torn covers, even the old black leather chair reserved for her husband had a light shadow from wear and tear. The children had stopped playing Ludo and were watching us. They'd heard every word we'd said. Hardship was not a good enough reason to smuggle drugs, their mother was saying. But not everyone was approached by a drug recruiter. If they were, how many would end up smuggling? How many would refuse?

"They are evil," Mama Chidi was saying. "Pure evil. God forgive me."

I had to leave. I could not sit there pretending.

"I just came to say goodbye," I said.

"Don't forget us," Mama Chidi said.

She was such a lovely woman, and she'd made me feel as worthless as spit. Back at my flat, I lay on the sofa. Morality was an easy friend to part with, yet so hard to avoid thereafter. It was hard to accept that I'd been a criminal. I got up and found a bottle of Star beer in the kitchen. I opened it, and the beer erupted. I licked my hands and drank the whole bottle clean.

At night my stomach rumbled. My mind was not settled. I could not stop my legs from kicking. I was hot and not quite dreaming when I thought I heard the front door click open. I imagined Rose had come back to say she had changed her mind. Then I thought of Sanwo coming to beg for forgiveness. I brought my arm out of my wrapper to scratch my neck. As I rolled over, a hand grabbed mine.

Armed robbers, I thought. I felt the weight of a body across my hips and an arm locked me down. I was about to scream. Another hand covered my mouth. I struggled and twisted my neck.

"Be still," a voice said. "Be still."

It was a man's voice. I nodded.

"Are you listening? Good. Your friend is dead. She died yesterday. Now, you must get out of this place. You understand? Disappear. I don't care where you go, just don't come back. I'm not joking. Do I sound like I'm joking to you?"

I shook my head.

"Good. No shouting, no screaming, otherwise I will waste you."

He released my mouth. My eyes watered from

shock. It was OC.

He stood up. "Don't try anything stupid."

My lips hurt. I wiped spit from them. "Rose," I managed to say.

"She was killed," he said.

"How?"

"Bag burst."

My hands trembled. "Raheem?"

"How do you know?"

"I saw. The woman in the newspaper. I knew. Something told me. She's dead?"

"I told her not to eat. Did she eat before she left?"

"No," I said, remembering her ginger.

"She's cost me."

My head felt as if I had a tiny ball bouncing inside. I sat up.

"Leave that lamp alone," he said.

I was reaching for my wrapper. I wasn't going to touch my lamp. I did not want to see his face.

He pushed the lamp aside with his foot. "She was a bad investment, a liability."

I found some courage. "Someone's daughter."

"I never forced her. If you're looking for someone to blame, blame yourself. You did not help. It was the nurse I wanted. You put too much doubt in her mind."

"Yes. For this." My voice was a whimper.

He hissed. "Look, I have no time to sit around talking. Get up, get dressed, do whatever you have to. By morning, you're out of here."

I thought of the fork by my mattress. If the fork were still there, I would bring it out and stab him in the arm, the neck, and the eyes.

"You're not answering," he said.

I hesitated. "I'm leaving tomorrow."

"Traveling up North? Rose said."

I didn't confirm. Rose had lied to him and that was good enough. I remembered her visit to Mrs. Durojaiye and her awkward attempt to recruit me. Was I her second choice? She was not as heartless as she should have been, not as knowledgeable, and now she was dead. The ball in my skull was now in my stomach.

"She convulsed," I said.

"That is what they told me."

The "theys" again. They, the mules, addicts, recruiters, barons, authorities, government, and newspapers.

Most people would turn a blind eye to Rose's disappearance, but the newspapers might try to trace her to her family. I rubbed my arms as if to ease the news of her death in.

"You're in shock," OC said.

I raised my head. He could waste me, and he cared about the state of my mind. Perhaps he'd watched too many American gangster movies, and now he was confused.

"I am," I said. "What do you think?"

"Pull yourself together. Here is her key. Just get out of here by tomorrow."

He threw her key at me and it struck my

cheek. My nightgown was wet and my hair was damp with sweat. I shut my eyes. Was it possible to hate a person I didn't even know, enough to wish him dead?

"God will punish you for this," I said.

He laughed. "Which god?"

I sat in the dark after he left. I smelled as bad as pus.

"Why didn't you listen?" I asked out loud.

I blamed myself. I should have stopped Rose and could have; instead, I joined her, then abandoned her. I doubled over from the weight of my guilt, or was it loss? I couldn't tell, but I'd felt the same heaviness before, when my father died. This was worse; I couldn't cry for Rose. I began to slap my arms until they hurt, trying to beat her death into my body, and the realization that I would never see her again made me gasp.

Was it possible, also, that there were no coincidences in life, that we came into the world with our fates already arranged? My father would say yes, absolutely. Why then did people suffer for their choices in life? The only justification was that they were paying for wrongs in their past lives. If their past lives were also predetermined, then why?

Shadows emerged in my room — my dressing table, my open portmanteau, my clock — it was almost three o'clock. I expected to see Rose's ghost standing before me, giving me answers.

Time itself was the worst of life's tricks, the

way it stretched and snapped in contempt of a person's will. I wished for the morning, and my wait seemed longer; a bag could not wait to burst inside Rose, and now her death was final.

"Why didn't you listen to me?" I whispered.

I stroked the floor, feeling the grains of sand on my fingertips, like crushed peppercorns, and smoothed them away. When the surface was clean, I began to smash my fist on it. I clenched my teeth and pounded until I thought my wrist might split.

PART TWO

I arrived in the mid-afternoon, the peak of market time. The bus had rocked me like a baby in a womb. Throughout the journey I'd thought about death. The greatest lie on earth was that people had to carry on after their loved ones passed away. Carry on for what? I thought. The world was cruel enough without having the option to choose when and how we exited it, so it was time that someone suggested mourners cried and cried until they dropped dead, or at least sat and watched their dead decompose.

The bus depot at Makoku was crowded when I arrived. I found a taxi with two other passengers: an old man who sat in front with his walking stick and a Celestial Church woman who sat next to me. She was wearing a white gown and kept glancing at my painted fingernails. The taxi smelled of lemon air freshener. The driver complained about his day's takings.

We drove through unused traffic lights at every junction. The taxi driver did not give right-of-way when he was supposed to and honked at every opportunity. Sometimes, he honked to greet another driver who honked back in return. I heard bicycle bells, motorcycle horns, car and van engines, and street traders calling out to customers: "Tang-erine!" "Fine bread!" T-shirts and underwear hung on chicken wire fences, shoppers and pedestrians crowded the streets. We passed smoking dumps, half-constructed buildings, petrol stations, piles of cement blocks, and kerosene tanks. My hometown was full of battered abandoned cars. They were propped up on bricks. Compounds were swept clean, but walls were defaced with signs: *Do Not Urinate*. *Post No Bills*. *Democracy is Dead*, one said, in bright red. Billboards cluttered the skyline: Coca-Cola, St. Moritz, FedEx. I noted the new businesses in the town center like Sunny Photostat and Good Times Beauty Salon.

We stopped at the marketplace, and the old man got out. He hobbled into the crowd of market shoppers milling around stalls of melon seeds, cherry peppers, cassava leaves, and farina. I remembered Sanwo saying that there was no reason for hunger in Nigeria.

The Celestial Church woman got off at Mount Olive Maternity. She struggled out of the door mumbling "Lord have mercy" to herself. After Mount Olive, the road became clearer, and I could hear juju music from stereos and radios. There were oil palms and banana trees. The soil was redder, and the houses were dingy pastels with rusty corrugated iron roofs. My mother's was a yellow bungalow with green wooden shutters. The taxi stopped at her compound entrance, and in my nervous state, I dropped the change he gave me. Coming home always required a transformation on my part. I felt obliged to assure the people who loved me, my mother in particular, that I was the girl they remembered.

"Stranger!" my mother said.

I found her in her kitchen, cooking on a keroscne stove. The onion fumes made me squint. My mother hugged me too tight, and in that moment I was happy. Nothing could replace her enthusiasm. Living far away, it was possible to forget her welcomes, and each time I returned, I asked myself how I could leave her.

"Mama mi," I said. "I can't breathe."

"That's good. Why didn't you write to me, eh? I'm very upset with you. I can't believe this. Let me see your face."

She lifted my chin, and her smile immediately turned. My mother was one person I didn't need to say a word to, and unlike me, she didn't hide her emotions. She had an expressive face, the face of a story-teller. She was wearing one of her fabric designs, a red and green wrapper, and rubber slippers on her feet.

"It's been terrible," I said, answering her unspoken question.

"What happened? Someone died?"

She patted my shoulders, and tears dropped from my eyes. My nose ran. I couldn't shut my mouth. The sound I made was dreadful.

"It's all right," she was saying. "It's all right. You came here. You had enough strength. This will not destroy you."

"What my eyes have seen!"

"You're behind the latest coup attempt?"

"No," I said, as if taking her seriously.

"Then what?" she asked.

"Too many things. Too many. I have not sent you money in months."

My mother tilted her head. "Did I ever ask you for money?"

"No."

"So. If I didn't ask for your money, I don't expect it. Anyway, who told you you were capable of looking after me? It's you that must be looked after, till the day I leave this earth. Yes, even if I can't walk or put food into my mouth." She was smiling, but I'd let her down, I was sure. She needed the money I'd stopped sending her.

"Mama mi," I said, wiping my eyes.

"Who passed away?" she asked in a serious voice.

I shook my head. "No. Not yet. I can't. I will, soon."

She nodded. "I'm used to waiting. Whenever

you are ready to talk. You're just like your father."

I began to cry again, this time silently. She could not liken me to my father anymore.

She forced me to eat. I didn't want to. I had a few mouthfuls of her *amala* and *egusi* stew and felt calmer. She ordered me to take a bath and sent someone in the compound to buy lemongrass. She brewed the grass for my bath water. I refused when she insisted that I rub shea butter and menthol on my chest.

"I don't have a cold," I said.

"It helps you sleep," she said.

"It smells bad."

"The smell is what helps."

I couldn't bear her concoctions. My mother was a collector of balms and ointments. She stored them in jars, and nothing pleased her more than curing someone, purely by chance. She claimed she was gifted and could have been a doctor had she been allowed to attend school and university. She enjoyed sickness because she couldn't wait to heal people. When no one was sick, she turned her attention to herself. One moment her back was aching, next her leg. She was healthier than me. I touched the shea butter lightly to appease her and rubbed the base of my neck.

"Now sleep," she ordered.

I lay on her bed and fell asleep.

When I woke up, I vowed that I would not cry for Rose anymore. She'd never cried for herself, and whom was I crying for anyway? For now, I was willing to accept that her death was not final and that her spirit was safe, whatever she had suffered before she died. I'd cried over my own loss, my own rage.

I ate and slept for two days straight. By the third day, the whole street knew I was back home. My mother turned visitors away. "They're looking for money," she said. "And gossip."

It was Wednesday morning, and she was there when I woke up. I was lying in bed. Through her bedroom window I could see a group of oil palms. The sun was a perfect yellow. I couldn't imagine a more peaceful view to wake up to.

"I should greet the compound people at least," I said.

"Why?"

"They will accuse you of hiding me."

"They accuse me anyway. Always a reason to criticize, those ones."

I smiled. "At least that is the extent of their meanness."

"What?" she said, distracted. She was searching for her slippers.

"The townspeople," I said. "They're not mean-spirited by nature."

"You must be joking," she said. "What town is this you're talking about? They've just kidnapped an albino in the marketplace and everyone is looking for him. Didn't you see the posters?"

I sat up in bed. "What albino?"

"One Bini man like this. He wore a hat and

glasses to protect himself from the sun. He disappeared last month on a sanitation day. His family believes they've taken him to harvest his organs, you know, for juju."

"Juju?"

"Yes. No one ever thought it would happen here. They say it happens only in cities like Benin. The police constable has been running all over the place. The *Oba* has called for a town meeting at his palace. His chiefs believe it's an out-of-town person. They say no one from Makoku would do that to an albino in this day and age. They say maybe it's the military that detained him, or the sanitation squad that picked him up. Me, I don't know. That albino knew not to wander during sanitation hours. He never attended any political rallies, never really did anything wrong."

I lay back in her bed. We'd shared it at night, and I was able to stretch once she woke up at dawn. The "theys" were here in my hometown.

My mother's stories were bizarre. I never knew how to react to them, and this one about the albino was more than I could take first thing in the morning.

"As for me," she was saying, "I can't stand the military. The one thing I praise them for is that at least we have electricity regularly now."

"You have electricity regularly?"

"Not one power cut in Makoku."

"In Lagos, we still have power cuts."

"Not here. Our governor has warned them that

if he hears of any such complaints, he will throw them in jail."

"All of them?"

"Yes, and they will rot in there, those National Electric Power men, from the messenger to the most senior in charge, he said."

"It worked?"

"Definitely."

I got out of bed and joined in the search for her slippers. I was sure they were in her main room.

"This world is a horrible place," I said.

"Prayer," she said. "It's all you can do, and read your Bible regularly. Do you read your Bible?"

"No. Let us look in the main room. You always leave your slippers there."

She eyed me. "Why don't you read your Bible, Tolani?"

"I don't believe in that anymore."

She followed me to her door. "What do you mean? At least you've been to school. At least you can read and write. Why don't you read your Bible?"

"Your slippers..."

"My slippers aren't running away. Why don't you believe in your Bible, I ask?"

"Praying to an *oyinbo* man? I don't believe in that."

"Pretend He's black! What does it matter? Have you seen God to know His color?"

I smiled. "She. And She looks exactly like me. That's the God I'm trying to believe in now."

"She? That is terrible talk. You can't make up your own god."

"Yes, I can. Every religion was made up."

My mother shook her head. "That is taboo."

"It isn't," I said. "Why should I have to believe in a god that speaks a different language and looks like someone else's fantasy?"

She was angry, but seemed resigned at the same time.

"Just tell me something," she said. "There is a new temple not far from here. They're indoctrinating young men and shaving their heads. They sing and dance around the marketplace, Hare Christians or something."

"Krishnas?"

"Whatever. They're strange. Are you with them? I hope you're not with them."

I laughed. "I don't know anything about Hare Krishna. This is my own belief."

She checked my expression for lies. "The whole point of being on earth, the whole point, Tolani, is that we worship Him. That is why we exist. That is why He created us. Do you believe that?"

"I can believe that."

"Can?"

"I don't know for sure."

"Hm, well, I know. There is no higher power than God. Let us assume you know for sure. So, you with your Tolani god, you're saying you exist solely to worship yourself?"

I hadn't thought my philosophy through.

Maybe God created us. Maybe we created God. Maybe we existed to worship God. I didn't even know for sure that death was final.

"I have a lifetime to decide," I said.

"Well, at least for now you're in grief," she said, and patted my shoulder.

After I bathed and changed, I went outside to greet the compound people. I felt as if I was walking under a spotlight. The sun was bright and the air smelled of burning firewood. The compound had several bungalows with narrow verandas and in the center was a yard. Most of the yard was red soil, but there were patches of grass and an old mango tree. A few dwarf goats and a mongrel rested on the red sand. Two children played by the tree. It was a school day, and they were about five years old. The boy was kicking a football, and the girl talked to a naked doll. The others, elders, who were no longer of working age, had such sharp bird-like eyes. They watched closely as I went from bungalow to bungalow. I could almost believe they knew why I'd come home. As usual, the greetings lasted longer than greetings in Lagos: "How are you?" "Fine, thank you." "Quite an age." "Is work going well?" "Watch your step." "Hope all's well."

For each elder, I knelt and smiled. I ended up in the home of a woman who was about my age. She was new to the compound and read my letters to my mother. Like me, Yoruba was her first language, but unlike me, she could read and write Yoruba fluently. She was a seamstress and worked from her veranda. I was surprised when she shook me with both hands as though I was a foreign dignitary.

"I've enjoyed reading your letters," she said.

"I've stopped writing them," I said.

"Well, you're here now. You can say what you want."

She had a tidy smile. As I left her veranda, a mongrel tailed me.

"Go away, you," I said, and shooed.

The little girl with the doll was watching me. "It's One-eyed," she said. "That's its name, One-eyed, not you."

"One-eyed?" I asked.

She poked her eye with her finger. "Yes. Because one of its eyes got blinded like this. It's a stray. It comes here to play with me."

Her voice was like an adult's, and she reminded me of Rose's niece, Ibimina. They had the same complexion.

"What is your own name?" I asked.

"Peju."

"And your doll?"

She looked at her naked doll. Half of its hair had been pulled out.

"She has no name."

"Why not?"

"She doesn't need a name."

"Yet One-eyed does?"

"One-eyed does."

She was a pretty girl and her braids suited her.

"She needs clothes, your doll with no name," I

said. "And she needs to have her hair combed."

"Her clothes have spoiled," she said. "She has no clothes and her hair has gone from stress like yours."

My mouth fell open. She smiled, unsure about why she was getting such a reaction.

"Yes," she said. "And you've lost weight and you're not taking care of yourself in Lagos and..." she hesitated.

"And what?" I said, looking around for the person who had told her this. They'd all disappeared into their bungalows.

"And your breasts are flat like an old woman's," she said, still smiling.

I walked back to my mother. One-eyed observed me. My mother was on her veranda, folding a stretch of dyed cloth. She'd spent the morning beating the cloth on a log to smoothen it. She had a neat pile of more cloth in purples, greens, yellows, and oranges. They were like fruits and vegetables. I touched the top one and it felt slightly waxy.

"A little girl has just abused me," I said.

"Who's that?" my mother asked.

"Peju."

"What did she say?"

"She said I'm not taking care of myself."

"Hm. She heard that from someone."

Peju was talking to her doll, scolding it from the sound of her voice. The boy was doing a fantastic trick with his football. He kicked it to his chest and then headed it.

"Peju does that," my mother said. "She repeats

things. I will tell her mother."

"Don't tell."

"Why not?"

"It doesn't matter."

"We have to correct her, don't we?"

"I do look ugly."

"Not possible. I'm a beautiful woman. How can you be ugly?"

I laughed. "What if her mother told her that?"

My mother finished folding and placed the cloth on her pile.

"Her mother is not like that. She's the seamstress in that house. Quiet, pays her rent on time, does her business. She reads and writes my letters. Peju must have heard it from one of the elders."

"She's about five?" "Not yet, but you would think she's fifty the way she carries on. The other day she told me, 'Mama, I don't want to hear your stories about the tricky tortoise again. I've never heard a tortoise speak.' Yes, just like that. You can't fool her. Peju only wants to hear gossip from adults and then she repeats what she hears, word for word."

"Her voice is quite clear."

"She was talking like that by age one. She started one day, without hesitation, she was speaking perfect Yoruba. Instead of calling her brilliant, her grandmother was calling her a witch."

"What kind of grandmother is that?"

"Ah, well, we all know."

"Who?"

My mother wrinkled her nose. "Sister Kunbi."

"Her?"

My mother nodded. "Never a good word from her. Her son is Peju's father. He is married, but he had a — what you call it — love affair, with Peju's mother. He denied that Peju was his child. Sister Kunbi too said the girl was not his child, but look at her, fair as Sister Kunbi with the same light brown eyes. They had to admit. All that hypocrisy when a child is involved. I told the woman to come here and stay."

Peju was throwing her doll in the air and catching it. There was more intrigue in our compound than I cared to believe. Hearing about Sister Kunbi reminded me of the questions I had about my own father. I was sure the tension between my mother and Sister Kunbi had something to do with the identity of my real father. Sister Kunbi was a bitter woman anyway because Brother Tade controlled her movements and encouraged her to be fat, praising her, while he took outside wives as his business grew.

"They've accepted the child at least," I said.

"They had no choice," my mother said. "She belongs to the family."

"The father didn't want to take Peju's mother as a junior wife?"

"She refused. The man insulted her and she doesn't want to be a junior wife anyway."

"You didn't encourage her to marry him?"

"Me? Why? It's up to each woman to decide if she wants to be on her own or not. Marriage is optional for a woman, motherhood is not. Now, if a woman neglects or mistreats her child, then I must talk."

"How come you never talk about when I was born?"

I slipped the question in. My mother's eyes widened. "Me? I don't know. Maybe it's because...ah well, that was the way it was in those days."

"How?"

"You weren't supposed to say when you were expecting. You were always being warned that someone might jinx you."

"Like who?"

My mother smoothed her pile of cloth. "I've mentioned one name already."

I was watching Peju; her arms and legs were like sticks.

"That's Sister Kunbi's face on the girl," I said. "But she is skinny."

My mother nodded. "She won't eat, Peju. You have to threaten her to get her to swallow her food. That's the main difference between her and her grandmother. One hardly eats, and the other eats too much."

"Do they ever visit?" I didn't say Brother Tade and Sister Kunbi.

My mother shook her head. "No, they stay in their town. I stay in mine."

Peju was singing a folk song I'd learned as a child, about dogs and how they became domestic pets. After a famine in the forest, all the animals agreed to eat their mothers. The dog was caught trying to sneak his mother into Heaven and was banished from the animal kingdom thereafter. Peju clapped and danced around One-eyed:

Everyone killed and ate their mothers
The dog sneaked his into Heaven

Peju and her nameless doll became my companions. I spent time with them as I began to accept that Rose was dead. At first, I imagined that Rose had never used the Sidi Raheem passport; that she'd exchanged hers with another swallower, or thrown it away because she'd decided to stay in England as an illegal immigrant. I even imagined her in Czechoslovakia.

Soon, I started picturing myself at Rose's funeral with Sisi and Violet. They were wearing black; I was in white. Sisi threw herself on the ground, beat the earth and the rest of her usual antics. Violet was telling me that, actually, white wasn't appropriate for a funeral. I screamed at her, "What difference does it make?" Violet accused me of not stopping Rose from swallowing and I pushed her into the grave. "I tried! She was my friend! What did you ever do for your sister?"

I eventually had to stop this kind of day-dreaming.

I concentrated on the clothes Peju wanted for her doll. She asked her mother to sew a small wrapper and top. Her mother cut and finished the outfit in an hour, using spare ankara cloth. Peju and

I put the T-shaped top on the doll, and I secured the tiny wrapper with a safety pin. Peju reminded me about her doll's messy hair, so I cut off the few long locks on the doll's head, and used a black dye from my mother's supply to color the cropped hair. Peju wanted two facial marks for her doll, so I made two short lines on the doll's pink cheeks with a black Bic biro. Peju decided she wanted henna for the doll's feet, so I found some brown dye and painted the doll's feet. These little projects occurred over three days. In between, Peju played with her doll, and when she had a new idea, she came to find me. She wanted more clothes for her doll, a head-tie, handbag to match, and so on. Her mother sewed them all.

I sat on the veranda and sometimes indoors while my own mother was away at work. I studied my face in the mirror; my hairline was broken, and my cheeks were dried up. I wanted to be ugly. I took pleasure in being ugly. My mother was still keeping people in the compound away from me. She was a little too direct. She arrived from work one afternoon, and I walked over to take a bundle of cloth from her. An old man who happened to be by the compound entrance was complaining to her. "We haven't seen Tolani," he said. "Since she came from Lagos, we haven't seen her."

He had seen me, but I had not personally been to his home to greet him.

My mother answered, "Baba, please. She's been around the place once already."

"*Ni suuru*," he said. "Have patience. I'm not fighting with you. I just want to see her. That's all."

As we walked away, my mother blinked fast to show she was irritated. "My only child comes home looking skinny and miserable, and I'm supposed to let her go around greeting all and sundry like a...like a first lady?"

She was normally patient with elders. She was trying hard to hide her fears, and she had attained the status of women her age within the compound. She was almost a man, now that she was past her childbearing years. People in the compound valued her knowledge and experience, and they respected what came out of her mouth. She settled arguments between neighbors, heard disputes over property and rent. Someone's grandson was accused of stealing a transistor radio earlier in the month. It was an outrage, my mother said. She discovered that the accuser, a young man from another street, was lying. She made him prostrate before the accused's parents. "We don't raise thieves here," she told him. "If you're looking for thieves, go to the state governor's house."

Another night, I was half asleep when I overheard her advising a husband and wife. "Both of you," she said, "it's enough. You, stop hitting. If it were the other way around, how would you feel? And you, stop crying all over the place. No one pities you. I'm telling you. They say sorry to your face, but the minute you turn your back, they're laughing at you. Take it from me. No one believes your wife is strong enough to beat you up."

There were so many people around my mother. She was not lonely or bored. She hissed when we reached her house. "That old man annoys me. What did he mean by that? Accosting me in public. I'm not going to treat his foot anymore."

"Take it easy," I said.

She was upset with me, not with the old man, and I would have to tell her why I came home, soon.

Early in the morning and late at night were my favorite times to take a bath. There was a cubicle behind my mother's house. It was cement with a wooden gate and built like an outside shower, except it had no ceiling or plumbing. Before I bathed, I fetched water in a bucket from a communal tap in the yard, cold water, and carried it to this cubicle. The water always straightened my back fast as a whip. It took three bowls to adjust to the temperature. After this, I watched the sky. In the mornings, the sky looked as if it were bleeding. At night, it was so dark I couldn't see a horizon. That night there was no moon, and all I had was a kerosene lantern but I was not afraid.

What scared me most? Ruin, of whatever was of immeasurable worth to me: the love of a parent, friend, boyfriend; trust; peace of mind and security. Yet I surrounded myself with people who risked losing everything, including my devotion and trust, their security, respect for themselves and even their own lives. Rose and Sanwo were people who took risks, and I'd remained close to them. That was not by accident. They were people I admired because they were naturally careless. I gave them what I craved myself: chances. Now, here I was with my mother. Would that too end in ruin?

Saturday morning I went for a walk. I had to leave the compound. I felt imprisoned inside. I went down the hill, past Mount Olive Maternity. To avoid the crowds on the busiest market day, I made a detour into a quieter street that led to the palace grounds. The street was not empty in the least. I greeted other pedestrians, and they greeted me. They knew I was from Lagos. I was wearing jeans, and jeans were considered childish over here, for teenagers only. Women my age wore wrappers and up-and-downs, or skirts and dresses. I noticed posters of the missing albino on walls. LAST SEEN WANDERING AROUND THE MARKETPLACE, the large print said under his photograph. People disappeared for all sorts of reasons; now, Rose was one of them.

My mother was already at the marketplace that morning. When I was a child, she'd taken me there while she carried on trading, but I'd also spent time with my father. We'd walk around town. He'd always walk by my side and keep his hand on my shoulder so I wouldn't stray. I ended up in places where children rarely went, palm wine parlors where men laughed so loud I had to block my ears. "Where's your shadow?" his friends joked whenever they saw him. Some scolded him for taking me around: "You want to spoil this child?"

They embarrassed me. As I grew older, I knew my father did not like the attention people gave him, and once I was around, he knew they would focus on me. Now, I could only imagine they must have known about him. Every man wanted a son. If his wife couldn't provide one, some other woman would.

I reached the palace entrance. Whitewashed rocks lined the grounds, about five acres, and there was an old colonial flag post at the beginning of the driveway. Within the grounds was a series of long bungalows. They were made of mud and cement. The three main bungalows facing the entrance had carved veranda posts. On the veranda floors were wooden figurines.

The present *Oba* was a descendant of the exiled *Oba* who had ordered my mother to report to the palace as a wife. This new *Oba* would give up his seat for only two reasons, my mother said: if a military man drove him out, or if an oil man bribed him. He was a coward, she said, and he loved money more than anything else. He had sold most of the palace figurines, precious and sacred relics, to dealers who sold them to art collectors overseas. They were now on display in foreign museums, and no one could reclaim them. He gave chieftaincy titles for favors and logging contracts for kickbacks. I remembered visiting his predecessor at the palace with my father. It was a huge ceremony and we stood with a crowd in the palace grounds and watched that *Oba* walk out of his palace followed by his chiefs, wives, and drummers. He wore a brocade gown and slippers. On his head was a beaded cylindrical crown. He carried a wooden staff. My father prostrated on the ground to greet him like everyone else: "*Kabiyesi Oba wa!*" Your Highness. I was about Peju's age, watching the colorful entourage, when a hand in the crowd grabbed my shoulders. "Get down lower," a voice whispered in my ear. I almost wet myself. The hands seemed to have come from nowhere. "She's just a child," my father said.

The sun became too hot. I decided to return home. I had one day left of my vacation, and walking around reminiscing was not going to solve my problems. The trouble was, I was not ready to hear the truth about my father either, and I was more nervous about this than I was about telling my mother anything about myself.

I was out of breath before I started to climb the slope from Mount Olive. The road had gutters on either side. A woman from a nearby house waved to me when I reached the top. "A man is looking for you," she called out.

She was my mother's friend. She had crates of empty Coca-Cola bottles on her veranda.

"What man, ma?" I asked.

"I don't know," she said. "But he's from Lagos."

I took shorter steps. Perhaps he was a policeman, or OC. As I walked into the compound, Peju collapsed in my path. She was chasing the little boy, who ran in bends like a wasp. He was dancing now, and taunting her, "You can't catch me! *Ho-bee!*"

"A man is looking for you," Peju said, patting her chest.

"Yes?" I said.

"Yes, and you've barely been here a week."

She coughed and continued her chase.

It was Sanwo. He was standing on my mother's veranda.

"You scared me," I said.

He smiled. "Why?"

His square-shaped haircut was leveled down. He was wearing a brown-patterned shirt and black trousers. He looked thinner and seemed shocked by my own appearance.

"Do I look that bad?" I asked.

"You've lost weight."

"You too. How come you found me?"

"The bank. I called them, and someone told me you were on vacation."

"Who?"

"Godwin. I used to call every now and then. This time, they said you were not there. I got worried. After I spoke to him, I went all over the place looking for you."

"Dear Sanwo," I said, holding his hand. It was possible to exhaust love. One disappointment and argument at a time. Even the fullest heart would eventually be empty.

"This Godwin," he said after a while. "You've never mentioned him before. Is he a friend of yours?"

"Godwin? No, not really."

I hoped he didn't think there was any reason to be jealous. He was watching Peju.

"Why?" I asked.

"I was about to ask you the same question."

"I mean, why did you call and never ask to speak to me?"

"I found a job."

"What!"

"Yes, and I was waiting to surprise you face-to-face."

"You? Where?"

"A consultancy firm."

"Doing what?"

"Spreadsheets."

That was hard to believe. He was working for a management consultancy firm owned by a man who had an MBA from an American university. The firm provided services to the newer private sector banks, and Sanwo worked in their financial planning department, training banking clerks to use spreadsheets. The new banks were the future, he said. The old banks would soon be obsolete.

"Spreadsheets," I repeated.

The job was perfect for him. As usual, I had my doubts about projecting beyond a second in the environment in which we lived, or trusting that the new banks would be any less fraudulent than the old, but I was impressed.

"Yes," he said. "Chief Mrs. found me the job. I told her I was ready to expose her. She was desperate to get me out of her house after that."

"You moved out of their quarters?"

"Oh yes."

I looked at him from head to foot. He was actually living on his own? Was it possible? His socks were silver, and his sandals were brown. I heard Rose's voice as clear as if she was standing behind me: "The *bobo* done craze."

It made me laugh to recall her voice so clearly.

Sanwo, too, was amused. "Be careful," he said. "Your people are watching us."

"Including that little one," I said, pointing at Peju. She was hopping around like a frog now.

Sanwo nudged me. "What happened? Godwin also said you'd lost your job."

My heart skipped a beat. "When?"

"For gross misconduct, he said."

"Lord have mercy," I whispered.

I hadn't thought Mr. Salako would sack me after I'd left. He was too cowardly to face me? I was not quite ready to lose the wretched job.

"What did you do?" Sanwo asked.

"I'm sorry, I can't tell you."

"What will you do now?"

"Stay here."

I decided as I said the words.

"Doing what? I thought I was the unrealistic one."

Peju laughed. I thought of her doll clothes and that image led to another.

"Me and my mother," I said. "We will do something together."

"Like what?"

"We will make clothes."

"What kinds of clothes?"

"We will make clothes and sell."

From my mother's cloth, I thought. I was a failure, a complete one. To come home without money was bad enough, and now I might have to depend on her.

Sanwo frowned. "Is that why you came back here?"

"No."

"What happened then?"

I touched his shoulder. "Please, don't be angry. I can't tell you."

"Me? Angry? It's you I came to beg." He reached into his pocket. "Here is your money. I wanted to give it to you all at once. That is why I took so long."

He tried to pass the money to me, but I was so overcome I covered my face with my hands instead.

"Take," he said. "Before the whole world sees us and thinks I'm bribing you."

I held the money as if it was heavy. "Thank you."

"I will give you more before the end of the month, for pain and suffering."

"No more. You've tried. Really."

I was not angry with him anymore. Dreaming of success wasn't a crime. Neither was dressing badly.

"I have to see your mother now I'm here," he said.

"No," I said.

He could not see my mother. He knew what that meant. His hands went straight into his pockets, but I was resolved. If he objected, I was ready to ask him to leave, but I had to know.

"Why did you drive me away, Sanwo?"

"Me?"

"You can't remember anymore?"

"When? I mean how?"

"You were being so difficult."

"That was you."

My behavior was deliberate; he was not as manipulative as I was. His bickering, running around for his uncle, traveling up North, even losing the money that was meant to be my dowry, were all attempts to be rid of me, I was sure.

"Did I harass you that much?" I asked.

"When did you harass me?"

"Come on, to marry."

"Marriage before forty is for rich men only."

"Is that really what you believe?"

"In this day and age? Of course."

For women, it was always the babies. No wonder so many of us were single. Our economy had fallen so far behind nature that eligible bachelors were as rare as essential commodities.

"So," I said. "Money was more important than me."

He stepped back. "That is not fair. You like fine things. You think I can't see that? What was I supposed to do?"

I moved closer to him and rubbed his shoulder. He was rejecting me and I would have to make it easier for him.

"Are we still together?" he asked.

"Marriage will not save us. That, I know."

"So I'm not needed anymore?"

"Who said?"

"I'm still needed?"

I eyed him up and down. "After all the trouble you've given me? You think I will let you go as easy as that?"

He laughed. "You this woman, what else do you want from me?"

Violet, I thought, our landlord, our furniture, and the bank. I had too many matters to settle. For Violet, I would have to write a letter; also, for our landlord. The furniture had to be sold, the remainder could come back to me. At the bank, I had to secure my severance check.

"I have to write it down," I said.

"I'll wait," he said.

"Can I trust you?"

I was depending on him again. Giving him a newborn to take care of would have been easier.

He put his hand on his chest. "I've told you before, I'm not a bastard."

Together, we found a taxi after I'd written my notes and letters. I asked Sanwo to deliver the letters. He could not tell Violet where I was. He would have to ask Mama Chidi not to say a word about my whereabouts. The furniture in the flat, he could send to me by lorry. For my severance pay, I would come to Lagos as soon as I was able. My thoughts were running helter-skelter, and I was worried that he'd gone around looking for me after speaking to Godwin. That would definitely arouse suspicion.

"What did Mrs. Durojaiye say?" I asked.

"She said you looked pregnant the last time she saw you."

"Eh? What did you say?"

"What could I say?"

"Hm. She's back to being a sergeant major, that one."

"Her union is still on strike, she says."

"I hope it ends soon. What about Mama Chidi?"

"Confused as usual. I mean, I asked her simple questions: When did Tolani leave? How did she leave? She kept saying, 'She's gone! She's gone! I wish I could go!'"

Mama Chidi had too many children for her own good. She could try going to her hometown, on her own, and leaving Papa Chidi to look after them.

"And Violet?" I asked.

Sanwo nodded. "You're right about that one. She's mad. She was trying to make me stay for a haircut. A Lionel Richie, she called it, and I don't care where she trained in Italy, even if it was in the Vatican. There is no way I would let her come near me with clippers."

"Vio, Vio," I said.

She was just trying to survive. They were my people in the city: she, Mrs. Durojaiye, Mama

Chidi, and Johnny Walker. We were from the same village in Lagos. I would have to see them again. It would be terrible, to face Violet especially, and tell her what had happened to Rose, but I had to.

"Where's Rose?" Sanwo asked, startling me. "Mama Chidi said she too had 'gone.'"

"Yes," I said. "Rose has gone home."

What a mess, I thought. What a disaster. I vowed to myself that Rose would have a decent burial, whatever lay ahead. I would not fail her in that way.

"Tell Mama Chidi I'll be back soon," I said.

Sanwo never traveled by bus. On our way to find a taxi, he kept giving me business advice. I needed a plan, a forecast, a feasibility study, a costing, and a budget. It made me sad to think that this was how our relationship ended, still talking about money. I heard Rose's voice whenever I thought I should stir the discussion in the right direction.

"Let him go, sister. What did he ever do for you?"

She made me laugh. She spoke at the wrong time and noticed what I tried to ignore, like his silver socks. She was unable to tell a single lie, and I began to take advice from her from then on.

"Safe journey," I said to Sanwo when we found a taxi.

"Good ridi-yance," her voice said.

"I'll see you soon," I said and waved.

"God forbid bad thing," she said.

Rose. Her death was too much for me. "Stay in this dry town of yours," her voice chattered on as

Sanwo's taxi drove off. "It will give you what you want right now, peace of mind. Start your business even. How did being cautious in life ever help you? You cannot hide. Your fear will creep up and bite your ass. Take care of yourself. Your hair looks awful. Yes, it does. You can't attract anything looking like that. One day you will meet the man you've wanted other men to be. One day you will find the work your hands were made for. Your whole life will be a psalm of thanksgiving thereafter. I promise you, and you know I'm not very religious. It won't matter how much time you've wasted doing the wrong things. God's time is best. Isn't that what the Christians say? Speak to me if you're unsure about what to do. What are you crying for anyway? You thought Rose was gone forever? Rose has just begun."

I waved to Sanwo until his taxi disappeared, thinking about how I'd almost paid him to marry me. I was not that desperate now, just grateful for his kindness. One day I might settle down, and it was typical that he would meet some woman, after me, and end up as her wonderful husband.

My mother returned later that evening with six yards of fabric for me. "Since you're leaving tomorrow," she said.

The patterns were maze-like, with red, purple, and yellow lines. "Thank you," I kept saying as I unfolded it to find more surprises.

"Because of a simple cloth?" she said, looking pleased.

"Beautiful," I said.

She'd made the cloth with raffia, stones, and hand-stitching. The method was her speciality. She'd stopped using the feather and cassava method when she gave up indigo for imported dyes. She rarely used the stencil and candle wax method now. The patterns were predictable, she said, and the wax was a nuisance. With the raffia method, her fabric ended up crinkled and bruised, but she looked forward to seeing the results.

"I don't know what I want when I start off," she said, pinching her fingers together. "Then I unfold it. The surprise at the end. That's what I like most. It's like a story."

I placed the fabric on my chest. "You love your work too much."

She shrugged. "It tires me, hurts my fingers, and business is not that good."

My mother's palms had never been the color they were meant to be. They were reddish-brown from dye, and her fingernails had the same stain, like henna.

"That bad?" I asked.

"That bad. No one is buying, except the rich, these days, and you know they prefer their imported laces and brocades. We thought they would buy more *adire* when imports became more expensive. Before it was all imports, imports. Now we have fewer imports and still, there is no business."

I put the cloth down. "At least there is food in the marketplace."

"Yes, from somewhere else. No one grows food here. You should see the farming settlements, what is left of them, and how little they produce. We are all traders now, or businesspeople in town."

"Have you ever considered making something out of your cloth?"

"Something like?"

"*Adire* arts and crafts. I see them in Lagos."

After Sanwo left for Lagos, I began to think up more ideas, not in a way he would approve of, with a feasibility study. I was thinking that I could design table spreads and mats. I couldn't make them myself, but finding people who could cut and sew would be easy. I could start a business in Makoku.

"That's Lagos," my mother said. "We have no use for *adire* arts and crafts here."

"But you can make them here," I said.

My mother shook her head. "Lagos tailors are trained. Here, they can only cut straight lines and a wide curve for a neckline. Anything else they ruin."

I laughed. "Tailors ruin cloth in Lagos too, and I'm not thinking of anything complicated."

She looked me up and down. "So why are you asking me this?"

"I've been thinking," I said.

"Of what?"

"Staying here."

My mother nodded slowly. "I see."

"What?" I asked. It was obvious she was not

taking me seriously.

"I hear a man was looking for you today," she said.

My voice rose. "Who told you that?"

"People have eyes."

"Yes, too much around here. They're all such busybodies."

"But you still want to stay here with us?"

I played with the edges of my cloth. I had to tell her something.

"He had news about my job."

"News about your job?"

"Yes."

"Is he your boss or what?"

"No."

"Then who is he to you?"

"A friend."

She shrugged. The gesture annoyed me more. She knew it was a personal visit.

"No one came to ask for my hand or anything," I said.

"Pity," she said.

"Why?"

"After all, you're not a child."

"I didn't say I was."

"You want to stay in my compound until you become an old woman?"

"Mama mi, I don't want to hear this."

She'd resisted marriage until she was twenty. Twenty was old to her.

"You'll be a lonely old woman," she said.

"Yes. Maybe that is my fate."

"Childless old woman. People will call you that."

She was taunting me and I tried to sound cheerful to irritate her.

"Let them," I said. "A woman doesn't have to be married to have a child anyway. Didn't you say Peju and her mother are doing fine?"

"It's not that easy."

"How do you know it will be difficult for me?"

"Because I raised you on my own."

"So. It is not impossible then, and anyway, I didn't come home over petty problems like marriage or having children."

"That's good," she said. "At least you're talking, even if it's nonsense."

My voice rose again. "I am not talking nonsense!"

She beckoned. "What sense are you making then? Tell me. That you left your job? That you want to stay here and make tablecloths? That you believe you're your own god or that you think you can continue to behave like a child, sitting around here, moping..."

"I am not moping."

She slapped her knee. "Yes, you are. Moping is what it looks like to me, and what became of you? You had a good head. You were honest. Yes, you were. Now you come home and spin tales to me, thinking I can't tell the difference. You can't even look me in the eyes. No, you can't." She pointed. "Who came to see you today? What news did he bring about your job? Who died? Answer me."

I stood up impatiently. "My life isn't simple like yours."

"Hm, simple. That's very good."

"Living here, being an elder in a compound, being respected. I had to look after myself in the city. I had no one. No one. Ruin around me. Living in fear, trying to escape one problem or the other. It caught up with everyone..."

How could I tell my mother?

"Go on," she said. "Hide it. After all, you are your father's daughter."

I could have ripped her cloth for saying that. One standard for herself and another for me. One rule for Peju's mother and another for me. If I didn't tell her the truth, I'd learned that from her. She was always hiding behind her bizarre stories.

"What father?" I asked. "The one I thought was mine?"

Words are like eggs.

My mother's face stiffened. I was not prepared for her reaction. I was trembling and my face burned. The nerves in my armpits prickled. Realization clouded her eyes.

"What did you say?" she whispered.

I placed my hand on my chest. "I'm sorry, but I am your daughter. Whatever happened between you and my father, you should have told me. You should have, Mama mi."

"And I," she said. "Am I not someone's daughter?"

Did you ever see adire *makers at work? Did you ever? The original* adire, *that is. There are many hands involved, women's, and they work in groups. They knead the clay with their feet, mold it into pots, dry it, fire it; soak the cassava tubers to remove their poison, peel them, squash them, dry them, shred them, and pound them. They cook the powder into a starch with alum and water, pound the* elu *leaves in mortars, dry out the mash until it blackens to indigo, burn the cocoa shells, strain the dye through the ash, stir it in bowls, taste it to test that it is ready, and within a week they must use it; otherwise, it becomes useless.*

Timing and harmony are of the essence. If the women get it right, the dye on the cloth will be the exact color of the sky at night. The cassava starch will resist the dye clear as the stars. The most trying part of the process is painting the starch on the cloth over and over, over and over, repeating the same patterns.

It was nighttime. The compound was dark, except for the kerosene lanterns visible from windows. We had not spoken for hours. I stayed in my mother's bedroom while she remained in the main room. I finally came out to join her.

"I saw Iya Alaro in a dream," I said.

The moon was a grayish yellow. My mother's face was as still as the night. I could easily mistake her calmness for anger, but I knew better. She was never angry for long.

"Iya Alaro," she said. "She appears to me, too.

She will come to warn you."

I rubbed my arms, though I was not cold.

"My father took me everywhere. I could tell he didn't like attention."

"He was what you call humble."

"Yes. He was fair."

My mother shook her head. "A woman makes more than her fair share of compromises. How fair is that?"

"That is the way of the world," I said.

"What way?"

"For a woman to compromise. Her worth, for one."

"Did I not raise you to value yourself?"

"I am not accusing you of anything."

"Then how come you've come to that sorry conclusion already?"

"Mama mi, I've lived hundreds of miles from you. I have discovered some things on my own."

"Like what?"

"I trusted a man who lost my money. You know what that means."

"You are not old enough to draw comparisons with my life."

"Forgive me, but you will have to decide if I'm too old or not old enough. It is no wonder I am confused."

"You will certainly never be old enough to speak to me that way."

"You can't continue to see me as your daughter!"

"I can't see you in any other way!"

"I'm not the innocent girl you think I am."

"You'd be surprised. I know exactly who you are."

"I've done things that I'm ashamed of. You think I am proud to admit that to you?"

She paused. "No, but I know what it is like to live with shame, and I did that when I was young, younger than you are. Are you old enough to hear about that?"

I sat by her side. I was not sure. If she confirmed my suspicions, then my father's way was revolutionary, and hers was sacrifice. She could have had more children. She could have exposed him. Instead, she enjoyed freedoms that other women envied, freedoms that belonged to her, and for what? The privilege of keeping his secret?

"I'm listening," I said.

My mother lifted a strand of raffia from the floor. "See this? I use it for my work. Every day. I have a way of tying knots so they do not come loose while I am dyeing. When I am through with dyeing, I cut the knots with a blade, clean, like so. It severs the strands. It is possible to undo a knot with your fingers, but it takes time, and you must do it delicately." She blew the raffia out of her palm.

"We Yoruba believe in a cycle of life. A person dies and passes to the spirit world only to return to the land of the living. I have struggled with this concept in many ways. The last and first breaths for instance, how much time is between? The knowledge acquired in one life, at what point is it forgotten?

"I certainly do not have a simple existence. Is this ever possible? It is more likely that a simple assumption has been made about my life. I have always said, in passing judgments on others, that if you want to know the best and worst a person is capable of, try and imagine their greatest fear.

"No story should remain untold. Death is the state that should follow the surrender of all the secrets we carry, and I have resolved that it makes no difference how much time there is between our successive lives anyway. What matters is what we learn whilst we are living, what we can teach. Therefore, we need not wait for the moment before death to look at each other and say, 'Listen to me. Let me tell you what has happened in my life so far. Let me tell you as I understand it now.'"

As my mother spoke to me that night, I laughed and cried, although I'd heard her stories before, about her childhood fight with my father, his dedication to work and careless generosity. She talked about her own work, her beloved Vespa and *esusu* investment scheme. She told me how her aunt had saved her, about an *oyinbo* man who brought her fame, and another local man who had made her infamous in town. As usual, she spoke with gaps, but the moment arrived when she said, "There is something you haven't heard before. Something I haven't revealed as of yet."

I remembered Iya Alaro's counsel.

"Mama mi," I said. "You don't have to say another word."

"But I have not finished," she said.

Lies hide between words and the truth need not draw attention to itself. I drew closer to my mother. Would I not let her rest?

"It's my turn to speak," I said. "Your story is already told."